PLEASE DON'T MARRY ME

The Alyssa Holt Story

A Novel

IRENE WILLIAMS

© 2025 by Irene Williams

Printed in the United States of America

All rights reserved. No part of this publication may be reproduced, stored in a retrieval system, or transmitted in any form or by any means—such as digitization, photocopy, or recording—without the prior written permission of the publisher. The only exception is brief quotations in printed reviews.

ISBN

978-1-7360803-4-4

978-1-7360803-5-1

Website:

irenewilliamsbooks.com

Email: irenewill2020@gmail.com

This book is a work of fiction. Names, characters, places, and incidents are products of the author's imagination or are used fictitiously. Any resemblance to actual events, locales, or persons, living or dead, is purely coincidental.

"Blessed is anyone who does not stumble on account of me."

Matthew 11:6

ACKNOWLEDGEMENTS

I give thanks to God for inspiring me to write this story, and I'm grateful for my husband Clive, who provides continuous encouragement and support. I'd also like to thank my friends and family for their support; especially my friend Robert, who has provided a tremendous amount of feedback and advice.

In his pride, the wicked man does not seek Him; in all his thoughts, there is no room for God. He says to himself, "Nothing will ever shake me." He swears, "No one will ever do me harm." His mouth is full of lies and threats; trouble and evil are under his tongue.

Psalm 10:4, 6–7

Pitway, California, September 13, 1985

The pillow over her head couldn't muffle the noise; she heard all the yelling, cursing, and screaming coming from the living room.

The first time Jason fought with her mother, Alyssa had been so scared that she'd run barefoot out of her bedroom window to the nearest neighbor's house, begging the man to call the police. Her heart had pounded loudly, just as it was doing now.

She remembered that the night had been unseasonably warm, yet she had been shaking so badly that the elderly man had wrapped a blanket around her shoulders. The television volume was low, and a reporter had been discussing a speech President Reagan made the previous day.

Alyssa and her senior neighbor had stared out of his living room window when the police lights flashed down the road. She had watched the officers escort her mother, who was doubled over in pain, out of the house and down the front steps. Jason, already handcuffed, had been seated in the back of the police cruiser. The nine-year-old had sighed in relief, thinking everything would be okay, then the police would put Jason in jail, and Mommy would be safe. Alyssa had returned the blanket to her neighbor and run down his steps toward her house, but she had stopped in her tracks, stunned, when she saw Jason exit the cruiser. He had held his arms out while the officer removed his handcuffs and stood back. Then, Jason had jumped into his two-seater convertible, backed out of the driveway, and sped off down the street. Her bruised mother had cried out for Jason to stay as he sped away. Confused, Alyssa had run to her mother and wrapped her arms around her. Linda had winced in pain and abruptly shrugged her daughter off, saying, "Alyssa, please go to bed; Mommy is in pain now."

That was last year. Now the fights had become a routine. Alyssa dragged a second pillow over her head. It lessened the noises but was not enough for her to sleep without fear. Three months ago, when Linda Holt received a terrible beating from Jason, she was rushed to the hospital. It was so severe that Hazel, Linda's older cousin, brought Pastor Darrel to the hospital to pray for her. Thankfully, Linda recovered. When Hazel drove them home from the hospital after Linda's discharge, Linda promised she'd never open the door to Jason again. Yet, here they were.

At ten years old, Alyssa was very familiar with the patterns of her mother's relationship with her abusive boyfriend. First, Jason would come by and knock on the door. In the beginning, Linda would tell him to go away; then, Jason would start apologizing, sometimes bringing flowers or gifts. Eventually, Linda would open the door, and the two would start with the lovey-dovey stuff. But, without fail, they would get drunk and start arguing in the middle of the night and the stressed little girl would stay awake, worrying about her mother. Sometimes, the two were so loud that the neighbors called the police, and though Linda would be weeping while gently cradling the newly bruised part of her body when they arrived, she never agreed to press charges.

Knowing she couldn't go back to sleep while they were fighting, Alyssa jumped up, threw back the covers, and pulled out the small duffle bag from under her bed. The bag was a gift from Hazel. Cousin Hazel welcomed Alyssa whenever she needed to escape the turmoil at home. One time, when the fighting started, Alyssa ran the quarter mile to Hazel's house in her pajamas, without any shoes on her feet or a change of clothing. These days, she kept a bag stuffed with clothing. All she needed were her shoes and school bag before jumping out the bedroom window—the safest exit.

The screaming and tussling sounds coming from the living room didn't seem as loud out on the lawn. With both bags over her shoulder, Alyssa walked backwards until she stepped onto the road. The quiet, moonless night seemed eerie. She turned around and walked down the dark asphalt-covered street. The neighborhood homes weren't close together, so only scattered porch lights illuminated her path. After crossing an intersection, Alyssa saw movement in the shrubs on the left side of the road and froze; she sighed in relief when it turned out to be a family of deer. She continued her hike to cousin Hazel's home.

Hazel's gate creaked as Alyssa walked through it and continued down the side of the house. She tapped lightly on the window pane until a light turned on; she then headed back toward the front door. No words were exchanged when Hazel opened the door. Alyssa walked in and wrapped her arms around Hazel as usual. The older woman ran a hand over the young girl's long brown hair. Together, they walked casually to the spare bedroom.

"Do you want me to call the police?"

Alyssa shook her head. "Momma gets upset whenever the police come." She entered the bedroom, kicked off her sneakers, and climbed into bed. Hazel wanted to ask more questions but instead pulled the spread over the girl.

"You know you can talk to me anytime, right?" Hazel asked softly.

Alyssa nodded, staring out sadly from under the covers.

Hazel hated the thought of the ten-year-old girl regularly walking alone to her house in the middle of the night. She returned to her bedroom but couldn't sleep. Her mind drifted to Pitway's child services department, which had shut down years ago. Now, any local child in need was sent seventy-five miles away to a disreputable city child services facility. There were rumors and accusations of abuse in the facility, yet the government apparently did nothing about it.

Throughout her career, the middle-aged teacher had witnessed several cases like Alyssa's. Eventually, someone would report the neglected youngster to child services, and the minor would be taken far away from their community and placed into the city child services facility. They were never the same when they returned home. Whenever she encountered parents who lost custody of their child due to neglect, she'd encourage them to find a safe relative to take in their child. If necessary, she described what the child would endure in the city facility. That knowledge usually made a caring parent scramble to find a suitable relative to leave their child with until they were allowed to return home.

Alyssa was family, and though Hazel would never call child services on Linda, she worried about some stranger making the call out of concern. It was almost two in the morning; the best she could do right now was keep Alyssa in a safe environment and pray that Linda would get her act together. She'd planned to have a serious talk with Linda when she sees her.

The next day, Hazel and Alyssa drove to school together. Alyssa was in good spirits; she liked staying with Hazel because her cousin always made sure she had breakfast.

The school facility building, which contained students from all the grades, had once housed over 2,000 students. That number had plummeted since the town's main source of employment, a pharmaceutical manufacturing company, closed. School services declined along with the fall in student population, but Hazel and other dedicated teachers tried to pick up the slack by prepping students for college exams and tutoring those who were struggling. Hazel made herself available for any task that needed to be done, so everyone knew Mrs. Cummings. With Alyssa safe in class, Hazel continued to the school office, both adults and students greeting her warmly as she walked down the hall.

Besides her school job, Hazel worked part-time at the Pitway Inn to make ends meet. She'd always been smart with her money, but over ten years ago, she married Albert Cummings. They were in love, or at least that's what she thought until Albert proved his first love was alcohol. When he lost his job after the factory closed, Albert desperately tried to persuade Hazel to sell her four-bedroom family home and move into a smaller two-bedroom house further from the town center. Hazel loved the home that her grandfather had hand-built and passed down to her, so the answer was always no. Finally, Albert took matters into his own hands. He tricked Hazel into signing a substantial loan against the home's value for a business he was starting, he then walking out of her life with a younger woman. Hazel's part-time job was necessary to pay off her ex-husband's debt and keep a roof over her head.

The school day went by quickly. Hazel had been calling her cousin between classes throughout the day. So far, all calls to Linda went directly to the answering machine.

Alyssa walked home anxiously after school, not knowing what she'd find after Jason and her mom's fight. Sometimes, the house was trashed with empty beer bottles strewn across the floor. Other times, she'd find them both in bed in the middle of the day. Alyssa never understood why her mother kept dating losers after her dad died. She decided that when she grew up, she was going to live alone forever with no boyfriends, they were nothing but trouble.

After the factory closed, Alyssa saw many of the men in town spending their days drinking in bars. Cousin Hazel said they used their unemployment checks on themselves instead of their families. Hazel had seen several of their wives using government food stamps in the market.

When Hazel took Alyssa to church, the pastor often spoke about men drinking too much. She liked Pastor Darrell and the children's ministry staff, even though sometimes Bible study felt like school. Alyssa had spent last Christmas with cousin Hazel. When Alyssa entered the children's ministry, all the children received Bibles with their names on it. Cousin Hazel told her that Pastor Darrell had paid for them with his own money after Deacon Bryant had said there were no funds available for such frivolous things. One day, when she saw Pastor Darrell giving sandwiches to the drunkards on the street, she asked him why he was doing this. He told her that Christians should be kind and loving to all people because Jesus wanted us to love our neighbors. When he made that statement, Alyssa felt bad for wishing something bad would happen to Jason because she didn't want him in her house anymore.

As Alyssa walked up to her house, the elderly neighbor across the street called her over. He asked if she knew that an ambulance had taken her mother away that morning—she didn't. He then asked if she had someone to stay with. Alyssa nodded though she had no intention of leaving home.

The living room was wrecked, but the old black-and-white television appeared to be intact. Alyssa stepped over the debris left from the previous night's fight and headed to the kitchen. There was no milk in the refrigerator, but the cans of spaghetti she'd hidden under the sink for times like these were still intact. Her mother had been in and out of the hospital frequently since Jason entered their lives.

The kitchen table was a mess. Alyssa emptied the ashtrays,

cleared the empty beer bottles, and removed the dirty dishes before laying out her dinner. As she sat down, Alyssa saw a picture frame on the floor. She jumped out of her chair and ran to pick it up. Alyssa exhaled in relief when she saw that the picture of her father in his military uniform remained undamaged despite the broken frame. As she carefully tilted the frame over the trash can to remove the broken glass, she recalled the days when her father was alive.

Alyssa loved the way her dad made grilled cheese sandwiches. He'd cut the brown crust off the sides and serve them with warm tomato soup. Her Native American father, John Holt, was taken away from his family at the age of two. Before the 1978 Indian Child Welfare Act, it was common practice for the government to remove Native American children from homes they wrongly deemed as neglectful and place them in non-Native homes. They placed her father in a foster home with people who knew nothing of his original culture or language. Somehow, all records of his original family and tribe were lost. He did conduct an exhaustive search for his family, but to no avail. With no idea who his parents were or what tribe he belonged to, John struggled in his adult life.

At eighteen, John joined the army and had a successful military career. He met Linda at the state fair. After the two married, they settled in Pitway because it was Linda's home town. John was dispatched to many foreign operations for several years. Then one day, her mother opened the door to casualty officers. They told her he had died valiantly, sacrificing himself to save others. Linda received his medals and heartfelt messages from many soldiers at the funeral, but becoming a widow at twenty-five changed Linda for the worse.

Jason, and all the other boyfriends before him, were rowdy drunks. They were nothing like her father. John Holt was a kind, gentle man who eagerly helped anyone in need, and he never struck her mother. Everyone loved him, but now he was long forgotten.

Alyssa carefully extracted the photo from the broken frame

backing board before taking it to her room, and hid it with her other cherished items. Afterwards, she sat on the yellow shag carpet in front of the large black-and-white television with her spaghetti. Jason's visits were so frequent that she couldn't remember the last time she was allowed in the living room to watch television.

Sleep didn't come easily that night. She lay in bed, waiting for the sound of her mother walking through the living room and tossing her keys on the table. She wondered if her mother would come home alone. Just in case, Alyssa got up and locked her bedroom door.

When her alarm went off the next day, she stretched. Her sleep had been peaceful. She quietly peeked into her mother's bedroom, but no one was there. Shrugging, she prepared for her usual school day routine.

Her morning class went on as usual until someone came to escort her to the school office. Inside, the principal was waiting along with Hazel.

"Alyssa, whom did you stay with last night?" Principal Jane Byrd asked.

"I didn't stay with anyone. I was at home." Alyssa frowned, noting the worried looks on their faces. "What's wrong?"

Hazel spoke softly, "Alyssa, your mother's been in the hospital since yesterday morning. She's not doing so well. So, I'm going to drive you over there so you can see her."

Her mother being in the hospital was nothing new. Linda was in and out so often that Alyssa could recognize most of the nurses who worked there. She didn't understand why this visit couldn't wait until after school. Without saying a word, she picked up her backpack and followed Hazel to her car.

Pitway present population was too small to have its own hospital. Any patient in serious condition had to travel over twenty miles to the closest hospital, which was in Exeter. Used to the long drive, Alyssa stared out the window as they passed through other small towns. She often wondered why they didn't appear as run-down as Pitway.

At the hospital, Hazel checked with the head nurse about Linda's condition. Alyssa overheard the room number and walked down the hall, until she stood in front of the correct door.

"Excuse me. Do you need help? Who are you here to see?" asked a nurse approaching from behind.

"I'm here to see my mother, Linda Holt," said Alyssa, slightly annoyed at being stopped.

"Well, I'd better go in with you. We can't stay long; your momma needs her rest to recover from the surgery," said the nurse.

The word 'surgery' caught Alyssa's attention. She followed the nurse into the shared hospital room and approached her mother's bedside. Alyssa had never seen her mother look so bad. She was pale, dark circles ringed her eyes, and her blond hair was matted with perspiration.

"Momma?" Alyssa called, as she lightly patted Linda's shoulder. There was no response.

Hazel entered the room and stood beside the nurse.

"Honey, your mother's resting; she had an emergency surgery," said the nurse. "They had to remove her spleen because it ruptured, but we're giving your mother medicine to make her better."

"Why can't she open her eyes?" Alyssa asked.

"She's very weak, sweetheart," Hazel replied softly. We'd better go now so she can continue to rest." She led Alyssa from the room and sat her down at the nurse's station before talking to the nurse some more. During the conversation, both women peered sadly at the young girl. Alyssa would never forget the look in their eyes.

CHAPTER
TWO

And He Himself gave some to be apostles, some prophets, some evangelists, and some pastors and teachers, for the equipping of the saints for the work of ministry, for the edifying of the body of Christ.

Ephesians 4:11–12

Seven years later, 1992

Alyssa fought hard to stay awake as Pastor Tim Bryant preached. She wished the church was full like it had been when Pastor Darrell was there, then her nodding off wouldn't be so obvious. But then, she probably wouldn't be nodding off at all.

These days, Deacon Bryant insisted on being called "Pastor Bryant" since he had taken over as interim pastor when the church board voted Pastor Darrell out. Their reason for ousting the head pastor was that too many congregants had left town, and the money being collected was not enough to support his salary. And though Pastor Darrell was willing to stay on with a severely reduced income, the board removed him anyway. Cousin Hazel said it was because Deacon Bryant told them that if he were made the new pastor, he would do the Lord's work for free. Conveniently, several board members received extraordinarily large discounts on cars from Tim Bryant's dealership while others were relatives of the deacon. So, after being voted in by the board, Pastor Bryant packed the former pastor's office items in a box the very day they let Pastor Darrell go.

Pastor Darrell was busy picking up trash from the church's

front yard when Tim handed him the box before demanding the keys to the church. Hazel and other church members felt so bad about the way their former pastor had been treated that they threw him with a huge going away party at Hazel's home.

Alyssa had previously asked Hazel if they could attend church in the next town, but Hazel quietly instructed her young cousin that they couldn't risk offending the new pastor. Besides, Hazel had grown up in Pitway Baptist. Therefore, every Sunday morning, they sat through what Alyssa jokingly referred to as "spiritless preaching."

A multitude of families fled Pitway Baptist church after the ousting of Pastor Darell, and attendance had been on a steady decline since the church installed the new pastor. Pitway's residents knew Pastor Bryant was behind Pastor Darrell's removal, but no one dared make an official complaint. The Bryant family owned most of Pitway's establishments, including the town bank that held everyone's mortgages and loans. The new pastor owned the only car dealership in the region, his older cousin owned the only gas station, and another cousin owned the only food market in town. People often joked that nothing happened in Pitway without a Bryant.

The Bryants were everywhere, including the town Chamber of Commerce board, which meant they had the power to veto any competing businesses that wanted to operate in Pitway. Several businesses were turned away despite the dilapidated town's need for commercial growth.

The only thriving business in town was the Pitway Inn, where both Alyssa and Haze worked part-time. Seventeen-year-old Alyssa was saving for college, and Hazel still needed extra funds to cover the loan her ex-husband took against her home. Since Pitway was near the tourist town of Three Rivers, where vacationers came to fish and admire the picturesque national parks, many who couldn't find rooms in Three Rivers stayed at the Pitway Inn.

At seventeen, Alyssa's choices of employment were limited, yet she persevered. Many at the church knew of her constant search for work. Over the years, she'd been a babysitter, garden assistant, and held countless other positions while going to high school.

Alyssa sighed in disappointment as she flipped through her Bible. Every Sunday, she dutifully brought it to church, hoping in vain that Pastor Bryant would quote scripture instead of pompously preaching sermons rarely sourced from biblical text. She missed Pastor Darrell's teaching—how he explained the scripture in minute detail, ensuring that everyone understood the meaning of each verse. She also remembered how people sat on the edge of their seats, listening intently and taking notes of his interpretations. Pastor Darrell constantly encouraged all members to read the Bible.

Since stepping onto the pulpit, the former deacon had treated the church as his personal kingdom rather than a refuge for followers of Christ. At his dealership, he made sure every customer knew he was the pastor of the only church in Pitway. His staff had to address him as "Pastor Bryant" whenever a customer was within earshot, and his office plaque read "Pastor" instead of Manager.

Under his leadership, Pitway Baptist saw many ministries shutting down. But today, when he announced the children's ministry would be closing next month, Alyssa jolted awake. She waited impatiently to hear the reason why the ministry was being discontinued, but no reason was given. Some of the attendees exchanged uneasy glances, but no one spoke up to question the pastor's decision.

When the service ended, the tall thirty-four-year-old pastor stood by the door, chatting with members as they exited, as was custom. Alyssa told Hazel she'd meet her at the car and then she stood in line with the other congregants, waiting for her chance to speak to the pastor.

"Good morning, Pastor."

"Good morning, have a blessed day," the pastor said, already turning to the next person in line. Alyssa didn't budge.

"Pastor, I want to ask a question. Can you tell me why the children's ministry is closing?"

"Well now, Alyssa, is it? Yes, we decided to end the Sunday school services. It doesn't make sense to keep it running for just fifteen kids."

"But, Pastor, the kids enjoy Sunday school. I know I enjoyed it when I was there. Is there any way to keep it running?"

"I think it's best that the children remain with their parents. We don't want to waste time on so few students, and Sister Mary has gotten older now. She doesn't have the strength to watch kids at her age."

"Well, maybe I can do it," suggested Alyssa.

Pastor Bryant laughed heartily. "Well, maybe you could one day; unfortunately, we don't have the resources to teach and support you for the position."

Before Alyssa could reply, the pastor quickly turned away, engaging in a conversation with another parishioner and completely ignoring Alyssa. Disgusted by his rudeness, Alyssa clenched her teeth as she slowly walked away to Hazel's car.

"Hey, what's with the mean face? Did something happen?" Hazel asked as Alyssa slid into the passenger seat.

"Yes, Pastor Bryant happened. I asked if I could teach the kids to keep the ministry open, but he dismissed me."

"I'm not surprised. He's all for closing ministries; keeps all the attention on him and his sermons. Well, you tried. We'd better head home." said Hazel.

Alyssa shook her head. "I'm not giving up so easily."

"Alyssa, you're leaving for college this fall. You can't go to school in Los Angeles and come back every Sunday to teach."

Alyssa frowned. "Oh... you're right," she replied dejectedly. "There must be something I can do to get it started, then someone else can take over."

"Have you looked around at the dwindling congregation lately? There aren't many people left to do that."

In the morning, Alyssa said her usual prayers of gratitude, but when she stood up, a thought came to her mind. She took Hazel's car and drove to the winery where her friend Sarah lived. Sarah's entire family worked at the family vineyards, and now that Sarah had completed high school and had no plans to go away to college, she worked alongside her parents.

The friends sat down together. Alyssa shared her plan to reopen the children's ministry and her idea of presenting it to Deacon Barry instead of Pastor Bryant. Sarah loved the idea. Both girls had great memories of the children's ministry and felt obligated to keep it going.

"I don't know where I'd be now if it weren't for Pastor Darrell and the kids' ministry teachers. They helped me get through everything that happened with my mother. At first, I was relieved to come home from school and not find my mother and her boyfriend there. But later, when they told me she'd had an emergency surgery and was suffering in pain while I was at home feeling happy, I hated myself for it."

"Then my mom was gone, and cousin Hazel let me live with her. I remember being sad and stressed all the time. I was also afraid Hazel would tire of taking care of me, and send me to child service. It was an unsettling time; whenever Hazel said we were going somewhere, I thought 'this was it; the day she was turning me over to child services.' The ministry teachers noticed something was wrong with my behavior. They sat me down and found out what was going on in my head. When they told my cousin what I was thinking, she got me counseling and made it clear that she wanted me to live with her permanently. If any of the kids in Pitway Baptist are going through some trauma like I did, they'll have no one to talk to because the pastor never talks to the kids, and now, there won't even be a children's ministry."

"I know what you mean. I remember Pastor Bryant becoming

indignant when my neighbor asked him to speak to her teenage son who was depressed. First, he asked if she was a member. She said she only occasionally attended. Apparently, that wasn't the answer he wanted to hear. He told her that he only counsels' adults, then he just walked away without offering any advice or referrals."

"Why am I not surprised?" Alyssa scoffed. "I tried to talk to him about the ministry, but he brushed me off. Sarah, you know my heart is set on going to college to get my degree in social work. I can help set up the ministry, but I won't be here after August. So, I was thinking that after we start, we can ask other teens to take turns helping so you wouldn't be alone. What do you think?"

"That sounds great! Also, I've decided to take courses at the community college after harvest time. I could probably take a child psychology or children's education course for my humanities requirements."

"That would be wonderful! I'll work on a plan to present to Deacon Barry. Although he's Pastor Bryant's cousin, I believe he cares about the church. Also, all the other board members respect him, so if he likes it, they'll probably go along with it." She leaned forward. "Cousin Hazel and I were at the last church member meeting when Deacon Barry became upset about how many members had left Pitway Baptist in the past year. Pastor Bryant became flustered when Deacon Barry turned to him and asked, 'What plans do you have to grow the church?'"

"Aren't you afraid Pastor Bryant will be upset because you're asking the deacon about the ministry after he told you no?"

"Not really. What's he going to do, yell at me in church? And if the deacon says no, Pastor Bryant doesn't have to find out about it."

Later that night, Alyssa stayed up, poring over books she had checked out from the library, searching for resources to strengthen her children's ministry presentation. In the morning, she visited Sister Mary, the retiring children's ministry teacher, to discuss her plans to keep the ministry open.

"I'm so happy Pastor Bryant changed his mind about the children's ministry," Sister Mary said with a relieved smile. "I don't want to quit, but my arthritis doesn't allow me to move like I used to, and all my helpers have left the church."

"Well, I haven't received approval yet. Sarah and I are working on a plan to reopen the ministry, and we're hoping the board will approve it. I'll be leaving for college in August, but Sarah and the other teens can manage the ministry after that."

"I'll tell you what I'm going to do. I'll call a few members and let them know how much it would mean to me if the ministry continues."

"Thank you so much, Sister Mary! I'd really appreciate that."

"Don't thank me yet, dear. There's no telling what's going to happen. But come with me. Let's invite the head of the church to intervene in this decision."

Taking Alyssa by the hand, Sister Mary led her to her special space for prayer. Together, they knelt and lifted their request to the Lord.

CHAPTER

THREE

Likewise, every good tree bears good fruit, but a bad tree bears bad fruit.

Matt 7:17

"Well now, it's about time you showed up. Where've you been?" grumbled Deacon Barry, who had been waiting impatiently in Pitway's battered diner for forty minutes for his cousin, Pastor Bryant, to arrive. The portly deacon, who also served as Pitway's only town judge, had already consumed a hefty serving of meatloaf and mashed potatoes before requesting two huge slices of apple pie.

The pastor motioned for the waitress before sliding into the booth. "Deacon, may I remind you that my struggling dealership demands many hours of my attention? You're the one with tons of free time now that you've retired and picked up the part-time judge job. I have many years to go before I reach your level."

Barry smirked. "C'mon, Tim, there's no way you're struggling. Aren't you the richest man in town?"

"Barry, do you realize how far the population in this town has dropped? We need to figure out some way to draw the old factory families back to Pitway where they belong."

"Those people are long gone. But Tim, if you felt that way, why in the world did you and your boneheaded Chamber of Commerce reject the mall project those contractors brought?"

"We had to reject it, those people planned to bring stores that would compete with some of ours. We must protect what we have."

Barry shook his head. "Tim, that mall would have brought so many jobs. More people would have moved into Pitway to be close to work. And it would have drawn tourists from Three Rivers and the surrounding national park area. There would've been plenty of business to go around."

"Ah, doesn't matter now," the pastor shrugged. Besides, we can figure out something amongst ourselves, we don't need outsiders."

Just then, the waitress approached their table to take the pastor's order. She patted down her hair as she spoke. "Pastor Bryant, it's so nice to see you! Sorry I haven't been to service lately; I've been away visiting my family."

The pastor flashed a plastic smile; "Well, now that you're back, I suppose I'll see you in the pew Sunday morning."

"Yes, you can count on me, I'll be sitting upfront for the first service."

"Oh, that must have been a long visit with your family; we only have one service now, and it's at 10 a.m. sharp. I'm looking forward to seeing you in the congregation." The pastor then placed his order with the waitress who promptly shouted the order to the cook. After the waitress walked away, a full-figured woman wearing a fitted dress entered the diner. As she passed their table and continued down the aisle, the pastor's head snapped around and watched the movement of her backside as the woman walked by.

Shaking his head, Deacon Barry admonished his cousin, "Tim, you really must stop that behavior. This isn't your home. You're out in public, leering at a woman's backside. You're a pastor for God's sake! You must lead by example." Barry shook his head disappointedly, "Let's get down to business. The board had a meeting to discuss ways to increase church membership. Here's what we have come up with."

Pastor Bryant groaned before stating, "Are we doing this again?"

"Yes Pastor, we must. Our church population is too low. I've never seen it like this before; and there's more, people are complaining."

"Oh, come on Barry. The church board always complains; that's just how it is, but hey, you guys voted me in so I can't be all bad." Deacon Barry lowered his head, recalling the day he encouraged the other board members to elect his cousin as the new pastor.

"Tell me, what is it this time?" Tim asked impatiently.

"Now, parents are upset because you're closing the children's ministry. Tim, we can't afford to lose more families. We're struggling financially as it is. Don't forget, the church needs a new roof."

"About that, I've been thinking... We should pass the basket around a few more times on Sundays. Some of our members still don't know how to give. Passing the basket around again will encourage them to put more money in. Either that or we lock the doors until everyone coughs up more money. As for the children's ministry—they use our side building. It's a separate structure we hardly use except for meetings and Sunday school. Why don't we put the building up for sale and use the money to upgrade the church and replace the roof? My office needs remodeling. I want the carpet replaced, and the walls could use a couple of coats of paint."

"Tim, how can we sell the building? It's on church grounds! We can't allow random people to live on church property, who knows how they will live? That money will run out eventually, so it's not a sound plan. Also, there's another issue: your personal life. Tim, it's been years since Jennifer left you, and it doesn't look good for the pastor to have so many different lady friends staying at his home. When you took this position, you told the board you were going to build a family. People gravitate more toward a pastor with a stable family life. Have you even considered marrying again?"

Tim began to protest, but the deacon interrupted him. "Now

hold on, Tim. Don't you miss having dinner ready and waiting for you at home? Wouldn't you like to have children who could run your dealership when you retire? What sort of future do you envision for yourself?"

Tim sighed. "Yeah, it would be nice to have a wife again, but the women I date aren't... wife material, if you know what I mean."

Barry shook his head disapprovingly.

Tim scratched his head, thinking hard. "I need someone who's... wholesome."

"Now you're thinking!" Barry said excitedly. "By the way, what do you think of that young widow, Louise Patterson? She has that wholesome look, she's pretty, and she's had her eye on you."

Tim frowned. "I don't want someone who's been married before. It's like buying a used car; you don't know how the previous owner handled it." He chuckled at his own joke.

Barry lowered his voice. "Tim, that's an extremely vile way for a pastor to refer to women," the deacon admonished. "I believe Louise would be a perfect fit for you. You've both been previously married, and you're still young enough to start a family."

Tim waved his hand dismissively. "I know you mean well, Barry, but she's not my type. I want a woman I can shape into a good wife. First, she must know her place and be compliant. I'm not getting stuck with another loudmouth who runs to her family whenever she thinks she's not treated well. The woman I marry must keep her business to herself. She must work by my side at church, take care of me at home, and keep the house in order."

Barry laughed. "It's no wonder you're still single. No woman I know will put up with all your 'wants.' You might as well look for one of those mail-order brides."

"Well, now you're talking. On second thought, those mail-order brides don't come cheap, and most can't speak English, so that's a no." He leaned back, drumming his fingers on the table. "Anyhow, you've got me thinking. When I stand at the door this

Sunday, I'm going to take a real good look at our female flock. There's got to be some wife material in there somewhere."

"There are different kinds of service, but the same Lord."

1 Corinthians 12:5–6

Alyssa phoned Deacon Barry and asked if she could meet with him to discuss the re-opening of the children's ministry. The elder seemed surprised to hear that Alyssa was considering it, but he eagerly agreed to meet the next morning at church. When she arrived, other board members were already seated around the table. Alyssa was acquainted with them as regular church attendees, but the familiarity did not lessen her nervousness when she presented her ideas. Nevertheless, the plan she laid out was favorably received, and the board loved the idea of having the teens work together in the children's ministry to help the younger kids. After the meeting, Deacon Barry told the elated teen that the board would be in touch after they discussed the matter thoroughly. Alyssa exited the building in good spirits, delighted that the church elders had taken her seriously.

The teen hummed a gospel song as she pulled the car into the driveway of her home. Outside, Hazel stood with a brush in hand, trying her best to paint the garage door, but her arthritic hands slowed her progress. Normally, she'd hire someone to do the job for her, but Hazel planned to gift Alyssa a sum of money on her eighteenth birthday to cover the first semester's tuition, which meant she had to cut back on expenses. Many items in the aged home needed fixing, but all except emergency work was placed on hold until she saw Alyssa off to college. Hazel was extremely proud of Alyssa's accomplishments and responsible character. She knew there wasn't much joy in the young woman's life and she hoped that life in college, away from their dilapidated town, would bring her some happiness. As her young cousin approached the garage, Hazel saw a joyful spirit in Alyssa and wondered what had put the smile on the teen's face.

"What's got you in such a happy mood?" Hazel asked.

"Victory! I had a great meeting with the church board, and I'm certain they'll approve my plan to keep the children's ministry open. It's going to take time and work to set up, but Sarah and I are ready for it."

"That's wonderful, honey! I can't wait to see you in action," Hazel exclaimed while flexing her fingers, something she did when in pain. Alyssa was quick to notice this involuntary action.

"Hazel, what are you doing? Leave the brush on the can; I'll paint the garage door."

"You don't have time to do that. You're going to work, remember?"

"It won't take me long. I'll change quickly."

Hazel sighed, thinking of how the home will feel empty once Alyssa left for college.

The next day, Deacon Barry phoned Tim about the board's decision to allow Alyssa and the other teens to keep the children's ministry open. They'd already informed some of the parents.

"You're doing what?! How did you know she spoke to me about that?" Tim questioned.

"Honestly, I didn't. This is the first I'm hearing about it. It doesn't matter anyway—Alyssa and her friends will start this Sunday. The board members will watch her in action, then we'll decide if the classes can continue and if she needs help in any area."

"Hmph, I'm going to watch too; I'll watch her fall flat on her face. That girl doesn't know anything about taking care of children. She's a child herself. Children need a firm hand, and Alyssa's too mousey, they'll walk all over her."

"I must disagree with you there, Tim. She may be timid, but she speaks up for what she believes in. The board and I were very impressed with her presentation."

Tim was furious with Alyssa for going behind his back to the board. However, he was so confident in her failure as a teacher, the pastor anticipated watching her failure on Sunday morning.

When Sunday arrived, Alyssa, Sarah and two other teens reviewed Alyssa's plan of action. Each had their own jobs to do. Before the children arrived, they held hands and prayed for the ministry's success.

As the parents brought their children in, Alyssa and her team introduced themselves and collected names and other information from the parents. This information was used to identify the parent when they return for their child, and to get to know the children better. They rearranged the seating, pushing back the desks and chair sets and leaving an open space in the middle for the kids to have free playtime before teaching began. Games and toys were laid out for the children. During this time, Alyssa and her staff assessed the age range of the children and divided them into three groups based on age.

At the end of the kids' playtime, the board members entered the children's ministry room with Pastor Bryant. They sat quietly in the back as the teens separated the children as planned. The team had each child introduce themself before the lesson began. After a while, a frowning Pastor Bryant had to return to the main sanctuary when he was notified that the choir finished singing and the church announcements were finished. Twenty minutes into the session, the board, satisfied with what they witnessed so far, quietly exited the room. Before walking out, Deacon Barry caught Alyssa's eye and gave her a smiling nod of approval.

When the service ended, parents flooded into the children's ministry to retrieve their child. Alyssa could not stop smiling when she realized many of the kids didn't want to leave because they were enjoying themselves. She had a wonderful time teaching, and could tell that the other staff members enjoyed it too. When the last child left, the crew gave each other high fives and praised the lord.

Alyssa walked triumphantly to Hazel's car while humming a hymn to herself. A few of the parents and children, whom she had never known personally before, waved to her as she crossed the parking lot.

"Well, look at you! I don't have to ask how your ministry fared. You're beaming from ear to ear," said Hazel, her face beaming with pride.

"We had a great time, and the children really enjoyed themselves. It was such an exhilarating experience! I only wish I had worked there earlier. When the board left, Deacon Barry smiled at me. You have no idea how good that made me feel."

"Oh, I have a pretty good idea; you're practically glowing. I've never seen you so happy."

When they got home, Alyssa quickly revised her plans for next Sunday's session before changing for work at the Pitway Inn. The manager had called the previous night and asked if she could cover a sick employee. Alyssa never turned down the opportunity to make more money for college.

The first room on Alyssa's cleaning list was filthy, but she wasn't bothered. She plowed through her work, ensuring the bathrooms were sanitized and the sleeping quarters were spotless. Though her body was sore from the work, the glow on her face lingered as she punched out to go home. The evening manager had never seen an employee so jubilant at the end of their shift!

The following Sunday, only Pastor Bryant continued to observe the children's ministry staff. The board was satisfied with what they saw and felt no need for further assessment. But Tim searched thoroughly for faults, and prepared to bring any short-comings he found to the deacon's attention. Although he found none, he continued to watch. He observed how the teachers inter-acted with the children, and soon, he began to focus on one member in particular. His eyes followed Alyssa, studying everything she did or said. Soon, the pastor found himself appreciating how hard the teen worked and how well she had developed into a beautiful young woman.

At the end of the day, Tim's thoughts continued to dwell on Alyssa. He returned to the children's ministry the following Sun-day, observing as long as he could before retreating to the pulpit. The young teen remained on his mind day and night. His current partner noticed Tim wasn't as attentive as usual. The woman had no idea she no longer appealed to him, as Alyssa was the only one he thought of now.

Alyssa was shocked when she received a call from Pastor Bryant Sunday evening. He had heard of her search for employment and asked if she could meet him at his dealership tomorrow morning. When she told Hazel about the call, The older cousin thought it was very odd that the pastor hadn't spoken to Alyssa about the job at the church. The teen shrugged off Hazel's bad vibes and con-templated the type of work she could do at a car dealership. Being an introvert, Alyssa wondered if she could ever make a good sales-person, but needing as much funding as she could get her hands on for college, she decided to push her timidity aside and make the best effort she could to convince the pastor that she was up for any task.

The next morning, Alyssa vigorously brushed her straight, long brown hair, inherited from her father, until it shined. The makeup applied around her large grey eyes, resembling her mother's, made her appear older than her seventeen years. The previous night, she thought about what a good saleswoman should look like, so she decided to look as professional and confident as she could. Alyssa had one good blue skirt suit; she decided that it would have to do. Looking over her resume, she realized the only experience she had in sales was at the movie theater concession booth, which had been a temporary job. Alyssa hoped the pastor would be happy with the limited skills she had and give her a shot anyway. Looking in the bathroom mirror, she practiced smiling frequently because she figured that's what salespeople do.

"Good luck honey!" Hazel called out. Alyssa gave her a nervous smile as she walked out the door. She hopped into Hazel's aged Pontiac and headed for the Bryant Car dealership at the edge of Pitway's downtown area.

Alyssa spotted the pastor waiting outside as she drove into the lot. Smiling, he greeted the teen with a hug before giving her a tour of the establishment. Alyssa could not remember the pastor ever being so friendly.

"You see those shiny new cars over there? They were delivered yesterday. Let's go over and take a look." Tim ushered Alyssa over to a sleek new red Cadillac sedan. He motioned for her to sit in the driver's seat while he entered the passenger side. Bryant described all the car amenities in great detail, then he discussed the luxuriousness and cost of the fabric on the seats. Alyssa breathed in the new car scent. She had never sat in a new car before, much less such a luxurious vehicle. She assumed the pastor was demonstrating how to sell a car to a customer, so she made mental notes of the car's description. When he was done, Pastor Bryant led her into an office. Alyssa immediately noticed the title "Pastor" prominently displayed on the window. A large nameplate reading "Pastor Tim Bryant" sat on his desk, matching the one on the door.

They sat on his office sofa while Tim continued their conversation, but he wasn't talking about cars anymore. Instead, the pastor began describing his vast array of assets, how powerful and important the Bryant family was to the community of Pitway, and how they looked out for one another. He reminded Alyssa that his father, Matthew Bryant, had been the mayor of Pitway for over thirty years. Alyssa nodded occasionally to appear interested. Tim then discussed his bank accounts and his custom-built home, designed exactly to his taste. Alyssa supposed the pastor was describing how wealthy he'd become from selling cars, but she hoped he realized she could only work for him until she went away to college.

Finally, the pastor paused and sat closer. "Alyssa, I can tell by your expression that you have no idea where I'm going with this. You see, I've been watching you, and I can tell you're a true Pitway girl. You love this town like I do. I remember you volunteering for the town square clean-up program and other events. So, when I heard talk that you were planning to leave Pitway to go to college, and you're looking for extra work to save money, I thought to myself, 'How can I help this girl?' Now, I know you haven't had much luck in the family department, and neither has Hazel. I remember when Hazel's husband left her; then she had major financial troubles. No, nothing good has happened to your family. There's just one disaster after another. I mean, even your mother ran off and left you to fend for yourself. And now your only kin is one poor cousin.

"The Bryants, on the other hand, have had nothing but favor and blessings. We all have our own businesses, and everyone in town respects the Bryant name. Now, I have a plan that involves both of us. We have history here; our grandfathers were buried in Pitway, and this is where your parents lived before your father died in the military. The two of us, we have strong roots here. So many of Pitway's young people leave, not because they want to, *but because they need money to live, right? But you, you don't have to leave because everything you need is right here. Pitway needs its caring residents to stay home, not flee! It's easy to run away, but I'm telling you now, nothing out there is better than what you can get in this town. I know Pitway has seen many hardships with the town's current economy, but all that will change. After the Chamber of Commerce, which I'm a part of, voted against that huge mall being built on the edge of our town, my family, the Bryant family, decided that we will build our own mini mall. Together, we are going to make Pitway grow again. You see, we'll create jobs and make our town attractive to shoppers and tourists. We don't need outsiders making decisions for us.*

"Yep, there are big plans in the works, and I'm making you a part of that plan." To Alyssa's surprise, the pastor grasps her hand before continuing. "You see, I need someone who's dedicated and willing to do whatever's necessary to restore Pitway to something better than what it was before. I need someone by my side who cares for this town like I do; someone who's willing to put their personal wants aside and sacrifice for the greater good. Well, in all honesty you wouldn't be sacrificing a thing, sweetheart; you'd be living in luxury. Those pretty little fingers of yours will no longer scrub hotel toilets or scrape gum off grimy hotel furniture. You'd have someone to clean after you! That car I showed you a while ago? That would be my gift to you! All you would have to do is take care of our home and church duties. Do you understand what I'm saying darlin? I'm asking you to be a Bryant, I'm asking you to be my bride...."

Alyssa saw the pastor's lips moving as he continued to talk, but she couldn't hear a thing. Her ears started ringing after he said the word "bride." Suddenly, she couldn't breathe. The pastor watched incredulously as Alyssa bolted out of the office. She ran down the steps and continued running until she reached her vehicle. Once there, Alyssa leaned on the car, lowering her head until she caught her breath. The pastor followed behind her.

"Um... Alyssa? Girl, are you alright?"

She looked up to see the pastor squinting at her.

"This must be too much excitement for someone like you to take in at once. It's like winning the lottery, isn't it? Don't say anything now, I know you're overwhelmed. Go home and get some rest. I'll start working on the arrangements. Oh, and think about this: as my wife, you will no longer be a financial burden to your cousin. I know Hazel loves you and wouldn't want you to worry, but financially supporting a second person with her small salary must be burdensome for the old girl." Tim lowered his voice. "I probably shouldn't tell you this, but sometimes her loan payments are very late. So, I'm 100% certain she'd be relieved to see her hapless ward married to a successful man so she could stop struggling financially.

When Alyssa still did not respond, the pastor sighed. "Well, I'll let you go now to think it over," he said and hugged a stiff Alyssa, leaving one arm around her waist. "I was thinking we could marry as soon as possible. I only need your cousin's signature on some paperwork. If I can't get that, we'll marry on your eighteenth birthday. That's coming up soon, isn't it? Call me soon so we can get this thing started."

Still in shock, Alyssa could only nod before entering the vehicle.

"Tell you what," he continued, pointing at Alyssa's car. "After we marry, I'll junk this old rusted heap and give Hazel a brand-new car. Wouldn't that be something? You doing something good for her for a change. She'd love you for that, don't you think?"

Alyssa silently nodded again and turned the key in the ignition. She drove for a few minutes before pulling over to the side of the road. The panic attack had hit when the pastor said the word "bride." She knew the faster she got away from the source of the attack, the better she'd feel. Alyssa sat there for several minutes, practicing the breathing exercises she had learned in therapy.

Why me? Why not ask one of the single women closer to his age?

Then another thought crept in, and it made her stomach twist. *Have I been a burden to Cousin Hazel all these years?*

Alyssa thought of Hazel as her second mother and couldn't imagine life without her. She knew Hazel occasionally sent her payments late, but her cousin never complained about money. Now, she worried about Hazel's financial status.

When Alyssa pulled into the driveway, her cousin was waiting at the screen door. The questions began as soon as Alyssa stepped inside.

"So... how was it? Why do you look so pale? What kind of job did he offer you? Did he discuss your pay? Now, don't assume a Bryant will pay you fair wages. I've heard many stories of them shortchanging people. Well? Did he offer you a job?"

"N–nothing has been finalized." She made it a point to not meet her cousin's eyes. "He wants me to think it over before giving him an answer. Phew, I'm famished. I'm going to make some lunch."

"I've already made lunch for you, dear. Sit down. I'll warm it up now, then you can tell me everything."

Alyssa excused herself to change into comfortable clothing. She knew that if she told Hazel the truth, the tough senior would march over to the pastor's house and give him a piece of her mind. Under normal circumstances, Alyssa would have been fine with it. But something about the way the pastor spoke of Hazel's finances made her worry. When Alyssa returned to the kitchen, she tried to steer the conversation into any topic but pastor Bryant; but Hazel wasn't having it.

"Well, the job Pastor Bryant offered involves long hours," Alyssa began, skirting around the truth, "and he will give me a car if I take this job, but I won't be able to go to college."

"Oh no! That won't do. Of course, you told him a flat-out no, right?"

"I... I wanted to tell him that, but he said to think about it."

Hazel placed her hands on her hips. "Alyssa, I know you don't like it when I tell you this, but you must speak up more. There is nothing to think about. I don't care how great the job is—you're going to college! When I see the pastor, I'll tell him myself."

"Oh no, that's not necessary, Cousin Hazel. I promise to tell him soon."

The following day, Pastor Bryant sat in his office, discussing his upcoming nuptials with his banker cousin, Ed.

"Yep, Alyssa was so shocked when I asked her to marry me that she lost her voice. My proposal took her breath away! I guess for someone like that, it's a fantastic dream come true. When the most influential bachelor in town asks you to marry him, and you're promised a brand-new Cadillac, it'd be too overwhelming for any girl. She's come a long way from pinching pennies and scrubbing toilets."

Ed raised an eyebrow. "Now, Tim, don't jump the gun. Did you hear her say 'Yes, I'll marry you?'"

"Of course she'll say yes. What other options does a girl like that have? She comes from nothing. Her father's dead, and her trashy mother's gone. Marrying me will make her somebody. No one will think of her as an abandoned orphan anymore."

"Tim, when you marry, don't be mean to Alyssa like you were to Jennifer," said Ed, folding his arms. "You don't want two wives running away from you. No woman would touch you after that."

Pastor Bryant's expression darkened. "Why do you keep bringing that tramp's name into our conversations? Jennifer wasn't fit to be a wife; always whining about me not giving her any money. What did she need money for? I gave her a home, credit at the market, and took her shopping for clothing every Christmas. All I asked was for her to take care of my home and my needs. When she took off in my car, I could have kicked myself for putting her name on the pink slip. This time will be different. Everything stays in my name."

"Anyway," Tim continued with a shrug, "Alyssa is different. I've been watching her. She's a good, quiet girl. Wouldn't stand up to a mouse. This time, there are no meddling parents to talk her into leaving me. The only person who could stand in my way is Hazel, but she should know better than to mess with me. And if she doesn't sign the consent for us to marry soon, we'll marry when Alyssa turns eighteen. I checked her contact details in the ministry file, her birthday's coming up soon. Maybe we'll have the ceremony on her birthday! That ought to make her feel special, right? She'll live with the best single guy in town in a well-maintained home instead of that rundown hovel Hazel calls a house."

"And just what are you going to do about your... lady friends?" Ed inquired.

Tim shrugged. "Well, I'll still enjoy their company. Of course, I won't bring them to the house anymore; wouldn't look right for a married pastor. The parishioners will expect me to show my wife some respect."

"But shouldn't you get rid of them when you're married? What if Alyssa finds out you're messing around behind her back?"

"What can she do about it?" Tim smirked. "Alyssa has no family outside Pitway, unlike Jennifer. Where would she go? Her cousin can't stand in my way."

Ed smiled broadly, "My goodness, Tim. Seems like you've thought of everything. Wow, a Bryant wedding in the summer! We haven't had a wedding for some time. I'll have to buy a new suit, I guess."

Tim grinned. "You do that, Ed. And buy it soon."

Later in the week, Alyssa and Hazel drove to the town market. While Hazel checked the frozen foods aisle, Alyssa went to the produce section.

"Oh, my dear!" Alyssa heard a familiar voice call out. It was Lucy, a middle-aged church sister and one of Pastor Bryant's cousins. She was beaming as she approached. "I heard the wonderful news. You will make such a beautiful bride! You must come by the flower shop to pick out the arrangements you want. Do you have an idea of how many people will attend yet?"

"Uh... b–bride?" the teen stammered.

"Why, yes! Tim told the whole family about the great news. We all think you'll be a great addition to the Bryant family. And with Hazel being a school teacher, she can help you teach the children when you have them. Yes, you will be a great young addition to the family." It was so good to see you dear."

And with that, Lucy walked off, pushing her cart along. Hazel walked over to the produce aisle to find a stunned Alyssa with her mouth hanging open.

"Alyssa, what happened? You look like you have seen a ghost."

"Oh! Uh... n–n–nothing. I was just trying to remember something," she lied.

"Well, try not to wear that expression on your face. You looked like you were having a medical emergency."

After purchasing their groceries, Hazel and Alyssa stopped by the town gas station on their way home. Before Hazel could slide her credit card into the pump, James, the station owner and another cousin of the pastor, approached them.

"How are you doing there, Hazel?" asked the plump father of five.

"Hi, James. I'm doing well. How are Annie and the kids?"

"They are doing great. Hey, I just wanted to come and say hello to my new cousin-to-be! Everyone is so surprised to hear about Alyssa joining the family." Perplexed, Hazel tilted her head to the side and looked questioningly at James.

"New cousin? Joining the family? What do you mean?" she asked.

James walked up to the gas pump and inserted his own card. "This one's on me, Hazel." Then, he strolled over to the car's passenger side and tapped the glass until Alyssa rolled it down.

"Alyssa, just wanted you to know that we are so happy to have you join the family!"

Before she could respond, James stood up promptly, walked to the pump and extracted his card before the tank filled, and gave a quick nod. "Yep, that's a wedding present from the family and me," he said with a grin and disappeared into his shop.

Stunned, Hazel stood with her hand over her mouth until Alyssa quickly exited the car and placed a steadying hand on her arm.

"I-I can explain Hazel," she began. Still, no words came out of Hazel's mouth. Alyssa retrieved the credit card Hazel had dropped on the ground. "Let's go home where we can talk in private," she said, gently leading her cousin to the passenger side. She then quickly slipped into the driver's seat and was ready to pull off.

Before they could leave, Annie, Jame's wife, came out the station door and stood in front of the car.

"Now, Alyssa, I know you're not going to leave without saying hello. Lucy just told me she saw you in the market and that you're coming to the shop to discuss flower arrangements for the wedding. I want you to know that I'm available if you need help picking out your dress..."

"There will be no wedding!" Hazel shouted before Annie could finish. "We must go now, Annie. Please step aside."

Confused and stunned, Annie did as told, but frowned at Hazel as the car pulled away. While staring at Alyssa in the car, Hazel's voice returned to normal. "That's the 'job' you discussed?! Let me get this straight in my head. You went to his office for an interview, then our pastor offered marriage as a job; and you're considering it!?"

"No! No, I'm not marrying Pastor Bryant! I'm just figuring out how to turn him down without offending him. He told me to think about it. I never told him yes. But it looks like he already told his family that I agreed to marry him."

Hazel forced herself to speak calmly. "Alyssa, when we get home, you call that... man, and you tell him a flat-out no! You will not marry him!"

A few minutes later, they pulled into their garage. Alyssa began unloading the groceries, but Hazel took the grocery bag from her. "Alyssa, stop. Please make the call now. I'll bring the groceries in."

Alyssa did as she was told and called the dealership's phone number as soon as she stepped into the house. The phone rang several times, but the call wasn't picked up. She exhaled, relieved she didn't have to speak to him.

"So, what did he say?" asked Hazel, walking into the kitchen.

"He didn't pick up the phone. I'll call back tomorrow."

"Tomorrow may be too late. You know how this town gossips. The quicker you stop their tongues from wagging, the better."

"You think he will be offended if I leave a message on his answering machine saying that I don't want to marry him?"

"Under normal circumstances, yes, a man may be offended, but this is by no means a normal circumstance. So yes, please call him again and leave the message," said Hazel, worriedly.

Seeing her middle-aged guardian's expression made Alyssa fret. "Cousin Hazel," she started hesitantly, "why... why do you think Pastor Bryant asked me to marry him? I never looked at him that way. I mean, I was only looking for a job. I don't want to marry anyone."

Hazel sighed. "Well, it's been years since his wife ran off. All the women in Pitway knew she had good reason to run. The decent single women left here are smart enough to avoid him. I guess he figures a young girl like you wouldn't know his history. There's that, and you're young and pretty. That probably put you at the top of his list."

Alyssa shuddered. "I'm going to leave the message right now so he can take me off his list."

"Yes, please. Then he can leave you alone, and things can get back to normal."

Alyssa grabbed a notepad before walking to the phone. She wracked her brain for the kindest message she could leave so that the pastor wouldn't become upset.

Hello, Pastor Bryant.

This is Alyssa. I gave great thought to your offer of marriage. It's a generous offer, and any woman would be happy to accept it—but I don't want to get married. I'm certain you will find a better prospect than me.

Have a nice day.

She took a deep breath and called the dealership again. Still no answer. This time, she left the message.

When she hung up, she walked over to Hazel. "Well, it's done. I've left the message. We shouldn't have any more talk about it from now on."

Three days had passed since Alyssa left the message for the pastor, yet she never received a returned call. Alyssa was working the Saturday morning shift at the Pitway Inn, serving breakfast to the guests. The dining room was busy, with few empty tables. Many of the guests were reading brochures about activities in the Three Rivers area.

Two young men ate their breakfast at a table near the counter. One wore a zip-up Stanford University jersey. They were engrossed in conversation as one twirled a fancy Mustang keychain between his fingers.

With no colleges or universities near Pitway, students rarely passed through the Inn. Most local kids who went away to college never returned after graduating because no jobs were available. Though Alyssa yearned to know more about college life, she never got a chance to discuss it with a current or recent student.

The teen hovered close to the young men, trying to appear busy with something behind the counter. All the while, her ears were tuned into their conversation. Disappointingly, the stocky, dark-haired one only grumbled about not trusting his grandfather's nurse, while the taller blond complained about the employees at his job.

"Alyssa, Alyssa? Can I see you over here?" Tammy Bryant, her manager, asked loudly.

Tammy waved her over and then pulled Alyssa to the other side of the counter. "Alyssa, sweetheart, it might not be a good idea for you to be so close to those young men. If Pastor Bryant walked in and saw his fiancée so close to other men, he might get a little upset."

"I don't understand Ms. Bryant; I told pastor Bryant that I don't want to marry him. I'm going to college."

"Alyssa, hush your mouth. You shouldn't say such things so close to your wedding day."

"W–wedding day? I haven't planned a wedding day!"

"Of course you haven't, silly." Tammy chuckled. "We know you and your poor cousin don't have any money. Pastor Bryant and the family are handling all the arrangements. You don't have to worry about a thing."

Before Alyssa could respond, Tammy walked away.

The young men halted their conversation when they overheard Tammy and Alyssa's exchange.

"What is this place?" whispered the blond man.

His friend shook his head. "Wish I knew Stan. Didn't realize forced marriages were a thing in California," he whispered back.

Alyssa felt so embarrassed. She knew the men had heard her conversation. Now, she was filled with fear. Pastor Bryant never returned her call, but she was sure he would have listened to the message by now. She felt nauseous and slightly faint. Her heart began pounding, preparing for a panic attack.

"Miss, are you alright?" asked one of the young men, both were staring at her.

"Oh... um, I'm fine. Thank you for asking. Can I get you anything?" she replied as calmly as she could.

"Just the bill please, thank you." As they paid their bill, she overheard them discussing their plans to return to Los Angeles early Monday morning. Alyssa and Hazel were supposed to drive to her college in Los Angeles before Labor Day, but now she wished they could leave sooner.

The next day, on her way to the children's ministry room, Alyssa said good morning as she walked by a small gathering of senior church ladies who were deep in discussion. A few turned around and replied in kind. When one whisper congratulations, her head began to pound. It seemed everyone believed she was getting married to the pastor. Another woman asks her to come to her dress shop asap otherwise she won't have enough time to make alterations. Alyssa stopped and addressed them. "There's been a mistake, "I'm not marrying the pastor, and I don't know why he's telling people this lie."

Some of the ladies gasped. "Oh dear," one murmured, while the others shook their heads sadly.

"Alyssa dear," began one of the women, "the pastor is a man of God. He told everyone that the lord said he should marry you. I'm sure in time, you'll be happy you did; and it's not a good idea to tell people that the pastor lies."

"Ethel! Why would you say something like that? If she doesn't want to marry him, she shouldn't be forced to do so," said another.

The two women continued to argue with each other, but Alyssa hurried away to the children's ministry room. She was experiencing a full-blown panic attack; the worst she's had in years. Feeling light headed, Alyssa was forced to sit just to catch her breath. Her hands trembled as she messaged her temples in an attempt to stop her pounding migraine. The attack symptoms took over her body. But when she heard the children's voices coming her way, she stood and pasted a smile on her face before greeting them cheerfully.

Once she and the other staff had them all seated with a project, Alyssa took out an apple to eat, just to keep up her strength. She hadn't eaten a full meal since Tammy chastised her the previous day in the hotel dining room. From the corner of her eye, she noticed Sarah and the other teens glancing at her strangely during the session. After the ministry service ended and the last child had left, Sarah approached her.

"Hey, Alyssa… are the rumors true? People are saying you're marrying Pastor Bryant."

Alyssa sat down with her head in her hands. "I don't know why he's doing this to me. Last Sunday, he called me about a job offer, so I went to the dealership the next morning expecting an interview for a real job. When I got there, he showed me around, started talking about what a great family the Bryants are, and then he asked me to marry him! I ran out as fast as I could. I called him a few days later and politely said that I didn't want to get married, but the pastor and his family are telling everyone in town that we're getting married. He hasn't called me back or anything. Everywhere I go, people are congratulating me. I don't want to marry him. Honestly, I don't even like him! These past few days have been a nightmare. I haven't slept since this happened."

Sarah exhaled. "Oh my goodness, I'm so glad to hear you say that! I don't want you to marry him either. But… what are you going to do? These rumors are everywhere."

"I don't know what else to do. I'm getting nauseous just thinking about it. And why me? There are plenty of single women in the congregation who are closer to his age. What made him choose me?"

"Hmm… Well, he was watching you a lot when you interacted with the kids. Maybe the idea popped into his head then," said Sarah.

"I think he plans to pressure me into it. He hinted that Cousin Hazel doesn't make enough money to support me and that I'm a burden to her. I never thought about the money she spends on me. Is that bad?"

"No, that's not bad. Hazel takes care of you because she wants to, and you're family. Don't listen to anything he says anymore. It's hard to believe a pastor would say something like that. That's evil!"

Alyssa hung her head. "Sarah, I may have to leave the church. That would mean stepping away from the children's ministry, and I don't want to walk away from it. I love these kids and what we're doing for them, but this is too much for me."

"Don't worry. I'll take care of the ministry. You must sort this marriage thing out, and quickly."

Alyssa left the ministry room after cleaning up with the other teens. In the parking lot, Hazel watched as Alyssa walked to the car with her head held low.

"Alyssa, these wedding stories have gone too far, and I do not want you stressing over this," Hazel said firmly. "I'm going to drop you home, take care of some errands, and visit Pastor Bryant to stop this nonsense. Don't worry. Everything will be like it was before."

Alyssa sighed in relief. "That would be wonderful. I don't want to see Pastor Bryant anytime soon."

That afternoon, Hazel parked her shabby four-door Pontiac in front of the pastor's elaborate ranch home. Tim was wearing an expensive bathrobe when he opened the door.

"Well, well, well," he drawled with a huge smirk on his face. "I was expecting you at some point. Why don't you come in and have a seat?"

This wasn't the greeting Hazel expected. She knew Tim Bryant disliked her ever since she had thrown a party for former Pastor Darrell when he was removed from the church.

Tim offered her refreshments before launching into his speech. He explained how he had heard from the Lord while observing the children's ministry with the elders. He believed the Lord impressed upon him to help Alyssa and the town of Pitway by offering her his hand in marriage. He also said that both her and Alyssa's hardships had grieved him. To Hazel's horror, Tim began discussing how this union would be a great financial advantage for her. He brought up her late payment problems, and lack of finances; information he could have only obtained from his banker cousin, Ed. He finally ended his monologue by stating that if Hazel signed consent to their marriage, the wedding could happen that very week; then he would reward her by paying off her loan and buying her a better car.

Hazel was stunned and repulsed by his offer. She had little respect for Tim Bryant as a pastor before, but she had never dreamed he would stoop this low.

"Pastor, didn't you receive Alyssa's call? She said she does not want to get married."

"Oh, that." Tim waved his hand dismissively. "Alyssa's young. She doesn't understand what a great opportunity this would be for her. You, on the other hand, know this union would only improve her life. She may protest at first, but with your signed consent and no place else to go, she'll have no other option but to marry me. In time, she'll understand how beneficial this relationship will be."

"Let me see if I heard you correctly; you're going to pay off my loan if I force my seventeen-year-old cousin to marry you?"

"Oh, let's not forget the new car!" Tim said with a grin while studying Hazel's expression. "Let's not also forget what a great advantage this would be for Alyssa. She'd have money to do whatever she wanted. She'd be living in luxury! I'm certain that if her mother were here, she'd be ecstatic at the idea of her daughter marrying the most powerful man in Pitway, don't you think?"

"But Alyssa doesn't want to marry you."

Tim sucked his teeth in irritation. "Yes, I know she said that, but she only said it because she's afraid of leaving you. You must impress upon her how great this offer is. Look, we both know a pretty girl like Alyssa shouldn't be cleaning hotel bathrooms on her weekends. She should be out somewhere having fun, but she doesn't know any better. She only knows that she must help you out financially because of your... problems. Think about it, Hazel—why would she want to stay in that run down house of yours, working her fingers to the bone at seventeen? Any girl in her right mind would kill to live here. Look at this place." Tim gestured with his arms as he looked towards the ceiling. "Those expensive exposed beams are hand hewed. Come, look at my `state of the art' kitchen; this place is a woman's dream."

"...hey Timmy, what's taking you so long sweetie?" said a woman from somewhere in the back of the home. Upon hearing the request from his companion, Tim took Hazel by the elbow and ushered her towards the door. "Uh, I have a few guests in the back watching a game. Now you go on home and think about what I said. Think about what's best for you and Alyssa; and get back to me quickly because this offer is not going to last forever," And with that, he shoved Hazel out the door.

Outside, Hazel shook her head in disgust. She thought of what kind of man offers money for a guardian to betray their child while at the same time have a woman waiting for him in the bedroom. Disgusted, she climbed into her car, gripping the steering wheel with white-knuckled hands. Then she closed her eyes, took a deep breath, and whispered, "Lord God, I need your help with this situation. I don't want this man to marry my cousin."

Back home, Hazel opened the door to find Alyssa in tears.

"Alyssa, what's wrong? Why are you crying?"

"Cousin Hazel," Alyssa said through choked sobs, "please tell me you got through to the pastor. Please tell me he's calling the wedding off."

"Alyssa, please calm down. Wait, why aren't you at work?"

Trying to compose herself, Alyssa explained, "Today, Tammy spent the whole day telling the guests and staff about my upcoming wedding. I didn't say anything because I knew we'd argue if I did. One of the guests asked me why I looked so depressed if I was getting married."

She swallowed hard and continued. "I kept my voice low when I told her it's because I already told Pastor Bryant that I didn't want to marry him, but he's still spreading rumors and telling his family otherwise. Somehow, Tammy overheard my reply. Her face turned red, and she started arguing loudly with me. Alyssa wiped her eyes. "She said I shouldn't say bad things about the pastor. I argued that I was telling the truth. She was furious and started calling me names like 'ungrateful trash' and 'worthless.' It got so bad that I just left. Tammy screamed at me not to walk away from her, but I couldn't take it anymore. And now, I don't have a job." She clutched Hazel's hand. "Please tell me you have good news."

"Oh, you poor thing," said Hazel, pulling her into a tight embrace. "This whole wedding fiasco has gotten out of hand. I'm so sorry, Alyssa. I tried to reason with that womanizing idiot, but he wouldn't listen. Don't worry—you're going to college as planned. There's no way I'm letting the Bryants bully you into this marriage. We'll think of something."

Later that night when Alyssa laid in bed, all she could do was think and worry. She reflected on past events, knowing that when the Bryants teamed up to make something happen, they usually got their way. The Bryants were responsible for kicking Pastor Darrell out of the church, and now they've teamed up to force her into marriage. With her eighteenth birthday coming next weekend, Alyssa feared they'd force her as an adult to marry the pastor because Hazel won't give them her consent; she didn't have much time.

At 3 a.m., Alyssa pulled back the covers. The teen got on her knees and asked God to bless what she was about to do. Alyssa then crossed over to the window to look out at the familiar mountain range, hoping the memorized image would give her peace in the days to come.

"Have I not commanded you? Be strong and courageous. Do not be afraid; do not be discouraged, for the Lord your God will be with you wherever you go."

Joshua 1:9

Benjamin scanned the room one last time, ensuring they left nothing behind. Once again, he lingered at the window to take in the remarkable view of the mountain range. The inn's décor was dated and the food ordinary, but he'd stay at the Pitway Inn again just for this view.

Benjamin wished his grandfather had a view like this to lift his spirits. The summerhouse where his grandfather was recovering from a massive stroke was beautiful. The ranch home was so close to the Kaweah River that he could walk to the lake's edge to fish daily if he wanted. However, being wheelchair-bound meant his grandfather could only look at the river water from his deck. Now, the strong patriarch with whom he had lived during his teen years was feeble and morose. The stroke left him without the ability to walk or write. For someone who had built a thriving commercial real estate corporation from scratch, this was a death sentence.

"C'mon, Ben. What're you waiting around for?" quipped Stanley. His blonde best friend was holding the door open with one hand while rolling his suitcase out with the other.

"I'm coming. Why are you in such a rush? It's not like you're going to work today."

"No, I'm not working, but I have other plans."

Benjamin smirked. "You mean you have 'plans' with Rosemary."

"Yeah, so what? What's wrong with looking forward to spending time with my fiancée? Don't you look forward to seeing Gloria?"

"Of course I do, but I'm not running to her like a puppy. I call when I'm ready to see her; she calls when she's ready to see me. We're not glued at the hip."

Stanley rolled his eyes. "Ben, you should really stop taking relationship advice from your father."

"What's wrong with my father's advice?"

"Oh, let's see—he's been through two bitter divorces and countless short-term relationships. Listen, your dad's great at his construction business, but personal relationships are not his expertise. Cmon, let's just go," said Stanley.

They checked out of the hotel and headed for Benjamin's two-door Mustang convertible in the parking lot. Benjamin threw his suitcase along with all his fishing gear and outdoor equipment into the back seat.

"You can throw your things into the trunk," he said, sliding into the driver's seat. "I took up all the space here."

Benjamin reached down and released the lever to open the trunk, while Stanley headed for the rear of the vehicle. But the trunk hood didn't pop up as usual.

When Stanley pulled up the trunk hood, he immediately jumped back when he saw what was inside. "Stan, what's taking you so long? Remember, Rosemary is waiting." A few minutes passed before Stanley gently closed the trunk hood and rushed back to the passenger side with his case. Ben looked at his best friend incredulously as he jumped into the car and stuffed his suitcase under his legs. Benjamin frowned. "What are you doing that for? Why didn't you put your case in the...?"

Stanley interrupted Benjamin before he could complete his sentence. "Ben, please just drive!"

Benjamin stared at his friend who appeared pale, "what's wrong with you? You look like you've seen a ghost."

"Please Ben, I'll explain later. Just drive!"

Benjamin shrugged his shoulders and drove off as requested, all the while taking quick peeks at his white knuckled friend. He wondered what happened at the trunk.

Five minutes later, they passed the "You are now leaving the Town of Pitway" sign.

"Quick, pull over here," Stanely demanded.

Before Benjamin came to a complete stop, Stanley pushed his door open, ran to the trunk, and opened it. The hood blocked Benjamin's view, but his mouth fell open when he heard the sound of a female voice coming from the trunk. Seconds later, standing before him was the young waitress who served them at the inn. She appeared tired, with beads of perspiration on her forehead, and her hair was matted from stuffing herself inside the hot trunk.

"Ben, this is Alyssa. Ah...she needed to escape her town without anyone seeing her leave." Ben stared with his mouth open while looking back and forth between his best friend and the Inn girl.

Alyssa shifted uncomfortably. "Um, I'm sorry to put you in this situation. Please, I just need a lift to the next town, which is fifteen miles away. I'll hop on a coach bus from there."

While she spoke, Stanley removed most of Ben's gear from the back seat and placed it into the trunk so Alyssa could sit inside with her large army-green duffel bag. When Stanley settled back into the passenger seat, Benjamin drove off without a word. Stanley, however, decided to gather more information from their stowaway passenger.

"So, Alyssa, where do you plan to go? Will you travel to a family member?"

"No, I don't have any family outside Pitway. I have my acceptance letter to Mount Saint Mary's University. The dorms aren't open yet, but I'll find a YWCA and stay there until I move into my dorm room."

"Oh, we're going to Los Angeles too. We can drop you off there if you like," replied Stanley. Ben turned his head and stared sternly at Stanley.

"That would be great! Thank you again for helping me," Alyssa said, sighing with relief. She noticed the driver hadn't spoken a word since she entered the vehicle; thinking it was a sign that he was not on board with driving her all the way to the city, she quickly added, "but if you're not comfortable driving me that far, it's fine if you let me out at the next town."

"Nonsense, we're going there anyway," Stanley assured her.

Benjamin said nothing but drove past the next town and continued down the highway.

Alyssa fought hard to stay awake and alert. The men seemed nice, but they were strangers. However, staying up all evening and sweating in a hot car trunk for hours had drained her. She began to drift off by the time they passed Bakersfield, which was the halfway point to Los Angeles. Minutes later, the men heard light snoring from the back seat. Realizing Alyssa was sound asleep, Ben decided to question his friend.

"Stan," he whispered, "what do we do now?"

Stanley raised an eyebrow. "What do you mean, what do we do?"

"I mean, we can't just drop her off on a random street in Los Angeles. Look at her; she's a country girl. It'd be too dangerous."

"I know what you mean. That and other thoughts crossed my mind. But here's the real question, do you think she's over eighteen?" Stan whispered.

Ben took glances in the rearview mirror and sighed. "Oh no, are we transporting a minor over county lines? We could be prosecuted for kidnapping!"

"Take it easy. You might be getting worked up for nothing. Here's what we'll do; let's pull over at the next rest stop and ask her more questions, beginning with her age. If she's under eighteen, we'll give her bus fare money and leave her at the depot."

"I don't know, Stan." Benjamin frowned. "Something bad could happen to her afterwards. What then? We would be the last known adults seen with her."

"Well, we could drive her to Los Angeles as planned and give her money to stay at a hotel?"

"Hotels don't register minors. We must confirm she's over eighteen."

"Okay, you come up with a plan then," said Stanley.

Benjamin thought hard until an idea popped into his head. "I know what we should do, we'll take her to Rosemary's. She'll know how to handle the situation, and she can also help Alyssa find a safe place to stay."

Stanley nodded. "Sounds like a plan. I'd better call her first—you know, to make sure it's okay to bring the girl there."

A few minutes later, Benjamin drove into a large, crowded rest stop. The enormous parking lot was filled with acres of cars and eighteen-wheelers. Benjamin stopped in front of the rest stop entrance to let Stanley out so he could find a phone booth inside, and then he continued through the parking lot in search of an empty spot. When he finally found one a great distance away from the rest stop building, Benjamin looked into the back seat after parking and turning off the engine. The girl was sound asleep, so he reached back and gently tapped her arm; this made her jump and bang her head on the window.

"Sorry, I didn't mean to startle you. We stopped here for food and gas. I'll walk with you to the rest stop."

Alyssa looked around at the sea of parked vehicles and wondered when Stanley had left. She exited the convertible and threw the large army duffle bag over her shoulders.

"I could squeeze your bag in the trunk if you'd like," Benjamin suggested.

"Thanks, but I'll keep it with me," Alyssa replied. They walked several minutes before arriving at the busy rest stop entrance. The moment they entered, a strong blast of air-conditioned air chilled Alyssa's sweat-dampened dress.

"I need to use the restroom," she said, looking around. Not used to being in crowded areas, she had no idea how to find it.

Benjamin pointed to the public bathroom sign. "It's over there. Please wait at the entrance when you're done so that we can find you."

Alyssa thanked him and haphazardly navigated her way through the throngs of people walking in different directions. Benjamin watched her maneuver through the crowd until she made it to the entrance; he then searched the row of public telephones against the wall until he spotted Stanley. His friend hung up just as he arrived by his side.

"I have good news," Stanley started, "I told Rosemary the whole story. She's willing to let Alyssa stay with her for the week. But if she's under eighteen, we have to get Alyssa's parents' permission. What do you think?"

"Sounds good to me, if she's eighteen; if she isn't, would her parents agree to their daughter living with strangers so far away? Or, here's a worse scenario; what if her parents want their daughter to marry the pastor. You know, there's no minimum age for marriage in California. If a parent or guardian consents, you can marry a 12-year-old girl to a 50-year-old man and it would be perfectly legal."

"Whoa, that's unsettling. I had no idea our state allowed that. Let's hope they agree with what she's doing. If they don't, I can't allow her to stay at Rosemary's, especially if the authorities are looking for her. But I'd also hate to leave her alone in Los Angeles."

"I feel the same way. Why don't we first sit her down and calmly ask about her overall situation?" Benjamin suggested.

Stanley nodded. "Agreed."

Meanwhile, Alyssa had already washed and changed. The first thing she did after exiting the restroom was call Hazel to let her know that she was safe.

"Oh, my goodness, Alyssa, where are you?!"

"Are you sitting down, Cousin Hazel?"

"I don't like the sound of this... Yes, I'm seated."

"I'm halfway to Los Angeles. I got a lift from one of the guests early this morning."

"What? How in the world did you arrange that, and why didn't you tell me?"

"Sorry about not telling you. I'd only planned to do it last night. That argument with Tammy scared me so much that I couldn't sleep. All I could think of was finding a way out of Pitway before the Bryants made me marry the pastor. Sneaking away was the only solution I could come up with because if they saw you drive me out of town, they'd come after you. I hope you're not upset. This was the only way I could think of."

"That's not true; it's not the only way. I would never let anyone force you into marriage, and... oh my goodness, you're traveling with strangers! No, no, this isn't right, Alyssa. I need you to leave those people and come back home right now."

"Cousin Hazel, please understand, I don't feel safe at home."

The two continued to go back and forth in their discussion until both were in tears. When Alyssa spotted Benjamin and Stanley heading her way, she quickly wrapped up their conversation. "I have to go now; I love you, and I'll call again to let you know when I reach Los Angeles." She hung up the phone quickly before the men reached her. "I called my cousin Hazel; she's my guardian. She told me to stay safe and call back when I can." Alyssa wasn't used to lying, she hoped the men believed her.

"Oh, good. It's important that your family knows you're safe," said Stanley. "Maybe one of us should speak to your cousin next time. That way, we can reassure her that you're alright,"

Ben didn't know what to do. The lawyer in him wanted to ask tough questions to verify Alyssa wasn't lying to them; but he could tell that the girl had been crying, so he decided to let it go for now. "I'm starving," he said instead. "I think we should get something to eat. There's seating over there."

Stanley picked up Alyssa's duffel and grunted at the weight. "Wow, how are you carrying this thing around? It's so heavy."

"Oh, Cousin Hazel's always telling me that I'm stronger than I look. The bag's heavy because I ordered a few textbooks early to get a head start on my classes. Sounds silly, doesn't it?"

"That doesn't sound silly at all. It sounds smart. I believe you'll do well in college," said Stanley.

"Thank you," Alyssa replied. She hoped she'd be around Stanley and Benjamin long enough to have conversations about college life.

After the three sat down at a table, Benjamin began to casually ask questions. "Ahh, can you tell us why the people in your town want you to marry the pastor? Sorry, it's been on our minds since we saw you at the Inn."

Alyssa told them about the children's ministry; how she and the other teens kept it from closing, and how the pastor began to make her uncomfortable by watching her work. "The Bryants run Pitway, they have their hands in all the businesses, and the mayor is the pastor's father. I'd ask around church if anyone knew of jobs available for the summer because I'm still saving money for college. I received a call from the pastor, and he sounded like he was offering me a job. He told me to meet him at his car dealership. When I got there, he started off as if he was interviewing me, then next thing I know he was telling me how the town would benefit if I married him. Initially, he asked me to think it over. Then he told me that cousin Hazel was struggling financially because she was supporting me, and my marrying him would make her life better. I called him to say that I did not want to marry, but it seem he'd already told everyone in town that I was going to do it."

"When I went back to work, I had a terrible argument with his cousin Tammy, she's the manager you saw arguing with me before. She was upset because I told a customer that I wasn't getting married. The arguing got so bad that I quit my job yesterday. Anyway, I know my cousin would never consent to my marrying the pastor, but with my eighteenth birthday coming soon, I felt I had to leave before the Bryants force me into the marriage when I become an adult."

Benjamin and Stanley exchanged glances at the mention of her birth date.

"How did the people in your town react to the news of your wedding?" Stanley asked. "Did anyone ask why you would marry the pastor?"

"Everyone seemed happy about it, but even if they disagreed, they wouldn't show it. No one in Pitway dares to go against a Bryant."

"Are you certain your cousin Hazel approves of you leaving home this way?" Stanley asked.

Alyssa didn't like the question Stanley asked, so she decided to embellish her lie to make it more believable.

"Cousin Hazel wasn't happy in the beginning, but she came around in the end."

After their conversation, Benjamin bought food for them, and Alyssa thanked him for the meal. When they were finishing, he announced he was going to the restroom and signaled for Stanley to join him.

He began their conversation once they entered; "So, what do you think? Do you believe the story of her guardian agreeing with her running off?"

"I want to believe it; there's no way to check her story without turning around, and speaking directly to her cousin. What should we do if her cousin files a missing person report?" asked Stanley.

"As a lawyer, I'm taking a huge risk here. Kidnapping charges can get me disbarred." He sighed. "I don't know what to do or say if we're stopped and questioned by the police, but I do know one thing: I'm not taking her back to a forced marriage, no matter what."

"I agree with you there. When we get to Rosemary's, I'll tell her everything, then she can decide if she wants Alyssa to stay."

"Use hospitality one to another without grudging. As every man hath received the gift, even so minister the same one to another, as good stewards of the manifold grace of God."

1 Peter 4:9–10

Benjamin drove into the driveway of Rosemary's affluent Santa Monica home in the afternoon. Alyssa was hesitant about meeting Rosemary in the beginning. Everything about the house indicated that the residents were wealthy, and she wasn't certain how she'd be received. However, Rosemary turned out to be a pleasant surprise. Alyssa thought Stanley's fiancée was very down to earth in spite of how she lived. After introductions, the three friends described their first college semester to Alyssa. They went over their experiences and the courses that challenged them. Alyssa was eager to hear more, especially from Rosemary, who was still enrolled.

"What degree do you plan to pursue?" asked Rosemary.

"Social work," Alyssa replied.

"That's interesting. What made you choose that subject?"

"I've always wanted to help people, especially children. I received a great deal of help when I was a child, and I want to help other kids get through their problems."

"I like that. I'm working on my PhD in psychology. You never know, we may work together one day in the future."

"That would be nice," Alyssa said with a genuine smile.

They continued their discussion while drinking lemonade by

the pool. Alyssa didn't want to be rude to her new friends, but she decided it was time to cut into their conversation and ask for the phone directory to look up the YWCA. It was already after 3 p.m., and she didn't know what was ahead of her.

"Excuse me, Ben, Stanley: thank you so much for bringing me to Los Angeles, but I think I should get going now."

"Wait, I thought you were staying with me for the week?" said a confused Rosemary.

"Oh, Alyssa, I'm so sorry we forgot to tell you. Rosemary offered to let you stay with her for the week," Stanley replied.

Alyssa turned to Rosemary hesitantly. "Are you sure it's okay Rosemary?"

"Of course it's okay! I'm tired of being alone in this big house anyway. My parents are in Europe most of the time. Please, stay and keep me company."

"Oh, I'd love to! Thank you so much."

Later, when Stanley and Benjamin rose to leave, Benjamin touched Alyssa's shoulder to get her attention. She flinched again.

"Sorry, Benjamin. I don't know why I'm so jumpy. Thanks again for everything."

After the men said their goodbyes and let themselves out, Rosemary took Alyssa upstairs to a large bedroom with its own ensuite and a phone. Alyssa called Hazel, letting her know she had a safe place to stay for the week. Hearing that Alyssa was staying with another young woman seemed to calm her cousin down. That night, Alyssa took a long, relaxing shower and slept soundly for the first time since the proposal.

The next morning, Alyssa woke up feeling refreshed and full of energy. She dressed in shorts and a tee and then checked for Rosemary, but her new friend was still asleep. Her restlessness prompted her to go for a walk and discover the neighborhood. She left a note in the kitchen before stepping outside.

Except for passing cars, there was little activity outside at 6:30 a.m. Alyssa walked several blocks past many wealthy Santa Monica homes. She took mental notes of the street names to familiarize herself with the area. After turning the corner onto a major thoroughfare, she trekked across a busy road where she caught a glimpse of the ocean in the distance.

Alyssa could count on one hand the number of times she'd been to a beach, so before she realized it, her feet headed in that direction. The downhill walk was long but worth it. The street was lined with beautifully blooming jacaranda trees. Their canopies provided just the right amount of shade as her feet crushed mounds of lavender colored petals discarded from the tree's enormous flower clusters.

When she reached the almost empty beach, Alyssa removed her shoes and sat on the sand with her legs folded. She positioned herself as close to the water as she could without getting wet. Closing her eyes, she listened to the waves lapping at the edge of the beach, momentarily forgetting her problems. Some time passed before she heard the voices of other beach visitors. Alyssa snapped out of her meditative state and looked around to find several groups of people on the beach. She stood, brushed the sand off, and started the uphill trek back to Rosemary's house.

The walk back was taking more time. More people were on the street walking towards the beach. Alyssa navigated her path around throngs of families holding beach towels and pushing baby carriages. The roads were now congested with commuters struggling to get to work on time. As she reached Rosemary's home, Alyssa thought it strange that Ben's mustang parked outside.

"There she is!" said Benjamin with a sigh of relief as Alyssa walked through the door. "I was going to grab Stan out of his meeting so we could start a search for you."

"Oh, my goodness! Alyssa, where have you been? I was worried about you!" said Rosemary.

Alyssa looked at their expressions and saw that they were genuinely concerned about her. "I'm so sorry. I didn't mean to worry you guys. I needed to take a walk, so I left a note. I'm very sorry. I won't do it again."

"Don't be silly! You can certainly go for walks. I read the note, but you were gone for hours. The security camera registered the door opening at 6:30. I was afraid you got lost since you're not familiar with the area. Why don't you freshen up, and we'll go out for breakfast?"

"Oh, please don't go to any trouble for me. I was going to change and start searching the newspaper classified ads for a job."

"Alyssa, there's plenty of time for that. We'll go get breakfast first, and then I'll drive you around your college campus so you can familiarize yourself with the area."

"That sounds great! I'll get ready quickly."

Benjamin and Rosemary waited until Alyssa went upstairs before speaking. "Whoa, crisis averted; she certainly has a sense of adventure. Not at all what you'd expect from a meek country girl." said Benjamin.

Rosemary chuckled. "You think Alyssa's meek? A meek person wouldn't climb into the trunk of a stranger's car. That's something I'd never have the guts to do."

"I disagree. You didn't see the argument she had with her manager at the Inn. Stan and I thought she was going to pass out from fear. There's no way she'd survive in this city with that mindset. But, no worries, we have a plan. Starting tonight, we'll take her wherever we go. She must adjust and toughen up; otherwise, she'll end up as someone's victim. Tonight, let's go out to dinner, then Stan can bring her to his Bible study class with you tomorrow."

"Oh? Does that mean you'll be attending as well?" Rosemary asked.

"No, that's not necessary. Besides, you know how I feel about those places."

"What I do know is that it would be great for you to come, even if it's just once, to Stanley's bible study sessions; he'd really enjoy knowing his best friend was there."

"Stan and I have an understanding. He knows how I feel about churches, so he doesn't expect me to ever attend."

"All the more reason for you to come and support him. You promised me that you'd try at least once."

"Yes, I did promise. But that day is not tomorrow." Benjamin checked his watch. "Well, I'd better get back to work. It's been rough trying to oversee grandad's company until he's back on his feet, and still please my father; feels like I'm being pulled in two directions."

"You know, your life would be much easier if you just told your father how you felt."

"He knows I have no love for the construction business, but my father's a master at manipulating people to do things his way. His latest move was hinting that my inheritance was tied to the company. If I walk away, I lose everything."

"That's coldhearted."

"Yeah, that's my dad. Anyway, I'd better get back. See you tonight."

Later that morning, Alyssa and Rosemary enjoyed brunch before Rosemary drove through various areas within the city to familiarize Alyssa with the different neighborhoods. Seeing her college campus for the first time gave Alyssa mixed feelings. Hazel was equally excited about bringing her to the university, and getting Alyssa settled in her dorm. Her cousin was to stay close by in a hotel for a few days; they planned to explore the city together. Running away meant they couldn't share that experience together.

"What's wrong, Alyssa?" asked Rosemary. "You look down."

"It's nothing, really. Seeing my school made me think about my cousin. She wanted to be here with me when I moved into my dorm. I didn't think about that when I left. Now I really regret leaving without saying goodbye."

"Don't worry. You'll see her again. I'm certain things in your hometown will change, and you'll be able to visit safely. But right now, you should be excited. You're starting college in a few weeks," Rosemary said cheerfully.

"You're right. I should stop sulking and focus on preparing for college. Tomorrow, I'll leave early in the morning to find a job and a place to stay next week."

"Oh no, I'm not letting you leave. I insist you stay until you move into your dorm."

"I can't ask you to do that. You've done so much for me already. Besides, aren't your parents coming home soon? What will they think about a stranger in their home?"

"I won't take no for an answer. As for my parents, they're hardly here when they're in town. They're always working, while I'm usually alone in this large house. You must stay and keep me company."

"Well, if you're sure it's not a problem, I'd love to stay. Thank you. This helps a lot."

That evening, they joined Benjamin, his girlfriend Gloria, and Stanley for dinner. Since Alyssa didn't bring many dresses, Rosemary went through her closet and lent her a few from her wardrobe, though they were a bit larger than her size.

As the group conversed, Alyssa got to know her new friends better. Stanley works in his father's finance company; his family belongs to a church where Stanley teaches bible study on Tuesday evenings. Rosemary's parents were lawyers who traveled frequently. As a child, Rosemary was often left behind with nannies. Benjamin's father owned a commercial construction company and expected Benjamin to take over one day, despite his son's preference to work at his grandfather's commercial real estate firm as a property lawyer. Gloria is the daughter of Ben's father's business friend. Both fathers had encouraged the two to date.

Somehow, the conversation shifted to parents, so Gloria asked Alyssa about her mother and father.

"My father was in the army. He was killed during a mission when I was seven," Alyssa replied.

"Oh, I'm sorry to hear that. So, it's just you and your mother then?" Gloria asked.

Alyssa hesitated. "No. Both of my parents are gone. I lived with my cousin."

Gloria frowned. "Ben told me about the situation you're in. I don't understand how your pastor can force you into marriage. I mean, am I missing something? Were you in one of those religious cults...?"

Stanley cut Gloria's conversation short, "Why don't we talk about something else?" "By the way, when do you turn eighteen, Alyssa?"

"This Saturday," she replied.

"Saturday, that's only five days away! Why didn't you tell me, we have to do something, "said Rosemary.

"No, Rosemary. You've done so much already, and you hardly know me."

"I agree," Gloria muttered under her breath to Ben. Then, she turned back to Alyssa. "So, didn't you have a boyfriend or a guy friend who could have stood up to this preacher for you?"

"No. I worked a lot and never had time for dating."

"What? That's crazy! You're almost eighteen and you've never dated? Don't you want to have a serious relationship or marry one day?" Gloria continued.

"Not really. I want to go to college and spend as much time as possible working to excel in my field."

"That sounds so silly. Why wouldn't you want to be with someone?" Gloria pressed.

"Well, relationships come with risks. You never know what's going to happen. My cousin almost lost her house after her husband left her. It was built by our great-grandfather. She had no mortgage, but her husband took a loan against it and left her drowning in debt. And my mother had a boyfriend who... well, I'll just say he was always mean to both of us. After the factory closed in my town, people were without work. Many of the men started drinking and became mean to their families; so, I thought a lot about not getting into a relationship." Everyone at the table fell silent after Alyssa's last statement until Stanley changed the subject to a lighter topic.

The couples sipped their cocktails, telling jokes, while Alyssa looked around at all the affluent guests in the upscale restaurant, and felt out of place. She didn't think she belonged and was intruding on her friends' dates.

"Excuse me, I'm going to get some air." Alyssa quickly got up and walked outside. She wandered down the busy street until she found what she was looking for, a telephone booth. Though she was comfortable in Rosemary's lavish home, not being with her cousin was tougher than she thought. Hearing Hazel's voice again brought her some comfort. Alyssa had missed sharing conversations and meals with the only person she believed truly caried about her. It's only been a day since Alyssa left home. So much had happened, and although she appreciated her new friends inviting her into their lives, she had never felt so alone. She longed to return to Hazel; however, just thinking about the confrontations she would have with the Bryants made her nauseous.

Before hanging up, Hazel and Alyssa prayed together. As she stepped out of the booth, Alyssa stared at the early sunset. She was close enough to the beach to see the ocean waves. For a moment, she considered walking in that direction until the water washed over her feet and ankles. But she snapped out of her daydream when she heard familiar voices calling her name. Her dinner party had exited the restaurant and was looking around, most likely for her.

Alyssa waved at the group until they saw her and responded in kind; then she proceeded to walk in their direction, remembering to smile before reaching the group so Rosemary wouldn't worry about her. Despite her homesickness, it was nice to have new friends who cared about her. She knew only God could have given her the courage to sneak into that trunk last night.

SEVEN

"A friend loves at all times, and a brother is born for adversity."

Proverbs 17:17

S everal days later, Alyssa called out to Rosemary before she closed the front door. She wanted to share the good news; she got the first job she applied for! It was a waitress position at a restaurant within short walking distance from her college. Alyssa was sure it wouldn't have happened without Stanley and Rosemary's help. Stanley and his Bible study group had prayed for her success, and last night, Rosemary had proofed and typed up Alyssa's resume into her word processor. She saved it on a floppy disk and printed several copies for Alyssa to hand out during her interviews.

Rosemary wasn't downstairs, so she called Stanley at his job to give him the good news, and thank him for the prayers. He was happy for her and promised to let Benjamin know. Hanging up, Alyssa thought of Cousin Hazel. She missed telling her cousin about her accomplishments and hearing her congratulations. Her big eighteenth birthday party was supposed to happen today. Hazel had planned to bake her favorite cake; lemon chiffon. It was going to be a special combination birthday and going away to college party. Sarah and her other friends were coming over; but Pastor Bryant ruined everything.

"Rosemary?" she called again. But there was no answer.

"Rosemary?" Alyssa continued searching the upper floor of her friend's home, but there was no reply. The security chime, indicating that someone had just entered the house. Alyssa immediately ran down, expecting her friend, but it was Rosemary's parents who entered. She'd briefly met them the previous day. The middle-aged couple was cordial but always busy and on the go. Neither showed interested in holding a conversation. She excused herself and retreated to her room; sulking because there was no one around to share her birthday with.

Sighing, Alyssa decided to take a nap. It had been a busy day. She had woken up early to make necessary purchases for her dorm before attending a second interview in the late morning. When the manager of the upscale restaurant had asked her to come in again, Alyssa assumed it was just to fill out paperwork, but instead, she was introduced to the staff and provided with lengthy training before the manager told her she was hired. The posh restaurant was a much different setting than the breakfast room she worked at the Inn. Some of the mandatory procedures were difficult to remember, but she was assured that it'd come to her in the end. Two hours later, she was on her way back to Rosemary's house.

The nap gave her the strength she needed. When she woke up, she decided to walk to her favorite place. This time, she wore the swimsuit Rosemary had bought for her to use in the home pool. She added shorts and a tee over the suit and left the usual note. Alyssa walked half way down the street when a familiar car pulled up beside her.

"Hey, just where do you think you're going?" Rosemary called out.

"Rosemary? I was looking all over for you. Guess what? I got the job!"

"That's wonderful! I knew you'd get it."

"I couldn't have done it without your help. You, Stan, and Ben have been such a huge support."

"Oh, stop before you make me cry," Rosemary said, waving a hand dramatically. "By the way... Happy Birthday!" She stepped out of the car and wrapped Alyssa in a huge hug. "Now get in."

Alyssa grinned. "Thanks, Rosemary! I'm so happy you remembered!"

"Of course I remembered. And if I hadn't, Ben and Stanley would've reminded me; mainly to tell me that I no longer have a minor living under my roof. They were really concerned about keeping you safe until you were an adult. Anyway, we must leave now."

"Really, they were worried about me?"

"Yes, but not in the way you think. Ben was afraid to turn you loose in Los Angeles. He said something bad always happens to small town girls in LA, and the authorities would question them as the last adults seen with you. Oh, and he said it would be all over for him because, he could never explain to the police why your DNA was found in his trunk. "

Alyssa burst into uncontrollable laughter, making Rosemary laugh too.

"Ben has a wild imagination," Alyssa said between giggles. "By the way, I thought we were headed back to the house; where are we going?"

"It's a surprise," Rosemary replied as she drove towards the avenue.

"I should change first. I'm wearing shorts over my bathing suit."

"You don't need to change. Come as you are."

"Well, ok." Rosemary drove close to the shoreline for about ten minutes before turning into a driveway of a huge Beach House.

"Whose home is this?" Alyssa asked.

"It's Ben's grandfather's house. Ben lives here most of the time: sometimes he stays with his dad." The women entered the spacious quiet home, with Rosemary leading Alyssa by the arm. They stepped onto the back patio when suddenly Stanley and Benjamin shouted, "surprise!" Stunned, Alyssa looked around at the gift boxes, balloons and cake with her name on it. She couldn't understand why she began crying. Her friends were startled.

Alyssa wiped her tears," I'm sorry for crying. It's just, you guys have been so nice. You hardly know me, but you remembered my birthday; Thank you," she said as she hugged each of her new friends. As they made their way to the patio table, Alyssa heard the waves before the beach came into view. The others assembled around a balloon centerpiece on the outdoor patio table while their young friend continued walking until she saw the wave's crashing on the sand.

"It's a pity we couldn't package the beach as a gift for you," said Benjamin, stepping up beside her.

Alyssa laughed. "Ben, you're so lucky to live on the beach. You can swim any time you want!"

He shrugged. "Eh, it's okay. I prefer to swim in my pool."

"The beach is so much better. You can listen to the waves all day long."

Benjamin leaned in slightly and whispered. "Listen, the beach can wait. Rosemary and the rest of us are looking forward to celebrating your eighteenth birthday. Aren't you excited?"

Alyssa turned and saw her cheerful new friends watching and waiting for her to join them. She quickly walked to the table and sat next to Rosemary, thanking them all for planning the celebration.

The four friends dug into grilled hamburgers and hot dogs. When it was time for cake, Rosemary lit the candles, and her three new friends sang "Happy Birthday" to her. Alyssa had a great time, so much so that she forgot about being homesick and thought of how blessed she was to meet these people when she needed them most.

After the party, Alyssa asked Benjamin if she could use the phone to call her cousin. She loved hearing Hazel's voice whenever she could. When her cousin wished her a happy birthday, Alyssa asked if she could come visit Pitway, just for a day or two. Hazel surprised her when she said that Alyssa leaving for college sooner rather than later was the best decision. And when Alyssa asked how she was doing, Hazel's only reply was that all was well in Pitway. Hazel's assurances that she was doing well gave Alyssa some peace about leaving the way she did, but she still missed being home.

Defend the weak and the fatherless; uphold the cause of the poor and oppressed. Rescue the weak and needy; deliver them from the hand of the wicked.

Psalm 82:3-4

But all was not well in Pitway. Hazel knew lying to Alyssa was the best thing she could do for the young freshman. If Alyssa knew what was happening, she would surely give up her education and return for Hazel's sake, and that would be the worst thing to do.

Hazel's problems began the very day Alyssa ran away. While worrying about the young girl hitching a ride with strangers to the city, she heard a loud, persistent knock on her front door. When she pulled the door open, a tall, stout, red-faced Tammy entered her home without waiting to be invited in.

"Where is Alyssa?! Why didn't she come to work today like she was supposed to?"

"Alyssa's not home. Didn't she quit her job?" Hazel replied.

"What do you mean she's not home? Is she working somewhere else? No, she couldn't have found another job that fast," Tammy said, reasoning with herself. "Wherever she's at, you tell that girl if she doesn't show up for work tomorrow, she'll lose her job permanently. I'll make sure the Pitway Inn never hires her again. And another thing, you'd better talk some sense into your cousin and make her stop humiliating Tim by telling people she's not getting married. She must be the most ungrateful orphan girl I've ever known." Tammy continued her tirade, berating every aspect of Alyssa's character in front of Hazel.

Hazel never really liked Tammy. Normally, she'd argue back and defend Alyssa, but she held her tongue because she was financially dependent on the work she received from the Inn. Hazel was amazed at how fervent the Inn manager was about Pastor Tim marrying Alyssa. The nonstop rantings ended with Tammy stating how Alyssa should be grateful that a good and successful man like the pastor chose to marry someone with nothing to offer, like her. Instead, she's disrespecting his request and was not showing any appreciation for the blessed offer before her.

After the uninvited guest stormed out, Hazel closed the door and wiped Tammy's spittle off her cheek. She thought Tammy's rant was the conclusion of the Bryant search. Unfortunately for Hazel, she had to endure angry Bryant family members all week. The pastor himself called on Tuesday morning, asking for Alyssa. Hazel gave him the same vague reply she gave Tammy. She received an angry response with words she believed should never leave a pastor's mouth.

When Hazel pulled into the gas station on Tuesday, she was met with angry stares from Annie and James instead of their usual gracious greeting. The couple whispered amongst themselves while Annie pointed angrily at Hazel before James approached the car, and demanded the return of his ten-dollars' worth of gasoline wedding gift.

At Pitway Grocery, Margie Bryant, the store manager, approached Hazel and asked where Alyssa was. This time, Hazel decided to tell the full truth. The reply she received was frightening.

"How could you allow that to happen?! You are her guardian. You should have called Tim immediately when you found out Alyssa had left town!" Margie shook her head disapprovingly. "Tim will be very cross with you."

The finale, however, happened on Thursday. As Hazel prepared to leave for work in the morning, she heard relentless pounding on her door. She opened it to find Pastor Bryant.

"Where is she?" was all he said before pushing Hazel's door open before she could invite him in.

"I'm telling you, no one has seen Alyssa this week," said Annie. Tim looked around Hazel before walking past her into the house.

His cousin Annie walked in right behind him and haughtily looked around at the well-worn living room furniture, before smirking. "Better watch where you sit Tim, this place is a dump. Then, turning to Haze, she sneered, "Alyssa hasn't been seen by anyone this week; where is she hiding?" Annie demanded.

Hazel was fed up. "Alyssa's not hiding anywhere; she's away at college! Now that I've answered your question, can you please leave so I can get to work on time?" she said exasperatedly.

Tim was enraged. He stepped close to Hazel's face. "You mean to tell me you let her leave town knowing that she was to marry me?"

"Pastor," Hazel began with her hands on her hips, "Alyssa never agreed to marry you. She told you that on the phone. She'd already planned for college, but even if she wasn't going to college, she wasn't going to marry you!"

"You see that, Tim? That's exactly what she said to me and James at the station. She told us, 'There will be no wedding!' She said it just like that. This is Hazel's doing. She sent Alyssa away. That girl wouldn't jump without Hazel telling her to do so."

Tim looked directly at Hazel and replied, "Well, if she knows what's good for her, she'd better bring Alyssa back." With that said, he stormed out of Hazel's living room with Annie on his heels. Hazel was happy to see them leave, but she sensed this wouldn't be the end of Tim's threats.

Previously, Hazel thought Alyssa's fear of the Bryants was caused by her anxiety and timidity. Now, she understood why Alyssa believed leaving town was her only option. She realized just how unhinged the Bryants were. Not only were they a group of self-serving egomaniacs, notorious for getting their way, but they were also a dangerous group of people.

As months passed, the townspeople believed the story Pastor Bryant spread to save face. He'd boldly claimed that Hazel had forbidden Alyssa from marrying him and that she had sent her away. However, while the pastor saw himself as the victim, the Pitway residents felt differently. Many who had heard of the pending nuptials felt relieved when it did not take place. Given what they knew of the pastor's previous marriage, none of them wanted to see the mild-mannered teen connected with Tim Bryant in any way.

Out of fear, Hazel did nothing to challenge the rumors, and she avoided as many of the Bryant-controlled establishments in town as she could; including Pitway Baptist, opting to travel to surrounding towns for her needs. Some Pitway Baptist members called to see how she was getting along, but because they too feared the wrath of the Bryants, they shied away from greeting her in public. It was emotionally a difficult time for Hazel, living without Alyssa and enduring the silence of fellow townspeople.

Though she wanted her cousin close, Hazel pleaded with Alyssa not to return for the Christmas break because she feared the Bryant family members would plot some type of ambush. The Bryants continued to show fervent animosity towards Hazel whenever their paths crossed, and Hazel didn't believe Alyssa could handle the continued pressure from the crazed family without spiraling back into frequent anxiety attacks. And because Tim and Annie told Tammy to reduce Hazel's hours at the Inn until she brought Alyssa back, the senior couldn't afford a trip to Los Angeles; her money was stretched thin.

During their phone conversations, Hazel fabricated a petty excuse for not coming to Los Angeles, for Alyssa's sake. She pretended to have friends coming over for the holiday, but it was the first Christmas Hazel planned to spend alone. The thought of it lowered her spirits, and hearing the disappointment in Alyssa's voice made her feel even worse.

The morning after Christmas, a knock at the door startled Hazel. It had been so long since anyone had visited Hazel that, at first, she thought the knocking sound was from the television she had left on all day. Seeing Alyssa's friend Sarah on the other side of the door was a pleasant surprise.

"Oh my, Sarah! It's so nice to see you! Please come in. I was just finishing breakfast. Would you like some flapjacks?"

Sarah smiled politely. "Good morning, Mrs. Cummings. Thank you, but no. I'm still full from Christmas dinner last night. I stopped by to bring you a jar of homemade strawberry jam that my mom made."

"Oh, I love jam. Please tell Sonia I said thank you. How are your parents?"

"They're fine. We had family over, so my mom's been cooking non-stop. How have you been? I haven't seen you at church in a while. But to be honest, I don't leave the children's ministry building, and my parents don't attend anymore."

"I know. I haven't seen many of my friends after I stopped attending Pitway Baptist," Hazel said sadly.

"Well... you're not the only person who's left Pitway Baptist. Some of the parents who used to bring their kids to the children's ministry haven't returned after Alyssa left. Other members are attending churches in nearby towns."

Hazel nodded, unsure of what to say.

Sarah hesitated before proceeding. "Umm... Mrs. Cummings, I wanted to check on something I heard. People are saying the Bryants cut your job hours at the Inn because Alyssa didn't marry the pastor. Is that true?"

All the color drained from Hazel's face. "Sarah, you must promise me something before I answer that question. Promise me you won't tell Alyssa any of this."

"But Mrs. Cummings, maybe Alyssa can speak to the Bryants and make them stop."

"No! I don't want her anywhere near those crazy people. My worst nightmare is her coming back here and being forced into marrying the pastor."

"But how can they force her if she says no?"

Hazel shook her head. "You haven't experienced the Bryants like we have. They don't take no for an answer. And Alyssa... she's too meek to stand up to them." Her voice hardened. "No matter what happens, you cannot tell her any of this."

Sarah nodded in agreement, and sat down when Hazel pulled out a chair for her.

Hazel exhaled and began to tell Sarah everything the Bryant's had been up to. Though Sarah believed her friend needed to know how Hazel was being treated, Hazel was adamant that Alyssa was safer not knowing. In the end, she made Sarah promise not to reveal anything to Alyssa.

After Alyssa's young friend left, a low-spirited Hazel remembered the worst event in her young cousin's life, the one that brought on Alyssa's anxiety problems.

Their prayers were answered, Linda had survived the life risking surgery that removed her ruptured spleen, which was caused by multiple beatings she received from her boyfriend Jason. The day before Linda was set to be discharged, she spoke to Alyssa on the phone. Linda promised her daughter that things would be different this time. She swore she'd never bring Jason back into their lives again.

Before going to the hospital to pick up her mother, Alyssa and cousin Hazel cleaned the mess left behind at the house when Linda and Jason had their major fight. Hazel swept and vacuumed the bits of broken glass left on the carpeted living room floor while Alyssa cleaned the kitchen. Then, Hazel cleaned Linda's bedroom before they left. On the way to the hospital, Alyssa made Hazel stop at the flower shop so she could buy her mother a single rose.

As soon as they pulled up at the hospital, Alyssa dashed out of the passenger seat even before Hazel could turn off the ignition. The ten-year-old ran to the elevator bank on the other side of the waiting area because she knew from her many past visits that it was never busy. With the rose in her hand, she dodged a parked gurney and a group of nurses before entering the hospital room where her mother was recovering.

But something was wrong, her mother wasn't there and neither were her things. A strange lady rested in her mother's former bed. The woman looked at her expectantly.

"Do you know where my mom is?" Alyssa asked.

The elderly woman shook her head and buzzed for the nurse. A nurse arrived quickly, one Alyssa recognized.

"Do you know where my mom is?" she asked again.

The nurse seemed at a loss for words. "Why don't you come with me, sweetie? Your mother is not in this room." She took Alyssa by the hand and escorted her to a seat behind the nurse's station. "Wait here. I'll be right back." A few minutes later, a different woman approached her; she wasn't wearing a uniform.

"Hello dear. My name is Mrs. Jones. What's your name?"

Alyssa looked up at the woman and the nurse standing beside her. She sensed something was wrong because neither of them had answered her question about her mother. Just then, Hazel stepped off the elevator and approached the nurse's station. She didn't understand why Alyssa was sitting there instead of in the room with Linda.

The nurse spoke first. "Hello," she said, relieved that the little girl wasn't there alone. "This is her relative, Mrs. Cummings," she told Mrs. Jones.

"Ah... is something wrong with my cousin? We thought she

was being discharged today," Hazel said, trying to gauge the expressions on the women's faces.

"Hello, I'm happy that you're here. My name is Mrs. Jones. Please come with me," said the woman.

Alyssa stood up to follow them, but the lady turned around and asked her to wait until they returned. It wasn't until Hazel entered the office and saw Mrs. Jones's title on the door that she realized the woman was a social worker.

"I don't understand what's happening. Why can't I see my cousin?" asked Hazel.

"I'm sorry to say this, but your cousin isn't here."

Hazel gasped, believing that Linda had somehow succumbed to her wounds. But then why would the hospital discharge her?

As if reading Hazel's mind, the social worker continued. "I was told that Mrs. Holt left a few hours ago with a man she referred to as Jason."

Hazel's face turned red. Linda had done many questionable things since the death of her husband, and each time, Hazel had taken pity on her cousin. But abandoning Alyssa for the man who had almost beat her to death? She could never forgive that. With tears in her eyes, she asked Mrs. Jones, "How am I going to tell that little girl her mother abandoned her?"

The social worker handed Hazel some tissues to dry her eyes. "Leave everything to me, Mrs. Cummings. I'll break it to the child gently." Mrs. Jones retrieved a document from one of her files. "In the meantime, I need you to fill out this form. I need the child's and the parent's full name." The social worker stopped, looked at the clock, and frowned. "I must call child services now before it's too late for them to transport the girl to the facility."

Mrs. Jones's last statement snapped Hazel out of her anguished state. "No! No one is taking Alyssa! She lives with me. She's always lived with me. That's the arrangement I made with her mother," she lied. "Whenever Linda goes away, Alyssa stays with me." Hazel was willing to say anything to prevent Alyssa from experiencing even one day in the child protective services system.

Mrs. Jones looked skeptical. "So, Mrs. Holt has done this before?"

"No, not exactly. Well, this is the first time she forgot to tell us that Jason was picking her up."

"Hmm... This Jason, is he the same man who abuses her? I have a police report here, it says Mrs. Holt refused to press charges."

Hazel stood up. "You'll have to ask Linda about that. I'm going to take Alyssa home now. When Linda calls, I'll tell her to call you." She turned and promptly walked out of the office, ignoring the social worker's efforts to give her a card.

"Alyssa, honey, we have to go home now," Hazel said hurriedly as she pulled the girl's arm to make her stand up.

"But what about Mom?" Alyssa asked tearfully.

Hazel glanced at the nurses. She could tell they were listening, so she replied carefully, "You know your mother. She'll call later."

Believing Hazel's statement, the girl happily left the hospital, fully expecting her mother to call and explain why she had left before they arrived.

Alyssa waited. Days went by, and every day, she'd ask Hazel if her mom called. The answer was always no. Alyssa insisted they drop by the house to see if Linda had returned and forgotten to call.

When they arrived at the home, Hazel could tell that most of Linda's clothing was gone. There was no note or any indication that the mother had thought of the daughter she had left behind. How could her cousin abandon her only child without so much as a phone call? The thought made Hazel fume. When Linda did call, Hazel planned to teach her how to be a responsible parent. Then, she had a frightful thought, Linda was with Jason. There was a possibility she was unable to call, or worse.

Days turned into weeks before she sat Alyssa down for the conversation she had hoped she would never have to have. Hazel was prepared for the tears but not the change in character. Knowing her mother abandoned her created a moody, unusually clingy, and anxious child. Alyssa threw tantrums and argued with teachers. Her grades plummeted because she no longer cared about doing her homework assignments. Pastor Darrell and the children's ministry staff brought their concerns to Hazel when they too noticed the negative behavior changes. They referred Hazel to a good Christian child therapist.

Therapy payments weren't something the divorcée had funds for. Hazel had to pull funds from areas she shouldn't have. But she wasn't alone in her quest to prevent her young cousin from continuing down a dark path. The children's ministry members made a concerted effort to help Hazel by monitoring Alyssa's behavior and reporting their findings. They were the first to notice the positive changes in Alyssa's behavior. Soon, Alyssa's negative traits faded, and most of the time, she behaved like any other child her age. At other times, extremely stressful events brought out the worst of her anxiety. Occasionally Linda would send Alyssa a birthday card, but they were all missing a return address.

Years have passed since that dark period, and Alyssa no longer exhibited those old behaviors. That was until the Bryants decided to bully Alyssa. Hazel had no idea how much stress the Bryants placed on the teen until she experienced it herself. More than anything, she wanted to see Alyssa, hug her, and spend Christmas together as usual. But it was too dangerous.

She feared the Bryants would discover her return and force the girl into marriage. No, she'd rather not see Alyssa again than risk her being wed to Tim Bryant.

"Better is a neighbor who is near than a brother who is far away."

Proverbs 27:10

Alyssa hung up the public phone and walked slowly through the empty hallway back to her room. Just last week, all the students had been excited about going home for winter break, Alyssa included. She'd packed and re-packed, all while stressing over how to avoid being seen by the Bryants and anyone else in town who would tell them she was back. She missed Hazel so much that she was willing to risk returning.

Alyssa had said her goodbyes to her friends and left presents for Rosemary, Ben, and Stanley. When she visited Rosemary the previous weekend, Benjamin had offered to drive her to Pitway and stay until she was certain of her safety. But Alyssa did not want to be a constant burden to her new friends, nor did she want to intrude on Benjamin's family holiday time. She knew he planned to spend Christmas with his grandfather. Her friends had already done so much for her, and she wished she could do something for them in return; however, they had no needs she could meet.

Hazel's insistence that she'd be safer in Los Angeles for Christmas was a shock she didn't see coming. Four months had passed, so she couldn't understand why Pastor Bryant would still be looking for her instead of looking for someone who liked him. Since her dormitory building was closing for the holidays, Alyssa had to request emergency special housing from the dormitory director.

This provision was mainly for international students who couldn't afford to go home or didn't celebrate the seasonal holidays.

She tried to make the drab temporary dorm room as homey as she could by putting up a string of Christmas lights. Alyssa's Christmas breakfast was a granola bar with instant hot cocoa. Christmas dinner consisted of Chinese takeout, Orange Tang, and moon pies for dessert. She laughed when she opened the gifts her friends had given her. Rosemary's gift was sunglasses, Benjamin's was a radio and cassette player Walkman, and Stanley's was a beach bag. In the evening, Alyssa spoke with Hazel on the phone until she ran out of dimes. Thankfully, the room had a television, and she watched all the Christmas movies she could to pass the time.

There wasn't much to do after Christmas Day. Occasionally, Alyssa worked double shifts at her waitress job to cover for other employees. The tips from this job were enormous compared to what she used to receive serving at Pitway Inn.

She was grateful to find that she wasn't the only student residing on the third floor. Mei Ling, a freshman student from Taiwan, knocked on Alyssa's door one day. She was frightened by the noises she'd heard from what she thought was an empty floor. Alyssa was so happy to have someone to talk to. They soon decided to visit tourist attractions in the Los Angeles area together. With work and school, Alyssa had never had time to visit them before. During one of their outings, Mei Ling spoke about missing her family; it was too expensive for her to return home for the few weeks they were off. Alyssa was too embarrassed to discuss her reasons for not being home during the break, so she changed the subject. They got along so well that when it was almost time for all the students to return, Alyssa and Mei Ling requested to be dorm mates for the semester.

"I don't understand why she did that." Rosemary sighed. "Why did she stay in a dorm room by herself when she could have called any of us? Just when I thought she was emerging from her timid nature, she goes and does this. Looks like I still have a lot of work to do."

"Rose, Alyssa's not one of your psychology projects; she's our friend," Stanley protested.

"I am not turning her into a project. I'm helping her to speak up, speak out, and be empowered."

"I know you believe you're helping, but Alyssa trusts you as a friend. She didn't ask for help to change her character, right Ben?"

"Actually, I agree with Rosemary. Even you must admit she's still passive around us, and she's known us for months. Alyssa does need help stepping out of her shell and speaking up for herself. I'm constantly encouraging her to do so when I can," said Benjamin.

"Have you ever thought she's happy with who she is? Not every woman wants to be like Gloria," replied Stanley.

"What's that supposed to mean?" Benjamin asked.

"It means your girlfriend not only speaks up and speaks out but she also speaks her mind too much, to the point where she's rude and unpleasant."

Benjamin began to protest but stopped himself, thinking of the many times he had wanted Gloria to filter her comments before voicing them.

"Alright, she doesn't have to be like Gloria, but even you have to admit that spending Christmas alone when she could have stayed with any of our families shows she's too timid. How will she ever survive in this city without us?" Rose replied.

Stanley exhaled. "Look, Rose, do what you want. But remember, she trusts us as friends. I don't want her to feel like we're not happy unless she's just like us. That will hurt her feelings and ruin our friendship."

"I'm not an idiot, Stan. I won't hurt her. It's just that for months she had been so excited about seeing her cousin Hazel and her friends at Christmas. I'm angry that their pastor and his family have ruined her holiday, and I don't want this to happen again next Christmas. I want Alyssa to be bold enough to look that bully pastor in the eye and tell him to get lost."

"That won't work. You don't know the dynamics of small towns. The most powerful guy gets what he wants, and few can or would stand up to him. Think about it. She was a seventeen-year-old teenager volunteering at church when her thirty-four-year-old pastor basically told her she was marrying him. When she told him no, that should have been the end of it.

"You weren't there when the hotel manager argued with Alyssa. When she told her boss she didn't want to marry the pastor, the woman told her to hush. This manager lady didn't want Alyssa standing too close to us because she didn't want to upset the pastor, and the man wasn't even in the building.

"Imagine you're seventeen years old; facing that kind of pressure without your lawyer parents, just you living with an older cousin as your only family member. Could you stand up to that?"

"No. I guess I'd want to run away too," Rosemary said dejectedly. "But why didn't someone help? Why didn't someone from her church stand up for her?"

"Aha, now you know why I don't believe in churches anymore," Benjamin said triumphantly. "Here's an innocent teen who dutifully goes to church every Sunday morning. She could've slept in on Sundays like many other teens who have jobs, but no; Alyssa got up and faithfully went to church every Sunday morning to volunteer her services. And how was she rewarded for her sacrifices? Her reward was being bullied into marrying a pastor twice her age. This guy wasn't looking for an equal partner; he wanted an inexperienced teenager he could control, and no one in the congregation stood up to say, 'This is wrong'!"

"Now you're making things up. She did not say it was like that," Stanley protested.

"She didn't have to say it," Ben continued. "A normal man, someone decent, would look for an adult and start with a date before proposing marriage. This guy didn't bother with any of that. I sense he feels entitled, most likely because he's the pastor. He believes that he's the king, not Christ. Therefore, the church is his kingdom, and the congregants are his subjects to rule over. No one dares to counteract any decision he makes because they fear him. And since it's his kingdom, he's entitled to whatever he wants. He sees a young, pretty, quiet girl that he desires in his congregation, so he aims to take her. Her interests have no bearing because it's his kingdom, and she has no say. I'm certain there were other marriageable women, closer to his age that he could have selected. But he didn't want an 'equal mate,' he wanted a pushover. Predators set their sights on the young, meek, and weaker targets. He figured he could force her into marriage because there was no father or family group to stand in his way. She was easy prey."

"These modern-day pastors are nothing like the early priests or disciples. The early Christians strived to live by the characteristics of Christ. Too many modern churches are filled with arrogant, self-serving people who pretend to be Christ-like while they sit in mostly segregated congregations."

"Ben, please," Stanley said, sighing. "Let's not go down this road again. We all know why you're against the church. Your father's construction company got ripped off by that pastor who waited until the roof was installed before saying he didn't have the money to pay for the work. Your dad had a bad experience with *one* church. Since then, your dad has condemned churches, depicting all of them as crooked and phony. You've listened to his rantings all your life. Now, his doctrine is part of who you are, even though your grandfather took you to church frequently until you protested as a teen. You've never opened your eyes to experience church for yourself as an adult. You shouldn't judge by hearsay alone."

"Since we're on the topic, why do you still refuse to attend Stanley's Bible study? Do you believe Stanley is crooked?" questioned Rosemary.

Benjamin threw up his hands. "Here we go again. I said I

didn't want to set foot in a church. I have nothing against Stan. I believe in God. I accepted Christ as my Lord and Savior. I believe Jesus was resurrected from the dead, but I don't take part in any church because they're all corrupt. They pretend to exhibit the clean, loving character of Christ while they practice the character of his enemy. There should be no theft or perversion in the house of the Lord. People should not be afraid to attend or leave their child alone with church leaders."

"All churches are not corrupt. You don't have to attend my church, but as a member of Christ, you should be a part of some church. I know you visited Gloria's church for her niece's christening. Why not continue attending there?" Stanley suggested.

"Are you kidding me? That wasn't a church; it was a country club. I tried sitting in the empty seats in the front, but Gloria pulled me back. Apparently, front seats are reserved for a few rich families. The same families have sat in those seats for years, and no one else dares sit in them. These people control how the church runs because they contribute the most money. As for the congregation, all the women wear Gucci and Chanel, and the men wear Armani. Gloria told me they ignore anyone who doesn't wear designer clothing. Those people are so phony. If Christ visited their church today, they'd kick him out for dripping blood on their expensive Persian rugs."

"Look, Ben," said Stanley. "I'm only saying you shouldn't condemn all churches because of the sins of a few."

Ben laughed bitterly. "Well, the few that I know of are so horrific that I refuse to step foot into any other. Why take the risk? Do you even listen to the news? Pastors with delusions of grandeur are all around, behaving as if they should be worshipped instead of Christ. Have you forgotten the Jonestown massacre? Hundreds of Christians were convinced they had to commit suicide because their lunatic pastor convinced them to do it. Or the priest in Louisiana who abused over thirty-seven boys? I could go on. Those 'few' have inflicted so much damage on the body of Christ that I can't imagine a non-believer stepping into any church without fear. I believe we should just pray in our own homes with our own families."

Stanley shook his head. "It really hurts when I hear people criticize 'all' Christians, and ignore all the good that has been done. Yes, there are people who should never be trusted with any congregation, and those congregations have paid dearly. But you cannot and should not condemn the good works of many thousands of churches because of the few. Also, you cannot rely on the media to report the works of good churches; that's not the type of story that increases viewership. They will, however, report any scandals they can find. Unfortunately, that's the information that sticks in people's minds.

"Ben, there are over 300,000 churches in America alone doing great work, like opening hospitals and running charitable organizations such as the Salvation Army. Did you know that Harvard, Yale, and Princeton were all founded by churches? Churches feed the hungry, rehabilitate individuals struggling with alcohol and substance abuse, and help the homeless rebuild their lives. And that's just what I can think of off the top of my head. There's an endless list of church ministries doing good work all over the world! Do you honestly believe these great works can be accomplished by individual families worshiping separately in their own homes? It's not possible, and it's not how Christians should behave. Hebrews 10:25 says we should not neglect meeting together. How can we spread the gospel if we don't have churches where people in need can just walk in and receive help? There's no way you can be for Christ yet be against the assembly that gathers in his name."

Benjamin sighed. "I know you're right, Stan. It's just that it irks me when innocent people go to church seeking God and end up being preyed upon instead of being prayed for by the pastor. There ought to be some form of oversight."

"Actually, there are guidelines in the Bible for church oversight," Stanley explained. "However, most people don't follow them because they fear their pastor, or banishment from the church more than they fear God. People rarely step forward and accuse a clergy member of misconduct. If you want to criticize the body of Christ on that, I'm with you. Too many remain silent when someone's being victimized. Denominational churches do have some oversight, but ultimately, the real power lies with the church members and elders."

Benjamin ran a hand through his hair. "Okay, Stan, I have other things on my mind, and I don't want to have this argument again. Let's agree to disagree. I have to drive up to see my grandfather this weekend. His nurse said he's had some setbacks in his health, and he's been asking for me."

"I'm sorry to hear that Ben. Do you think you'll see Maureen when you're there?"

"Nope. I always check with the nurse before I leave to ensure there's no chance of bumping into her."

"You know, your grandfather might enjoy seeing the two of you together. It may lift his spirits," Stanley replied.

"He'll have to find another way to lift his spirits because there's no way I'm staying in the house when she's there," said Benjamin.

"Ben, isn't it time for you to let go of your anger and reconcile? I think…"

"Sorry Stan, I have to get back to work," Benjamin said abruptly. He kissed Rosemary goodbye on the cheek before heading for the door.

Rosemary sighed and looked at Stanley. "Well, you tried babe. He's just not ready."

Stanley sighed as well. "Ben's not a kid anymore. He needs to see the reality of his family, not just his father's distorted view. I guess all I can do is keep praying he'll come to his senses one day."

"We'll both keep praying, and believing our prayers will be answered," said Rosemary.

"One who has unreliable friends soon comes to ruin, but there is a friend who sticks closer than a brother."

Proverbs 18:24

"I'm so sorry, Ben. You know we're here for you. I'll help with the arrangements in any way I can," said Rosemary as she embraced Benjamin. Rosemary and Stanley drove over to the beach house when they heard the news of Benjamin's grandfather's passing.

"Thanks, Rosemary. That means a lot to me. I knew I had to prepare for this day, but knowing doesn't make it any easier. I'm upset with myself for getting so busy with work. I was making plans to visit him next weekend on Father's Day, but then I got the call from the nurse," Benjamin said gloomily. "Maureen arranged for Grandad to be buried at the family plot, and the service is set for this Sunday. I'm driving up in the morning to settle some accounts."

"Tell me the time, and I'll drive you there," said Stanley.

"You don't have to do that, Stan. I know you have work."

"My work can wait. I'm driving, and I'm not arguing about it." Benjamin sighed, giving in. "Thanks, buddy."

The next morning, Benjamin and Stanley took their usual route to the picturesque small town where Ben's grandfather had resided for his convalescence. Suddenly, Benjamin had an idea.

"Stan, would you mind if we took a detour through Pitway?"

"Not at all. Looking for anything in particular?"

"Not really. But we didn't explore the town when we were there last year. I'd like to take a closer look since we're in the area."

They drove down the town's main street. Many of the buildings were in need of repair or fresh paint. There was a movie theater that appeared to have been closed for some time. A few vagrants sat on the sidewalk in front of it. A few more loitered near the grocery market, their hands stretched out whenever a customer opened the door. Stanley steered the car into a large rotary at the town center. The roundabout encircled a huge, unkempt memorial ground covered with overgrown shrubbery and trash.

"How did we miss seeing how rundown this town was? Why don't the people clean it up?" Benjamin asked.

"Have you really looked at the townspeople? They appear just as worn down and grungy as their surroundings. Also, we never had a reason to drive through before. The Inn is located on the edge of town. We knew this wasn't a tourist area, so there was no need to drive through Main Street. Have you seen enough yet? This place is depressing."

"Yeah, let's move on."

Two minutes later, Benjamin shouted, "Slow down! Look, there's Alyssa's church."

Stanley pulled over in front of the church steps and stepped out. "It's much larger than I expected it to be for a town like this."

As they walked up the steps, Benjamin noticed how unkempt the church landscaping was, but he gawked at the building's impressive architecture. "Whoever built this church invested a lot into the details. Look at how ornate the façade has been decorated."

Before Benjamin could stop him, Stanley opened the door and peeked inside.

"This is a beautiful church," Stanley whispered as he entered.

Benjamin followed, whispering, "What are you doing? We shouldn't be in here." But then he looked up at the intricately decorated domed ceiling and the huge stained-glass windows. "The people who built this church cared a lot about the design of this structure. But I bet if they were alive today, they'd wish it was moved out of Pitway to a more deserving town. Hey, Stan, we should get going before we're late."

They arrived at Ben's grandfather's cabin that afternoon. When the caretaker let him in, Benjamin headed straight for his grandfather's room. The cabin had been impeccably cleaned after the patriarch's passing. There was nothing left to do.

Benjamin scanned the nightstand for the family photo his grandfather kept beside the bed; it was the only picture they had taken together while fishing when he was a little boy. But it wasn't there. He returned to the great room where the caretaker was located.

"Excuse me, did you pack the picture away? You know the one that was in my grandfather's room?"

"Oh no, that was the first thing Maureen took when she came by."

"You saw her take my picture?" Benjamin asked.

"Yes. Do you want me to call her about it?"

"No, no. That's fine, thank you. I'll contact Maureen myself," he said through a forced smile.

At the funeral repast, Maureen observed Benjamin from a distance. He stuck close to Gloria and his group of friends; his father hovered near them at all times. She tried approaching Benjamin when he was alone, but he must have sensed her watching him because he walked off in the opposite direction, and began a conversation with someone else.

Stanley, noticing the snub, walked over, hugged Maureen, and offered his condolences.

Benjamin's family was small. Most of the attendees at the late Raymond Fritzmann's funeral were acquaintances and employees from his real estate firm. Through conversations with some, Maureen found out that Benjamin told the company employees that he was running the business temporarily until his grandfather was back on his feet. None of the workers knew of their employer's declining health. His death was a complete shock to them.

Maureen knew Benjamin would inherit most of Raymond Fritzmann's realty firm, and she had no problems with that. Her concern was that Benjamin's father would persuade him to sell everything and work exclusively for his construction company. Raymond Fritzmann had built his fifty-employee firm from scratch, and she knew his dream was to have Benjamin, his only grandchild, take over the business.

"Maureen...? You're not listening to me, are you?" Maureen's attentive husband tried his best to appear concerned for the departed, but he was mainly worried about the emotional turmoil Maureen endured whenever Benjamin was nearby.

"Sorry, Nicholas... I have a lot on my mind." Noting the deep frown lines on his face, she made a suggestion. "Nick, you should go to the hotel. I don't want to leave while so many people are still here, it would be rude of me to do that."

"You shouldn't worry about that, and I don't want to leave you by yourself." He held her arm reassuringly. "Maureen, you made all the arrangements on your own, I know you're tired. The staff here will take care of everything, please come with me and rest."

"No, I'll be fine. I cried all my tears while I watched him slowly slip away. Please, go to the hotel and wait for me. I won't be long."

"Alright, I'll leave. But call if you're too tired to drive." They kissed before Nicholas stepped away. Benjamin's father sneered as he watched them.

Another hour passed before Maureen instructed the staff to put away the food and alcohol. One by one, the mourners took the hint and left the dining hall. She noticed Benjamin watching her before his father escorted him out the door. His sad expression filled her with remorse as she realized that the only person who had truly tried to reunite the family was now gone.

CHAPTER
ELEVEN

An inheritance gained hastily at the beginning will not be blessed in the end.

Proverbs 20:21

"Hello, Benjamin. I hope you've been keeping well these past few months, I know you were close to your grandfather," said the elderly lawyer as he shook Ben's hand. Benjamin took a seat across the attorney's desk.

"You'll be happy to know we're at the point of distributing your grandfather's assets. All the creditor accounts have been settled equitably. Your grandfather had a lot to do with that, he settled many accounts before he passed so that you and Maureen wouldn't have to wait long for your inheritance distribution."

"That sounds just like Grandad. He never liked to leave a mess. He'd already shown me the will. He told me about my inheritance after I finished law school. I get 100% of the company, but everything else goes to Maureen."

"Oh? So, you're not familiar with the changes he made to the will last summer?"

Benjamin frowned. "Changes? No, Grandad never mentioned any changes to the will."

"Oh yes, he contacted me last September, you know, when he received the bad news about his health. He said he needed to change the original into a contingency will, and he was going to discuss it with you and Maureen together."

Benjamin shook his head. "Well, I made a point of not visiting when Maureen was present; so, I guess I missed the family meeting. I'm not sure why he never mentioned the change to me, though."

"I'll get right down to the basics then. First, full control of the company has been given to you, but ownership is split 80/20. Eighty percent goes to you, and Maureen keeps a twenty percent stake. If she passes away, that twenty will go to your children. If there are no great-grandchildren, the twenty percent will go to charity."

Benjamin gave the attorney a confused look when he heard the word 'children,' but the lawyer held up a hand for Benjamin to be patient. "Moving along, the rental properties in San Francisco, which are currently managed by Maureen, go to her. Also, all liquid assets, including your grandfather's stock portfolio, go to Maureen. Of course, you're aware of that because it was in the original will."

The attorney paused before making the next statement. "Here's the contingency: the following properties were previously going to Maureen—the three-acre mansion property on the beach you're currently living in, the Sierra Nevada Chalet, and all rental properties in Lake Tahoe. Though currently managed by Maureen, these may be inherited by you... after the sixtieth day of your marriage."

"My what?! Did you say marriage? What on earth made Grandad put that in the will?"

The lawyer removed his glasses and shrugged. "Benjamin, you know your grandfather was a very religious man. That's why he took you to church as often as possible when you stayed with him. He believes your parents' divorce and your father's lifestyle has turned you away from traditional family values. This contingency was his way of guiding you back."

"I don't understand. I'm only twenty-five. Since Grandad got sick, I've been running his business without any help and visiting him as often as possible. There wasn't much time for me to spend with Gloria, and now I'm supposed to marry her, just like that?"

"Benjamin, you've been working your job as a real estate lawyer and covering your grandfather's job for two years. Why haven't you hired more staff to help out? You had the resources to do it."

Benjamin placed his face in his hands. "I don't know, I guess I was trying to prove to everyone that I could handle everything on my own. How am I going to do this? If I ask Gloria to marry me, she'll want it to be permanent."

"Is that a bad thing? You've been together for some time now. Last year, your father told me you'd be marrying soon."

Benjamin sighed. "My father's been pushing me to marry Gloria because he wants more contracts from her father, but Gloria and I don't always click well together. I don't want to take marriage lightly and end up like my parents. Marriage is a huge step, and I know I'm not ready."

"Well, no one has a problem-free relationship. There will always be hiccups along the way. Tell Gloria how you feel. If the two of you plan to marry in the future, surely she'll want you to have those assets. Maybe you can come to an understanding."

"Humph, you don't know Gloria." He paused before muttering, "I guess I have no choice but to give it a try. I'll ask her to marry me temporarily and see what happens."

The lawyer chuckled. "Good luck with that. And remember, you only need to be married for sixty days. The will says nothing about being happily married."

"We shouldn't be here," Rosemary whispered to Stanley as they entered the popular restaurant.

"Shh, I promised Ben we would stay until it's done."

"Stanley, you know what Gloria is like. She'll make a scene. Do we want to be here to see that?"

"Ben needs us here for moral support."

"Moral support? Ha! He wants us to protect him when she has a fit."

"I'm certain it won't come to that—"

Stanley was cut short by a loud commotion from the dining area. He and the maître d' in front of them stood frozen as a red-faced Gloria stormed out of the dining room. Like the other guests, they immediately stepped out of her path as she approached. Rosemary watched in disbelief as Gloria shoved past entering guests on her way to the exit.

Stanley entered the dining area and found Benjamin on hands and knees, searching the carpeted floor as astonished guests looked on. "Ben, what are you doing?" whispered Stanley as the other guests continued to stare.

"Oh, now you're here? I told you 7 p.m. sharp!" said Benjamin.

"We're only fifteen minutes late. What happened? And why are you crawling on the floor?"

Benjamin didn't bother to look up when he spoke. "As we were seated, Gloria saw the bulge in my pocket and immediately knew it was a ring box. She got excited before I could explain my plan. Gloria started talking a mile a minute, then she started kissing me. She put the ring on her finger and just stared at it. The longer she stared, the redder her face became. Then she said, 'Tell me this isn't cubic zirconia.' Of course, I couldn't tell her that because it would have been a lie... Oh, found it! Thank goodness."

Benjamin stood up and walked to his table where Rosemary was already seated, enjoying a glass of the untouched celebratory champagne.

"How did the ring get all the way over there?" asked Rosemary.

"Well, Gloria aimed for my head, but I ducked just in time. Someone behind me yelled 'ouch,' and then you guys showed up."

"Oh, she must be really mad at you. What are you going to do?" asked Rosemary.

"I'll give her a day or two to calm down. Then, I'll try to explain over the phone that the diamond isn't real because the wedding isn't real."

"Ben, this is something you should discuss directly, not over the phone," Rosemary suggested.

"Will you come with me if I do?"

"Okay, over the phone it is," Rosemary quipped. "Tell me again, how long do you have to stay married?"

"Sixty days. Also, I checked the details of the will with a family lawyer. I don't have to file the marriage license. I only need to have the ceremony and remain married for sixty days. Since there are no references to my needing to register the marriage, I'll keep the license in a safe until I receive the title to my properties, then I can destroy it."

"Sounds like a simple plan. I hope it plays out that way," said Stanley."

"If you're worried about Gloria, don't be. She loves staying at Grandad's chalet. The thought of owning it when we have the real marriage will guarantee she'll be onboard."

"Personally, I'd marry you for the mansion on the beach," said Rosemary.

"Yeah, I love that place too," Stanley added. "What does your father think?"

"He thinks I should marry Gloria for real and get it over with. But of course, he has his own reasons, doesn't he."

"Hasn't he already obtained construction contracts from Gloria's father?"

"Yes, but he's not content with those small jobs. Dad believes once I marry Gloria, her father will give him the larger, more profitable contracts."

"So, when do you plan to marry Gloria for real?" asked Rosemary.

Benjamin sighed loudly. "You know, I'm not sure. The constant pressure from Dad and Gloria is exhausting. It's sort of turned me off from the idea of marriage. I don't like being manipulated... Hey, Rose, pour me a glass of that champagne. It's been an extremely stressful evening," said Benjamin.

Benjamin checked his watch again. He had been waiting for Gloria for over forty minutes in the elaborately decorated foyer. He called last night, and said exactly the time he wanted to see her. Gloria acknowledged over the phone, but she's intentionally making him wait. Ben knew this was her way of punishing him for the cheap ring, so he endured the wait.

"So, what do you have to say that was so important?" Gloria's voice, seemingly coming out of nowhere, startled Benjamin. He turned around to see her standing in the middle of the room with her arms folded and a pout on her face.

"Don't I get a good morning or some sort of greeting?" he asked in vain. Gloria responded with a mean face.

"Ok, fair enough. First, I should tell you about Grandad's will." He explained everything—why they must marry, what properties were involved, how this marriage was not the official one, and the reason for the cheap ring.

"You should have told me this plan before buying that stupid ring."

"In retrospect, yes, I should have. But now that you know the truth, let's start planning."

"I'm not planning anything with you! Do you know how it would look? Marrying you with my friends and family in attendance at some cheap wedding? I would be a laughing stock. Then, we'll get an annulment in a few months, and they'll laugh at me all over again," she said, leaving the foyer.

Benjamin followed her. "Gloria, please. This is the only way I can obtain my full inheritance."

"That's your problem! No self-respecting woman would enter a joke wedding like that. Here's an idea—hire an escort to do it."

"An escort? You want me to hire a prostitute as my wife?"

"Yes, rent a fake wife. You need someone who doesn't care about her reputation. An escort fits the bill."

"And what if she refuses to give me an annulment? She could later drag me through a divorce and take half of my inheritance as community property."

"Hmm, I didn't think of that. Well, you'll have to find an escort you can trust."

Benjamin laughed. "You know there's no such thing. Gloria, I need you to help me with this. We don't have to marry in L.A. We can have a quick wedding in another state." Benjamin sighed. "There must be something I can do to convince you. I don't want to lose the beach house. That's my home."

Gloria's eyes lit up. "I have another great idea! You can make Alyssa do it! She owes you for saving her from that cult she belonged to."

"She wasn't in a cult; it was a church. And no, I can't ask her to do this. I'm not taking advantage of her misfortune. She doesn't owe me anything. It was Stanley who kept her secret until we were out of town. I'm not sure what I would have done if Stanley hadn't been there."

"Well, if Stanley's such a good friend, he'd let Rosemary marry you temporarily."

"No, I won't insult Rosemary by even suggesting that."

"Oh, it's okay to insult me but not your friends?"

"You know that's not what I meant. Rosemary is engaged to my best friend, and she's the only child of lawyer parents," Benjamin threw up his hands. "That's it. I'm not going to stress over it anymore. If Maureen wants the properties, she can have them."

Gloria's jaw dropped. "No, Ben, you can't just give up the chalet! You worked so hard for your grandfather, while Maureen did nothing. It's not fair. You own eighty percent of the company now. I'm certain she wants more than twenty percent, so meet with her and negotiate a deal."

"I'm not meeting with Maureen!" Ben shouted. "Let's just forget it. I'll move in with my dad until I find my own place."

He got up, kissed Gloria on the forehead, and left before she could say anything more.

Alyssa's spring classes had finished but she continued to stay in Los Angeles. Hazel told her it still was not safe to return home. She wasn't happy about her situation, but the extra time spent in Los Angeles brought her closer to her new friends.

Stanley's Tuesday bible study class had just finished. Alyssa and Rosemary were discussing the last scripture he'd quoted while most of the other Bible study attendees prepared to leave. A few men kept Stanley engaged in conversation, delving deeper into his last statement that Jesus' treatment of women, as equal and respected individuals, was against the culture of that time. Stanley discussed the Samaritan woman's interaction with Jesus and the woman who touched Him despite suffering from a continuous menstrual flow. In those times, women were not allowed to touch men when they were menstruating. He highlighted the fact that Jesus first revealed Himself to women after he had risen, and He told the women to go and tell his brethren where to see him. Some of the men disputed these statements, claiming that women had no place in the church.

Stanley countered with 1 Corinthians 11:5, which states that women were *"praying and prophesying"* in the church.

Alyssa and Rosemary were just exiting the room when they spotted Gloria waiting for them in the foyer.

"Gloria? Hi! This is a surprise. Were you here for the Bible study?" asked Rosemary.

"Hello, ladies." Gloria walked over and gave them air kisses on each cheek. "Sorry, I came just as Stanley was finishing up. I'll come early next time. Umm, I really wanted to spend some time with you, Alyssa, but I didn't know how to reach you. Ben told me you attend Stanley's Bible study every week, so I came here."

"You want to spend time with me?" asked an astonished Alyssa.

"Sure! We haven't seen each other for some time. Are you free now?"

"I was heading back to the dorm, but we can get some coffee if you'd like. Rosemary, would you like to join us?"

"Oh, sorry, I should wait for Stanley, and he may be here for a while. You go ahead. We'll catch up on the weekend."

"Alright, I'll see you then," Alyssa said.

"Great! I know this place on Wilshire with the best biscotti and cappuccino you've ever tasted," said Gloria.

"What's biscotti?" asked Alyssa.

Gloria laughed. "It's a dry Italian cookie that you eat with coffee or wine. I grew up on them."

"I'm looking forward to trying them then!"

Gloria drove them to the high-end Italian restaurant and waited until they ordered before speaking. She began with small talk before saying "You know, I was a little upset when I heard what Ben and Stanley did for you. It's not because I didn't want them to help you, but Ben took a huge risk transporting a runaway minor out of the county. If your guardian had called the police, Ben could have had his law license suspended. A lot of people wouldn't have done what he did for you."

"Oh, I'm sorry," apologized Alyssa, a sudden sense of guilt making her flush. "I had no idea they could've gotten in trouble for helping me."

"Don't worry. It's no big deal now. Those two are always helping people." She paused to sip her cappuccino. "So, how has college been for you so far?"

"It's been great. I love my classes," Alyssa replied cheerfully. She was going to continue when Gloria cut her off.

"Actually... I've wanted to speak to you because I need a huge favor. It involves helping Ben out of a terrible bind," she began.

"Well, I'd do anything to help Ben. What's the problem?" Alyssa asked.

"Hmm, it's a bit complex. I don't know how to start. Let's call it a two-month-long project or job that he needs help with at the beach house," Gloria replied.

"Sounds serious. I'd have a long commute to my dorm. What kind of project would it be, and how many hours per day will this job take? Is this some type of secretarial work?"

"No, you'd do a little hosting, and that's it. You would have to live at his house. Most of your day would be yours to do whatever you want. By the way, if you don't mind my asking, how are you paying for your tuition and residential fees?"

"Oh, I don't mind. I'm paying with student loans and a few scholarships, but my jobs help. I'm guessing I'd have to leave my current job to work on this project?"

"Yes, but you'd be compensated for that. I'm sure Ben would cover your tuition and board for the rest of your degree."

"No, I couldn't take that much money from Ben—he's my friend. Would I really need to live at his house? Also, will you be there too?"

"Yes, you must stay at the house. And no, I won't be there. Alyssa, Ben's really counting on you to help with this project. So, are you on board?"

"Um, I guess so... If Ben really needs me, I'd be happy to help."

"That's great! He really does need you. He's in a legal bind. And out of all his friends, I think you're in the best position to help him. Ben will be so happy that you said yes!"

The next morning, Gloria visited Benjamin at work and told him that Alyssa had agreed to their plan.

"You asked her? Why did you go behind my back to asked her!" Benjamin snapped.

"I went behind your back because you didn't have the guts to ask."

"I find it hard to believe she said yes to marrying me after what she's been through."

"I know right? I was shocked myself. Personally, I think she really needs the money."

"She does? Alyssa never told us that she was in a financial fix. Maybe we should have asked how she's getting along. Gloria, I don't know if I can do this. It feels wrong. I feel like I'm taking advantage of Alyssa's situation," he protested.

"No, it's not wrong. And she's the type who wouldn't take money without earning it. So, this is the only way you can really help her financially."

Benjamin exhaled sharply. "We'll have to sit down together to discuss this. I need to be certain she understands what she must do."

"Hey, I did my part, the rest is up to you," Gloria said, preparing to leave.

"You're not coming with me?"

"Listen, I did the asking. You must work out the minor details on your own."

Benjamin sighed. "This still feels wrong... But if she said yes, maybe it won't be a bad thing, especially if this is the only way she'll take money from us."

He reluctantly called Alyssa and asked if she could meet him at Rosemary's later. She agreed, but he thought it strange she didn't ask him why. Benjamin hated having to make the next call. "Hey Stan, I have to talk to you and Rosemary tonight. I've asked Alyssa to join us."

"This sounds serious, buddy. What's up?"

Benjamin exhaled audibly. "Gosh, I don't even know where to start. Okay, remember how I wanted Gloria to marry me temporarily for the properties, and she turned me down?"

"Yeah, go on."

"Well, she decided to ask someone else to do it as a job, in exchange for tuition money."

"Oh no. Please tell me she didn't ask Alyssa."

"Yes, she asked her. And Alyssa said yes."

"What?! Are you sure she understood what Gloria was asking her to do?"

"I'm not 100% certain of that, which is why I've asked her to meet me at Rosemary's tonight." Benjamin paused, waiting for a response. "Stan, you're still there? What are you thinking?"

There was a momentary silence on the other side of the phone before Stanley's sharp exhale was heard.

"Yes, I'm still here; my mind's grappling with what you just said. Ben, Alyssa looks up to us, and I know she trusts you. To be honest, as her friend, I'm hoping she didn't understand what Gloria was asking and that she turns you down."

"Why would you want that?"

"Ben, she's been through a lot, and she's vulnerable right now. What are you going to do if, after living together, she falls for you?"

"There's no way that will happen. She doesn't look at me like that. But if you're concerned, I'll try my best to not let that happen."

"I'm going to hold you to that. I don't want Alyssa to get hurt in your charade. This doesn't feel right to me. But if she wants to go through with this fake marriage, I'll support her decision. Just know that Rosemary won't take this lightly—she's not exactly Gloria's biggest fan."

"Yeah... let's just see what happens tonight," said Benjamin before hanging up.

Later that evening, Stanley opened the door for Benjamin to enter. Just as he walked into the family room, Rosemary stormed up to him.

"Is this some kind of sick joke? You're making Alyssa marry you to obtain your million-dollar properties? I don't understand how you could do this! She risked her life running away from an unwanted marriage. Why would you get her mixed up in yet another marital scam? When did you even ask her anyway?"

"Please calm down, Rose. I didn't ask her—Gloria did. And Alyssa told Gloria that she'd do it."

Rosemary groaned and slapped her forehead. "Of course, I get it now. I wondered why Gloria came to Stan's Bible study. She just wanted to trick Alyssa into your scam."

"Wait, Gloria came to my Bible study? I didn't see her," said Stanley.

"You didn't see her because she wasn't there to listen to you. She claimed she wanted to spend time with Alyssa and suggested they go for coffee. I should have known she was up to something."

"You're jumping to conclusions. Maybe Gloria does want to spend time with Alyssa, and yesterday was a start," suggested Benjamin.

"Ben, I know you don't want to hear this, but I came to a conclusion about your girlfriend a long time ago. Do you know what she is?"

And with that, Rosemary and Benjamin began a long argument, only interrupted when they heard the doorbell. When Stanley led Alyssa into the family room, she sensed the tension between Benjamin and Rosemary.

"Hi guys, what have you been up to?" she asked. They all greeted her warmly before sitting down.

"So, Ben," Alyssa began, "tell me about this job you need help with."

Now that he was facing Alyssa, Benjamin struggled to get the words out, but Rosemary jumped in.

"Alyssa, what did Gloria tell you about it?"

"Um, she said I will have to work for at least two months. I'd have to live in Ben's house to do the job, and he insists on paying my tuition and residential fees for the rest of my degree." Alyssa then turned to Benjamin. "Ben, you don't have to pay my tuition and fees. You're my friend. You need help, and I'd like to help you out."

"Alyssa, I don't know what to say. Thank you doesn't seem like enough. The least I can do is pay your tuition and...," Ben had begun but Rosemary stopped him with a gesture of her hand.

"Alyssa, did Gloria tell you what the job is?" Rosemary asked sternly.

"No, she was vague on the details. Gloria said I would do some hosting, but most of my time would be free."

"Did she ever say you would be, married?" asked Stanley.

Alyssa's eyes widened. "Marriage? I don't understand, who's getting married?" She looked around at her friends, Stanley and Rosemary were speechless, while Benjamin stiffened in his seat.

Shifting uncomfortably in his seat, Benjamin said, "I'm so sorry, Alyssa. It seems that Gloria didn't tell you the full truth. Let me start from the beginning." He then explained his grandfather's will and what he must do to obtain his inheritance.

Alyssa's mouth hung open. "Why didn't she tell me this?" she asked.

"I don't know the answer to that. It's a difficult thing to ask someone." Benjamin sighed. "Don't worry, I won't let you do this. I had asked Gloria to marry me, but she turned me down, so that's it. I'm so upset with Gloria right now; I need to calm down." Turning to Stanley, he said, "Hey, let's watch a movie or something. The atmosphere is too serious in here."

"Sure, I'll find something on cable."

Both Benjamin and Stanley tried their best to be cheerful and upbeat during the movie. However, Alyssa's mind was restless. Halfway through the movie, she took Rosemary aside to the kitchen.

"What's wrong, Alyssa? You look so distressed."

"I can't stop thinking about what Ben said. Will he really lose his home if he doesn't marry someone?"

"Yes, but that's not your problem. Ben will figure something out."

"But he doesn't have much time left. I don't want him to lose his home, and he really did help me when I needed it."

"Alyssa, I know Ben. He wouldn't let you do something just because you feel obligated to."

"I know, and I appreciate Ben and all you guys looking out for me. But this is something I can do. It's just... pretend. And it doesn't hurt anyone, right?" She paused for a moment. "I think I should do it."

Rosemary scrutinized Alyssa's face, trying to process what her friend had just said. "Alyssa, are you absolutely certain? Think about it, you will be legally married to Benjamin for two months. Even after he annuls the marriage, people may still remember the two of you being married at the ceremony. Are you certain you're okay with that?"

"Yes. I'm not worried about a few people, none of my friends will know and I'm sure Ben would keep the ceremony small. Also, I can use the extra time to study for my courses."

The women returned to the family room. When Rosemary turned down the volume on the TV, both men looked up to see what was happening.

Alyssa composed herself. When she started speaking, her voice was steady. "Ben, I'll do it. I'll marry you. Just tell me what information I need to know in case someone asks me questions about you."

The two men gaped. They exchanged confused glances, before Ben stammered the next question. "Are... are you sure about this?"

"Yes, I'm sure. It's only for two months, what could happen?"

"Oh, thank goodness!" Ben replied, relief washing over him. "I don't know how to thank you for this! I promise to make this as easy as possible."

"Okay," said Rosemary, clasping her hand in joy. "As a psych grad student, I nominate myself as project manager for this... sham. I'll give you two tips on how to act and think like a couple so no one will become suspicious. I'll also arrange the wedding process. This will be good practice for us, Stan." She turned to the others. "First, you two should get familiar with each other's background."

The four friends stayed up late while Alyssa and Benjamin exchanged personal details to memorize.

The following day, they met at a restaurant, where Benjamin and Alyssa practiced being a couple in public.

"Alyssa, you should sit closer to Ben. And Ben, you should look at Alyssa more. Initiate small talk. Remember, you must look and act like a couple."

"You're right, Rose." Benjamin turned to Alyssa and took her hand. Alyssa flinched at his touch, prompting Benjamin to apologize.

"No, no, no!" Rosemary groaned. "Alyssa, you have to stop recoiling whenever Ben touches you. And Ben, stop saying sorry when she flinches. We'd better order our food now. Stanley! Stop laughing, you're not helping the situation."

"Sorry, I can't help it! This is so funny. They look so uncomfortable sitting next to each other." Rosemary rubbed her forehead in frustration.

"You're right, Stan." she turned back to Benjamin and Alyssa. "You two look too uncomfortable sitting next to each other. I have an idea that could help with that. I want both of you to turn and look into each other's eyes while Ben's hand rests on Alyssa's. You can blink, but don't break eye contact. I'm going to set my timer for two minutes. This will help you feel and appear more connected. Alright, start now!"

Alyssa tried to stay as calm as possible as she stared into Ben's brown eyes, but she noticed the corners of Ben's mouth turning upwards. This only made her want to laugh, so she tried her best to focus only on his eyes, but the prolonged staring was awkward. Two minutes felt like two hours. Suddenly, Ben burst out laughing, and Alyssa followed suit. Though Rosemary complained that they had only lasted eighty-five seconds, the exercise did reduce their anxiety. They took a much-needed break when their dinner arrived.

As they finished their meal, Alyssa asked, "so, what exercise are you planning for tomorrow?"

"Tomorrow's Saturday, we have a list of items to complete before the wedding next weekend. For now, continue to hold hands whenever you re in public, and walk together."

"Next weekend?! So soon? Surely there's more time before I move in, right?" she directed her question to Ben.

"Well, um, for it to look like a real marriage, you must live with me from the wedding day; sorry." he said.

"I must let Mei Ling know I'm moving out of our dorm room early. She's returning to Taiwan for the summer break."

"Why don't you invite her to the wedding?" Stanley asked.

"I can't tell my friends I'm getting married! What will they think when I return to the dorm unmarried in the fall?"

"You're right. I didn't think of that."

The group of friends stood to exit the restaurant. As they walked past the tables, a handsome young man watched disapprovingly as Benjamin grasped Alyssa's hand and led her through the narrow walkway. This time, Alyssa didn't recoil at his touch.

CHAPTER
TWELVE

"Faithful friends are beyond price; no amount can balance their worth. Faithful friends are life-saving medicine, and those who fear the Lord will find them."

Ecclesiasticus 6:5-6,14-17

"I don't like this one, the sleeves are too puffy; I look like a clown," Alyssa complained as she looked at herself in the mirror.

"But it's a good price! I want this one," Benjamin said enthusiastically to the sales lady.

"No, Ben. This wedding must look legitimate. You would never marry someone wearing 'that,'" whispered Rosemary.

Benjamin sulked. "This wedding is costing too much. First, we overpaid for the wedding bands. Why do we need real gold rings? Now, you want me to overpay for the wedding dress as well? She'll wear it for a few hours and never again. What's the point of paying so much?"

Overhearing Benjamin whine, the sales associate shook her head sadly, quietly wishing the beautiful bride-to-be would leave this jerk for a man who truly appreciated her. Suddenly, she came up with an idea. The associate excused herself and rummaged in the back storage area. She smiled to herself when she found it. The garment was an exquisite satin form-fitting dress that would make the bride-to-be look like a movie star. She carefully tucked the price tag where it would not be seen, then the associate removed the protective plastic and proceeded to the bride.

"Oh, miss," she said, motioning Alyssa closer. "Try this on. I think it will look wonderful on you."

Alyssa was happy to escape her bickering friends for a few minutes. She followed the sales associate, who helped her into the dress. When Alyssa turned to the mirror, the associate's mouth fell open in astonishment.

"That dress was made for you, miss! Just look at it."

Alyssa couldn't help but smile at her reflection. She'd never worn anything so elegant in her life.

"I love it!" she squealed. Alyssa hurried back to her friends. Stanley looked up first. He set his newspaper aside and stood.

"Guys, look," he said, gesturing toward Alyssa.

Rosemary and Benjamin turned and gasped.

"That dress, it's picture-perfect! This is the one!" Rosemary exclaimed excitedly.

Benjamin was at a loss for words. "Alyssa, you look wonderful in that dress."

"So, you'll take this one?" asked the saleswoman.

Alyssa and Rosemary said "yes" in unison, but Benjamin hesitated.

"Umm, what's the cost for this one?" he asked warily. Benjamin gasped again when he heard the price. "Rosemary, I'm sorry, we can't buy this dress—"

Rosemary cut him off and lowered her voice. "Ben, think about it. Pictures will be taken. The media may show up. This is a big deal. You can't stand next to Alyssa in an expensive tux while she wears a cheap rag. People will talk."

"Umm... the media? Do they have to be there?" asked Alyssa.

"No, Alyssa, we won't need the media." Benjamin turned to Rosemary. "You hear that, Rose? Strike that off your list. And by the way, the tux is a rental," Ben continued his dispute with Rosemary, but she cut him off again.

"This, is an Oscar De La Renta dress, and it will carry a great resale value; you can sell the dress after the wedding and recoup a good portion of your money back, cheapskate."

The saleswoman gasped. "Oh, dear girl, please don't let your fiancé sell your wedding dress. Don't you want to pass it down to your daughters?"

"Um... we're not having any children." Alyssa stated.

The woman shook her head disapprovingly. "Don't tell me he won't let you have children because he thinks they're too expensive!"

Alyssa laughed. "No, Ben's not as bad as he seems."

Later in the car, Rosemary reviewed the wedding plans with Benjamin and Alyssa. The caterer, florist, and seating arrangements were complete. Not only did she win the dress argument but she also convinced Benjamin to give her money for a new wardrobe for Alyssa to wear as his wife.

"The night before your wedding, movers will transport Alyssa's belongings to your beach house. Alyssa will stay with me that night. In the morning, I'll take her to the salon for hair and makeup before bringing her to the beach house. You'll be married by a retired judge officiant since Alyssa does not want a real minister involved in your fake marriage."

Listening to the details made the wedding feel too real for Alyssa. She rubbed her temples to alleviate her increasing migraine pain —an all-too-familiar precursor to her anxiety attacks.

When they arrived at Rosemary's, her friends sat around the table, preparing to eat together, but Alyssa excused herself, saying she was tired. She went upstairs and laid down but instead of sleeping, she shivered with cold sweats. Alyssa's anxiety tormented her, but she was too embarrassed to tell her friends about her condition.

One of her calming techniques was practicing self-kindness by saying positive statements to herself, so she sat up and began the exercise.

"I am strong, and I can get through this."

"There's nothing for me to be afraid of."

She repeated the statements until the anxiety subsided. Alyssa reminded herself that she was helping a friend whom she trusted—someone who would never take advantage of her. She took a few cleansing breaths to relax her mind. That's when she heard a knock on the door. Benjamin entered with a tray of food.

"Thanks, Ben. I was just thinking of coming downstairs for dinner."

"Don't mention it," he said, turning to leave, but he stopped. "Alyssa, I know today has been very difficult. I really appreciate what you're doing for me, and I promise there'll be no more stressful situations after the wedding."

Alyssa thanked Ben, but as he left the room, he felt guilty for putting his friend through this ordeal, especially after he overheard her reciting the positive statements to herself when he stood outside the bedroom door.

On Friday, the movers arrived early. All the items were packed and out the door in less than thirty minutes.

"Mei Ling, I promise I'll stop by before you leave for Taiwan."

"I will hold you to that. Have fun staying with your friend!" said Mei Ling, hugging her goodbye. She didn't understand Alyssa, who was so lucky to be invited to stay the whole summer at a beach house. To Mei Ling, the place sounded like a dream, almost like a resort vacation. But she couldn't grasp why Alyssa seemed anxious about leaving the dorm.

Rosemary arrived just after the movers left with Alyssa's things. "So, it's the night before the big day. How do you feel?"

"I'm fine," Alyssa said with a tense smile.

"You know, you're not a very good liar. I can tell you're nervous. Try not to worry—Stan and I will be standing beside you and Ben. Everything will go as planned."

"I know, and it's reassuring that you'll both be there. But I can't shake the feeling that I'm doing something wrong."

"I think I understand. Your mind knows the wedding is a lie, and you're not used to doing things like this. Just keep telling yourself that it'll all be over by this time tomorrow."

Without thinking, Alyssa brought her finger to her mouth to bite her nails, forgetting they were freshly painted. The damage was minimal, but it was just one more new thing that she wasn't used to, as she rarely painted her nails. Turning to the mirror, Alyssa didn't recognize the image looking back at her. Rosemary's cosmetologist and hairdresser had transformed her into a different person.

There was a knock on the door, and the elderly house manager returned with the glass of water she requested. "Oh, you look so beautiful in that dress!" the woman said warmly. "I wish Benjamin had brought you to the house more often so we could've known each other better."

Alyssa thanked the lady, and while she drank the water; there was another knock.

"Hello?" a man's voice called out as he opened the door. "Good morning Agnes, nice to see you again," said the middle-aged man.

"Hello, Phillip," Agnes replied, but when she turned her back to him, she rolled her eyes. Turning her attention back to Alyssa, she asked, "Is there anything else I can get for you, Ms. Holt?"

"Um, no. Thank you for the water."

Phillip introduced himself as Benjamin's father.

Alyssa stood as he extended his hand. "It's great to finally meet you," she said.

"Thank you. It's great to meet you too. You look like the perfect bride, by the way, very beautiful." He looked over his shoulder, making certain that Agnes had left before saying, "Thank you so much for doing this for Ben. It's unfortunate Gloria didn't come though like we thought she would; so, we're truly grateful to you for stepping in like this; we won't forget it."

Before Alyssa could respond, a harried Rosemary entered the room, slightly out of breath. "Whew, I made it in time! Oh, hello, Mr. Hallerman. I had to rush to the florist to pick up the bouquet. Alyssa, Mr. Hallerman will walk you down the aisle." Rosemary checked Alyssa's dress and straightened her veil before handing over the bouquet. "You look fabulous! Are you ready for this?" she asked, smiling.

Alyssa took a deep breath. "As ready as I'll ever be. Let's get this over with."

"Great! I'll go cue the music while you and Mr. Hallerman wait arm in arm by the door."

Alyssa heard the music play a few seconds after Rosemary left. Mr. Hallerman promptly opened the door and escorted her from the library through the expansive entryway toward the back of the home. They walked in step with the wedding march, emerging onto the decorated patio. Rows of guests were seated on both sides of the aisle. They stared at the unknown bride as she passed by. Alyssa had no idea so many people would be there. Looking around, she estimated the total number of guests to be at least forty or fifty. *So, this is Benjamin's idea of a small private wedding?*

The anxiety attack came on suddenly. Alyssa's rapid breathing made Mr. Hallerman whisper, "Are you alright? There's nothing to be nervous about." She fought through the anxiety, successfully suppressing her emotions as she stood firmly next to Benjamin under the flowered wedding arch and stared at a spot over Ben's shoulder. She didn't look into his eyes until it was time to kiss. Luckily, Rosemary made them practice beforehand. Alyssa knew to just close her eyes and let Benjamin kiss her lightly on her lips, as they had rehearsed.

She sighed with relief when the ceremony ended. Rosemary came over and hugged her while at the same time whispering, "you have to smile, try to look like a happy bride." Alyssa obliged and allowed Benjamin to lead her by the hand through the crowd of guests. So many strange people smiled at her, commenting on what a beautiful bride she was. Alyssa smiled back dutifully. Some stopped Ben, congratulating him and patting him on the back.

When the newlyweds reached the entrance to the home, the young man who'd watched the couple at the restaurant last week, seemingly appeared out of nowhere. He jumped in front of their path and punched Ben so hard, the newlywed groom fell backwards to the ground. Alyssa screamed and ran in the opposite direction down the beach stairs as the man yelled, "That's for my sister, you punk!" He then made a swift exit down the same stairs. All the guests stood out of the way of the tall athletic man.

As the young man walked through the gate onto the beach, he stood a few yards from Alyssa. His nostrils flared with anger as he stared at the bride. Wracked with fear, Alyssa took off her heeled shoes and ran as fast as she could to get away from him. Several beach visitors gawked at the young woman in the wedding dress running down the shoreline. She looked back repeatedly, though no one chased her. Others looked around for a camera crew, believing they were witnessing the filming of a Hollywood sketch. Benjamin's attacker watched her with amusement before sauntering off.

Back at the beach house, Rosemary brought Benjamin an ice pack for his jaw as he sat on the couch with Stanley.

"Well, apparently someone didn't get the memo," said Stanley.

"Stan, this isn't funny. I can't believe Gloria didn't tell her idiot brother about *her* plan. Now Ben's wedding will be the topic of all the office gossip for the rest of the year," said Rosemary.

"Hey Ben, maybe next time don't coerce your employees into attending your *fake* wedding just to make the wedding pictures look legit," Stanley quipped.

Benjamin rolled his eyes.

His father joined them on the couch. "Hey, did you see how scared Alyssa was when she ran off? I thought foster kids were tougher than that."

"Yeah, I'm not surprised she took off. Alyssa has these fears, and she's easily scared. I'm trying to help her to not let fear stop her from living. We're still working on that," Ben replied.

"Oh, by the way," Mr. Hallerman whispered to Ben. "Listen, I know Alyssa's doing this for you as a friend, but make sure she doesn't fall in love with you or anything. She's a pretty girl with no money, and you're a good catch. Also, I found out she didn't tell you the whole truth about her parents being dead."

"What do you mean 'found out'?" asked Benjamin.

"Yes, well, I figured my gullible son wouldn't think of running a background check on his 'friend' before committing to a fake marriage. Did you know Alyssa's mother is alive and living in a small town outside Henderson, Nevada? From the look on your face, I'm guessing the answer is no. Look, if this thing blows up in your face, you only have yourself to blame. I still don't understand why you didn't give Gloria a legitimate proposal—that's what she expected from you."

Benjamin was stunned. "Alyssa's mother is alive?"

"Yes, she lied to you about that. Who knows what else she's lied about? You don't know this girl. What'll you do if she refuses to annul the marriage after sixty days? She could lie and claim the marriage was consummated and then demand a divorce settlement. You could lose half your assets."

Benjamin shook his head. "You're wrong, Dad. I trust Alyssa. She would never do that." Then, a new worry crept in. "Oh no... Alyssa! Do you think Gloria's creepy brother could be harassing her? Stan, we must find her," Benjamin said, standing up.

"No, I'll go find her. If she sees your swollen face, she may run again," said Stanley, rising from his seat.

Once he was on the beach, it wasn't hard to determine what direction his friend ran in. Sunbathers were still gawking, and pointing down the shoreline. Stanley walked in that direction for a few minutes before he spotted Alyssa sitting on the sand, hugging herself, clutching her heels in one hand. Her expression was the same as when he had found her in Benjamin's trunk, stressed and on edge. So, instead of calling her name, he sat quietly beside her.

Alyssa glanced up. "Stanley? H–how's Ben?"

"Don't worry about him. He'll be fine. Ben sent me to find you. That was Gloria's little brother who decked him. She forgot to fill him in on the wedding being fake." He exhaled. "We were all worried about you. C'mon, let's head back."

Alyssa sighed. "Stanley, I don't want to face those people. They must think something's wrong with me for running away and leaving my husband behind."

"Trust me, no one thinks that. We were all shocked to see Ben get decked, and you were standing next to him when it happened, so you had every reason to be frightened. Her brother's gone now, so it's time for you to return." Stan held out his hand, and Alyssa took it; they stood up together. "Hang in there. I promise this will all be over soon," he said.

When they returned to the beach house, the guests were seated with their meals. Some looked up when Alyssa returned, but no one said anything.

Rosemary had a worried look when Alyssa and Stanley arrived. "There you are! How are you feeling? I missed the attack when I checked on the caterers."

"I'm better now, thanks. My face must look a mess. I'd better go clean up."

Alyssa made her way to the master suite she and Benjamin would be sharing for the next sixty days. Benjamin had hidden a cot for himself in the walk-in closet because Agnes would get suspicious if they slept in separate rooms. Alyssa walked in on Benjamin in the en-suite. He was standing over the sink holding an ice pack to his cheek.

"Ben? Sorry, I should have knocked. How are you feeling?"

"Like an idiot for letting Andrew sucker-punch me in front of all the guests," he muttered. "Sorry. I know this was more drama than we planned for, but I promise it will be over soon. The guests will leave in a few hours. Tomorrow, we leave for the honeymoon in Acapulco—that's a two-week break from prying eyes."

"I'm looking forward to it. I've packed my books for my correspondence courses to keep me busy. I should get a lot of studying done. Are you bringing anything important?"

"Sort of, my Nintendo and some account books from my grandfather's company."

"Isn't it *your* company now?"

"You're right. I guess it hasn't sunk in yet. Maybe spending two weeks reading these accounts will help with that. Listen, Stan, Rosemary, and I want you to branch out and try new things during these two weeks. I don't want you locked in the hotel room studying the entire time. We're going to a resort. Push yourself to try new activities and meet different people. I promise you'll have fun there. There are plenty of water sports and beach events. I want you to relax and enjoy yourself."

Alyssa hesitated. "I'm not sure I'll have a lot of spare time. My correspondence courses are intense. I'm scheduled to take finals before the fall semester begins; If I don't pass, they don't give me the credits."

"You've done very well with your grades so far, I'm certain you'll pass without any issues."

"Thanks Ben, I hope you're right."

CHAPTER
THIRTEEN

"But by the grace of God, I am what I am."

1 Corinthians 15:10

Acapulco, Mexico

Alyssa gripped the armrests tightly and took deep breaths as the plane bounced through turbulence.

"Is this your first international flight?" asked Ben.

Alyssa nodded. "It's also my first flight." She hesitated before adding, "Ben, I must confess something: sometimes, I struggle with anxiety."

"Oh, I wish you had told me earlier. We could have driven to the resort instead of flying."

"But I wanted to fly. It's one of the fears I plan to conquer. Stanley said I should remember Isaiah 41:10 whenever I'm afraid."

"I know that one: 'Fear not, for I am with you; be not dismayed, for I am your God.'" Ben paused, smirking at Alyssa's reaction. "What? Why are you looking at me like that? I know the Bible. My grandfather took me to Sunday school whenever he attended church, and he never missed a Sunday. I believe in God; I believe Christ is my Lord and Savior. I've read the Bible several times, so it's not difficult for me to remember scripture"

"Wow! I had no idea you were a believer. Tell me something: why don't you ever go to Stanley's Bible study?"

"Because I don't like churches. Also, I know Stanley. He

wouldn't be satisfied with a one-time visit. He'd want me with him every week."

"Well, what's wrong with attending church services?"

"There are many reasons, but the number one reason is that I don't trust pastors. There are too many bad apples out there doing things they shouldn't. Well, you've experienced that for yourself, haven't you? Churches have minimal to no oversight. Clergymen misuse their influence to do whatever they want while the congregation turns a blind eye. Just listen to the news, pastors are telling us who to vote for, even though Jesus wasn't political. They steal money from church offerings, commit sex crimes, and take advantage of people who trust them. That's what really gets me angry. Why would I want to be a part of something like that?" Benjamin noticed Alyssa's sadness. "Alyssa, I'm sorry if I've upset you, but this is how I feel."

"No, I'm not upset with you, I'm upset with myself. I'm one of those congregants who turned a blind eye. I knew Pastor Bryant had a reputation for doing things he shouldn't, but I kept my mouth shut like everyone else. Maybe if I had spoken up earlier about some of the things I knew, he wouldn't have tried to force me into marriage."

"Hey, I wasn't referring to you when I said congregants turn a blind eye. You were in no position to go up against your morally corrupt pastor. You were a minor. But tell me something, why did you keep attending that church when you knew the pastor's reputation?"

"I wanted to leave and try a new church because Pastor Bryant never quoted scripture when he preached, and some of his statements even seemed to contradict the Bible. But Cousin Hazel was afraid to leave. Also, she has sentimental ties to Pitway Baptist. She grew up attending that church and was baptized and married there. Her friends also go there. In the beginning, the church was a blessing to me too. When I was a kid, Pastor Darrell was in charge, and even you would have loved his sermons. He was a genuine man of God.

"I was young when my mother... well, when I no longer had a mother. After that, I started acting out. I didn't care about anyone because I believed no one cared about me. I did everything I was taught not to do—I cursed, started fights, and did other things I'm ashamed of. If it weren't for the help I received from Pastor Darrell and the children's ministry staff, you'd never call me a friend today. I loved working at the children's ministry as well, and I wanted so much to be someone the children could come to for help."

When the plane lurched through another series of bouncy, turbulent jolts, Alyssa grasped the armrests again. Benjamin stood and rummaged through his carry-on bag.

"Here, play with this to keep your mind off the flight."

"What is it?"

"I'll show you. It's called a Game Boy. This game is called Tetris. Watch me play the first game, and you'll get the hang of it."

Almost an hour passed before Alyssa managed to pry the Gameboy from Benjamin's grasp.

He sighed as she tugged it away. "Guess I got carried away. My dad's always yelling at me when he sees me playing it."

Alyssa played the game until the plane began its descent, hitting more turbulence. She handed the game back to Benjamin and gripped the armrest until they landed.

Their taxi passed many scenic resorts before arriving at the Palacio De Los Sueños. Like the others, it was a gated resort. As they waited for the gates to open, young, impoverished children approached the car with their hands outstretched, begging for money. Alyssa reached into her bag and handed money to the children closest to her.

"Please don't do that, Señorita," the driver cautioned. "You'll only encourage them to come back. We're trying to keep them away."

Once the gates opened, the taxi rolled forward. Alyssa was amazed by the beautiful, lush resort grounds. Numerous flowering shrubs and plants surrounded decorative fountains. Tennis courts and pools were located behind a line of palm trees.

"Wow, Ben! This place looks expensive. You must have paid a lot!"

"I did, but I think we both deserve a good break after the wedding. Next time you speak to Rosemary, please tell her all about this place so she stops calling me a cheapskate."

"I don't understand... You didn't want to pay a lot for this wedding. Why overpay for a fake honeymoon?"

"I love this place," Benjamin said excitedly. "My parents brought me here a lot when I was a kid. The resort has changed a little, but the layout is the same as I remember. I haven't been back since my parents' divorce."

"Um, I know you're close to your dad, but you never talk about your mom. Where is she?"

Alyssa waited for an answer, but it never came. The driver stopped at the entrance and removed their bags. They checked in and received their room key before a porter escorted them to their suite. The large suite contained one king-sized bed and a sleeper sofa.

"You take the bed; I'll use the sleeper sofa," said Benjamin. "I'm going to shower and head to the pool. Are you coming?"

"No, I think I'd like to explore the grounds and see what's available."

"Oh, I'll come with you if you want me to."

"No, I'll be fine."

"Alright, let's meet back here in two hours for lunch, okay?"

"That's fine by me," she replied.

Alyssa had never been to a resort before. As she walked, she studied every detail. There was a golf course and other sports areas. Food and drinks were available everywhere at the all-inclusive establishment. On her way back to the room, a maid greeted her in the hallway.

"Mrs. Hallerman? Mrs. Hallerman?" the maid called out twice, but Alyssa continued to walk to her room, unfazed. It was only when the maid called out a third time that she remembered Hallerman was now her surname.

"Oh, I'm so sorry! I'm not used to hearing my married name yet."

The maid politely asked if she needed any toiletries, but Alyssa declined. Once in the room, she repeated her new name over and over under her breath as a reminder to respond to it.

Benjamin, who was already in the room, laughed. "Why are you repeating 'Mrs. Hallerman?'"

"I'm hoping that repeating it will help me remember to respond. The maid called out to me just now, but I thought she was calling someone else."

"Don't worry too much about that. No one here knows who we are. Let's go eat, I'm starving."

An hour later, Benjamin pushed his chair back from the table. "That was a wonderful steak—medium well, just how I like it." He noticed Alyssa pushing the food around on her plate. "You know, if you don't like your food, you can order something else. What's on your mind?"

"Well, with all the fake wedding stuff, I forgot to call Cousin Hazel before we left. If I call from here, the Mexico number will show up, and I have no idea how to explain that to her. So, I guess I'll have to wait until I'm back in Los Angeles to call."

"You worry too much. Your cousin knows you're safe as long as you're far away from that pastor. She's probably hoping you're enjoying your time away. I have an idea! Since you promised to try new things, tomorrow I'll teach you to water ski. That should take your mind off worrying. This is your first time in Mexico; remember, I don't want you wasting time studying in the room every day. Have some fun and relax. When we return, we'll have to keep up appearances until the sixty days are over."

***

"I'm so sorry, Ben! I should have been more careful," Alyssa said.

"Please, stop apologizing. It was just an accident," Benjamin assured her. He limped along the resort path with a crutch under one arm and Alyssa under his other arm as support. They had spent most of the morning at the beach, where Benjamin had given Alyssa brief instructions on how to water ski. She enjoyed it tremendously, but when the motorboat turned around, she lost control and crashed into Benjamin. His minor ankle sprain was more of an embarrassment than anything else. As they entered their suite, Alyssa directed him toward the king bed instead of the sofa.

"What are you doing?" he asked.

"Ben, you must take the bed. It's closer to the bathroom."

"No, it's only a slight sprain. This isn't necessary," he protested.

"I'm not taking no for an answer," she replied, pulling back the covers. She propped up his ankle with pillows and placed an ice pack on it. "I'm going downstairs to get your lunch."

"You don't need to do that. We have room service."

"The room service menu is limited. I'll see if they have a steak for you." Alyssa was out the door before he could protest. Benjamin sighed in frustration; all his watersport plans were now on hold. The doctor had instructed him to stay off his feet for at least three days. He decided this was a good time to review the company accounts. The books, however, were far away on the sofa bed. Benjamin hopped to the sofa to pick up the ledgers. On his way back, he tripped over his slippers and crashed to the floor; experiencing excruciating pain as he landed hard on his sprain.

Alyssa returned to find him sitting on the bed massaging the swollen ankle. "What happened? What did you do?"

"I didn't see the slippers when I got up, and my crutch slipped on them."

"Oh, Ben, you're in a lot of pain!" Alyssa said, rushing to the bathroom. She returned with pain relievers and placed them in his hand before removing the glass of wine from the tray she had brought.

"Wait, where are you taking that?" Benjamin protested.

"Don't you know you're not supposed to drink alcohol with medicine?"

"Oh, yeah, I forgot. Thanks for bringing me dinner. I suppose you're going down to eat yours?"

"Nonsense, I'll be back with my tray, and I promise to try something new. You go ahead and start without me. I'm not sure how long I'll be."

After their meal, they discussed what they would do when they returned to Los Angeles.

"I know there's a ton of work for me to catch up on and I'll work late most days. Some business decisions were left hanging, and they'll need immediate attention when I'm back in the office. I'll come home to sleep and eat, that's about it. I told Agnes you'll be doing a lot of studying, and she promised not to get in your way. Also, Gloria called before we left. Unfortunately, her idiot brother insists on apologizing to you in person for scaring you, so he'll be dropping by."

"Can't you tell Gloria it's not necessary? I don't need an apology. Besides, you're the one he decked. Shouldn't he be apologizing to you?"

"I'll try, but Andrew's thick-headed. Maybe it's all those punches he takes as an amateur boxer. Anyway, he doesn't like me for some reason, so any apology I receive will not be sincere."

"Hmm, is he really thick-headed, or are you just saying that because he decked you?"

Benjamin smiled, "It's a little of both, but you'll see for yourself when we return. Hey, let's watch some TV or something before we're buried in our work."

"That's fine with me." Alyssa sat on the bed as Benjamin turned on the remote. "What's on that's good?"

They settled on an intense family mystery movie that held their attention until the end. "That was a great movie. I felt so sorry for the little boy losing his family," said Alyssa.

"Yeah, I know what you mean. Hey, can I ask you something?"

"Sure."

"Um... do you mind talking about your parents?" Benjamin immediately regretted asking when he saw how Alyssa's expression changed. "Sorry, I didn't mean to pry..."

"No, it's fine," Alyssa sighed. "I'm used to keeping my personal life to myself, but you're my friend. Well, I'll start from the beginning. My father grew up in foster care from the age of three. The government took him from his family's reservation, claiming he was neglected. When my dad turned eighteen, he searched for his real family. Unfortunately, the government didn't maintain their records well. No one knew who his birth parents were or what native tribe he belonged to.

"I was very close to my dad... Wait," Alyssa grabbed her wallet and passed a photo to Ben. It showed a much younger Alyssa and a handsome Native American man. They were smiling cheek to cheek. Benjamin instantly saw the resemblance. Father and daughter had the same straight nose and rounded lips.

"My dad was a member of the Army Special Forces unit. They'd send him on occasional unscheduled events, and he'd always come back. When my father was home, he took me wherever he went, even if it was just to fix something in a neighbor's house. It was his way of making up for lost time. One thing I could count on whenever he returned was a trip to the beach. We'd go early in the morning and spend hours swimming and playing.

I remember the last time he left for work. A long time passed, and I kept asking my mother when he was coming back, but even she had no answer for me. One day, two army officers came to the door, and my mother started crying. I didn't believe my dad was dead until the funeral." She paused, "I really miss him a lot."

"I'm sorry you had to experience that at such a young age," said Benjamin.

"My mom was never the same after that. She'd get drunk and hang out with different boyfriends. I was ten when she took off with her abusive boyfriend. She didn't say goodbye or anything, no calls. I've lived with Hazel since then."

"I'm so sorry, Alyssa," Benjamin said softly. "I thought you told us she died."

Alyssa broke eye contact before explaining. "That's what I let people believe. I never know what to say to people when they ask where my mother is. At school, my friends would ask, 'Where's your mother?' and I'd just say, 'I don't know.' This went on for a while. At parent-teacher conferences, Cousin Hazel would show up. One day, someone asked, 'Is your mother dead?' and I said yes because I didn't want to talk about my mom anymore. At first, I felt bad for lying, but then I realized it worked. People stopped asking about my mom and I let everyone think she had died.

Alyssa stood up and looked out the window. "In a way, she is dead to me because her leaving meant she didn't want me any-more. Truth is, I honestly don't know whether she's alive or dead; her boyfriend used to beat her so badly that she was constantly in and out of the hospital. If she were dead, it would explain why she never contacted me."

"I'm really sorry, Alyssa. You went through a lot. Listen, if you ever want to find your mother, I could help you. Would you like that?"

Alyssa sat down on the bed and went silent for a moment, thinking. "I'm not sure. If she's alive and hasn't contacted me or Cousin Hazel all these years, it means she really doesn't want me in her life. I don't know if I can handle that. But... a small part of me would like to see her again."

"That's understandable. We'll leave it alone then," said Benjamin as he put an arm around his friend's shoulders and wiped her tears with a napkin.

In the morning, Alyssa returned to the suite with Ben's breakfast just as he stepped out of the bathroom.

"Alyssa, I appreciate you looking after me, but I don't want you stuck inside just because I'm stuck here. Go out and enjoy yourself. I know how much you love the beach. Go, have fun."

"I don't know. It doesn't feel right leaving you by yourself. What if you need help?"

"I'll call the desk if I need help, but I don't anticipate any problems. This is only a mild sprain. I'll be back to normal in a few days."

"Well, okay then. I did want to explore all the areas of the resort. I'll grab a muffin or something and find a nice place to eat. See you in a bit."

Alyssa strolled into the dining area, where she saw couples and families seated together, enjoying breakfast. She noticed that no one sat alone. She took a muffin, an apple, and a small juice before moving to the outdoor tables.

She'd forgotten her beach hat, and the sun was relentless. Alyssa walked close to the resort walls where the trees provided some shade for her path. She saw movement on the other side of the resort gate as she passed by and had a feeling she was being watched. When Alyssa turned around, she spotted them: two young boys on the other side of the gates. Their clothes were torn and filthy. They looked at her but said nothing; she assumed they feared she'd chase them away. Though they didn't ask, she walked to the gate, took the breakfast items out of her bag, and passed them through the iron gate bars. They ate hungrily and shared the juice. When they finished, she asked their names and where their parents were. The older boy's name was Emilio, and his younger brother was Antonio. With the little Spanish she knew, Alyssa found out that their father went missing when they were younger, and their mother didn't have enough food for them to eat. Hearing this, Alyssa told them to wait for her. She returned to the dining area and filled her beach bag with fruit, muffins, and small packs of cereal and milk.

The boys were overjoyed when she returned; they stuffed the foods inside their shirts and pants pockets; they carried what didn't fit in their arms. Both thanked her profusely with huge smiles before retreating up the hill across the road from the resort gates. Alyssa returned to the suite feeling elated. She asked Benjamin if he could give her some money to buy a few necessities. He happily obliged, glad that something had made his friend smile. Alyssa promptly went to the resort shops and purchased shorts and t-shirts for the boys.

For the next two days, Benjamin noticed a pattern. After dropping off his breakfast, Alyssa would disappear until lunchtime. Whenever he asked about her morning, he only received positive, one-word replies. Curious, he called Rosemary and asked if she'd ever seen Alyssa *really* happy.

"Hmm, sounds to me like she's met someone she likes. Does she wear the ring?"

"Nah, I'm certain it's not that. At least, I don't think she would see someone. She asked for money to buy some things. I thought she'd purchase clothing or jewelry, but I haven't seen a shopping bag or anything new."

"Now you've got me thinking—maybe she goes to the casino!"

"No, no, Alyssa would never ask for money to gamble. But I need to know what she's doing and why she's keeping it a secret. I won't tell her my ankle's better. I'll keep that info to myself and follow her tomorrow."

"Are you sure, Ben? Remember, Alyssa's there because she's doing you a favor. Shouldn't you respect her privacy?"

"I know that; but if what you say is true, and she's meeting someone; I must make sure she's safe, right? Acapulco's not what it used to be; they have a serious crime rate now. I didn't know about that until I began reading the local newspapers while I was resting."

"You're scaring me now, Ben. Please make sure Alyssa's safe."

"I will. And if she's meeting someone harmless, I promise not to interfere."

The next morning, Benjamin lay in bed with his eyes closed when Alyssa returned with his breakfast. She hummed to herself as she trekked out their suite and locked the door. A fully dressed Benjamin whipped the covers off and waited by the door until he heard the elevator ding. After waiting a few seconds for the door to close, he exited the suite and pressed the button for the next elevator. It took longer than expected, Alyssa wasn't in the dining area when he arrived.

Scanning the outdoor area, he spotted her moving along the resort wall, heading for the gate entrance. Benjamin followed as quickly as he could without running. He watched Alyssa looking around before squeezing through the shrubbery next to the gate. She then looked up and down the road before crossing it. There was nothing on the other side but rugged terrain, trees, rocks, and shrubbery.

He was surprised when he heard her call out, "Antonio? Antonio?"

Shocked, Benjamin shouted her name. "Alyssa, what are you doing?"

Alyssa jumped in fright. Confused, she walked slowly across

the road to a furious Ben waiting at the gate. "Ben, you're walking? And you followed me?!"

"It's a good thing my ankle's healed enough for me to follow you. What are you doing, and who's Antonio?"

"First, *you* tell me why you're following me," she replied angrily.

"I'm following you to make sure you're safe. I was concerned. You've been unusually happy the past few mornings, and I wanted to know why."

"And I want to know why you didn't tell me you could walk! When I brought your breakfast, you were asleep. How were you able to get dressed and follow me so quickly?"

"I–I wasn't exactly asleep," Benjamin replied apologetically.

"Excuse me, Señorita y Señor," an unfamiliar voice called out. A staff member then walked to where they were standing. "Are you looking for the children who stayed at the gate?"

Alyssa's eyes widened. "Yes! Do you know where they are?"

"Ahh, you're the one! Señorita, the manager was walking the grounds when he saw you feeding the kids. He chased the boys away, saying, 'Children begging at the gate doesn't look nice for business.' He told them they're not allowed to come back."

"Oh no! Can I talk to the manager and explain that it wasn't their fault? I was the one who looked for them."

"I'm sorry, Señorita. The manager won't change his mind. He hates when they come to the gate."

"This is terrible. Tell me, do you know where they live? I want to see them," she asked imploringly.

"Señorita, those kids live in the slums, high in the mountains. It's a very dangerous place. Even I would never travel in that area. Strangers are kidnapped or shot. The place is filled with murderous drug dealers; you cannot go there."

Disheartened, Alyssa thanked the man for the information and slowly walked away. Benjamin caught up to her. "Alyssa? Alyssa, I'm sorry for how I behaved," he said, trailing behind. "I had to make sure you were safe."

"Benjamin, please leave. I want to be alone right now," she replied, continuing to walk away.

Benjamin paced in their suite. Several hours had passed, and Alyssa still hadn't returned. He tried working on the accounts while he waited but gave up when nothing he read made sense. It was late in the afternoon. From his window, Benjamin watched guests strolling with their partners to the dining halls. He scanned the crowd, but Alyssa wasn't among them.

Growing more anxious, Benjamin finally left the suite and searched the beach, checking every cabana and anywhere else she may have gone. Ben treaded through the resort gardens and pool areas with no luck. Thinking of the things Alyssa loved, he returned to the beach. By then, most of the guests had retired to dinner. When he spotted a figure sitting alone at the far, less populated, rocky end of the beach, Benjamin instinctively knew who it was.

When he reached her, he immediately abandoned his plan to admonish her for making him worry. She sat hunched over, wearing the same troubled expression she had when they first met at his car.

"Alyssa, you've been out here too long. Let's go back to the suite, please."

She said nothing when he pulled her up and led her by the hand back to the resort building.

When they headed toward the dining hall, Alyssa pulled away. "I'm too tired to eat. I'll just go to the room and lie down."

When Benjamin returned to their suite with trays of food, he found her lying on the sofa bed, staring into space. "Alyssa, I'm very sorry for the way I behaved earlier. I don't know why I shouted at you. Talk to me, shout if you must, but say something, please," he pleaded.

"I'm not angry with you, Ben."

"Then what is it? Do you miss those kids that much?"

"It's not just that I miss them. They trusted me, I got to know them. They told me how their father went missing and then their mother found out a drug dealer killed him because he didn't want to work for them. Since then, they've come to the resort gate to collect coins from the guests. When they go home, they give the money to their mother to buy food. I thought I was helping by bringing them food, but my meddling caused them to be banned from the resort. They'll go hungry, and it's all my fault."

"No, it's not your fault the hotel manager doesn't have a heart. You did what real Christians do. When they can, they feed the hungry."

"Why did I intervene? They would have been better off if I had left them alone. Why do these things keep happening? I try to do something good, and then it backfires. This time, children are going hungry because of me. If only I knew how to find them, maybe..."

"No! Don't even think of doing that."

"But I failed them... just like so many other things in my life. Take the children's ministry. I started well and got my friends committed to working there. The kids were enjoying themselves there. Then I ran away, leaving my friends behind to do the work without me. Unfortunately, that didn't work. I spoke with my friend Sarah last week; she told me Pastor Bryant convinced the board to shut it down."

"Alyssa, you didn't fail. Your pastor did. He was more concerned about forcing you to marry him than he was about the children's ministry."

"Ben, you don't know about other things I've tried and failed at. I started a town cleaning brigade, and it was going well. Then the town mayor shut us down because it was just us high school kids and he was afraid one of us would get hurt and sue the town. We had an elderly blind woman who lives in town. Her seeing eye dog was sick at the vets. Sarah and I saw her attempting to cross the street; so, we took her arm to help her, but she shouted and yelled 'thief.' Later we learned that we should ask permission first before touching someone. Anyway, bad things happen when I'm involved. Take our first day here, I injured you when you were trying to teach me to water ski. Maybe Pastor Bryant was right. Maybe I am hapless."

"Don't do this. You're tearing yourself down because a few bad things happened. Guess what? Bad things happen to good people all the time. Don't give up being the great person you are. You've succeeded in so many things that others in your circumstances would have given up on. Why do you think Rosemary loves you so much? She admires you and considers you a great friend even though she's only known you for a year. We all care about you. Don't believe anything your pastor said about you. As for him, I'll just say that manipulative, false men of God who put their desires above their congregation are exactly why I don't attend church. But you are not hapless."

Alyssa sat up. "Thanks, Ben. I know you're trying to cheer me up, but I know the truth. I'm not great or special in any way. If I were, my mother would never have left me behind."

Benjamin tried to think of something that would disprove Alyssa's comment, but nothing came to mind. There were no easy quotes or phrases to bring his friend out of her depressive state. He sighed as he sat next to Alyssa and put his arm around her as she placed her head on his shoulder.

When they first began this faux wedding plan, Benjamin had told Alyssa he'd tell her everything she needed to know. But now, his conscience reminded him of information he'd purposely withheld. Benjamin felt awful for keeping a large part of his life secret when he knew all about Alyssa's life. But the fear of not being in control of the emotions tied to his story kept his mouth shut. He didn't know for how long he sat deep in thought, but when he finally looked down, Alyssa was nodding off.

He gently laid her down on the sofa and covered her with a

blanket. Sleep never came for Benjamin that night. Instead, he was haunted by old painful memories.

"Rose, I need your help. She's so unhappy. What can I say to fix things?"

"Ben, there's no quick fix. She's had a rough life. It looks like bad events like this one make her reflect on her past. For now, I'll say you should just be there for her in this moment. That said, I know Alyssa. She's very resilient. I'm certain she'll be her old self again in no time. I just wish I could still be here when you guys get back, but you know I'm going away with my parents. All I can say is, keep being a good friend."

"Wait, she's at the door. I'll call you back." Benjamin hung up just as the door to their suite swung open. "Good morning! How are you feeling today? You were gone when I woke up, I was worried about you."

"Sorry Ben. I should have left a note. I woke up at around 5 a.m. and couldn't go back to sleep. So I decided to walk on the beach to clear my head."

"It's almost eight o'clock. That must have been some walk."

"It was. I read some scripture before leaving, particularly Psalm 34:18: 'The Lord is near to the brokenhearted and saves the crushed in spirit.' I thought, that's me, crushed in spirit. So much has happened in the past year, and I realize that I haven't been truly happy since I left home. When I was with Antonio and Emilio... I don't know how to explain it, but I felt at home with them. Does that make sense?"

"Sort of. Whenever you talked about working with the children's ministry, your face lit up. Maybe that's your calling."

"I don't understand. What does that mean?"

"Well, the Bible says God gives everyone a gift or talent. A calling is something you do that makes life meaningful to you. It doesn't have to be something that everyone sees, like musical talent. Some people have gifts like communication, teaching, business, or art. Your talent may be in working with children."

"I never thought of it like that, but I do enjoy helping children." She paused for a moment, deep in thought. "Ben?"

"Yeah?"

"I want to go back home."

"We're leaving in a few days. You'll be back home in no time."

"No, not your home. I'm want to go back to Pitway, but after I finish working for you. I'll have some time between then and the day I start my fall classes. I need to go home and face whatever I must face."

"Look, you're very emotional now, so it's not a good time to make this kind of decision. Let's discuss this when we're back in L.A. We'll make a plan so that Stan and I can accompany you because there's no way I'm letting you go alone. In the meantime, try to enjoy these last days at the resort before we have to live among prying eyes."

"Sounds like you don't trust your house staff. But you've lived there with your grandfather. Don't you get along with them?"

"Yes, they're great and have always treated me well. It's just that they gossip. Some things they see or hear don't stay private. We'll have to keep up appearances as if we really are married."

FOURTEEN

"Can a woman forget her nursing child, that she should have no compassion on the son of her womb? Even these may forget, yet I will not forget you."

Isaiah 49:15 ESV

When they returned to Los Angeles, Benjamin received numerous messages from the office. He dropped his luggage and rushed to work to handle projects that couldn't wait. Meanwhile, Alyssa received a warm welcome from Agnes as soon as she stepped into the house. Agnes showed her all the wedding gifts that were stacked in the library, along with Alyssa's forwarded mail. She quickly opened a letter from her dorm friend, Mei Ling.

Hey friend!

Soooo, I decided to stay in L.A. to take summer courses, and someone showed me the newspaper with your wedding picture. Congratulations! I can't believe you got married during summer break! How come you never mentioned your engagement? Are you coming back to classes in the fall? You must be on your honeymoon now, but call me as soon as you're back.

Mei Ling

Alyssa felt terrible that Mei Ling and her dorm mates had discovered her secret marriage. She wrote back to her friend and promised to tell her everything when they meet up. Somehow, she'd have to stall the meeting until after the sixty-day wedding was over; Benjamin had made her promise not to disclose the reason for the wedding to anyone.

Cousin Hazel was at the top of her list of calls to make, but her messages indicated that Sarah had called several times, so she decided to make that call first.

"Alyssa? Hey, I've been trying to reach you for days. Where have you been?"

"Oh, I was offered a job, and it took me out of town. How are you? How's everything back home?"

"Well, you know. It's the same, day after day. Have you spoken to Hazel lately?"

"No, I was going to call her now. Is everything alright?"

"Oh, yes, everything is fine. I was just wondering because... I haven't seen her in a while. I'll get off the phone so you can give her a call. It was great hearing from you, Alyssa. Talk soon."

Alyssa sensed that Sarah wasn't telling her something. She called her cousin, but no one picked up, which was odd because they had an answering machine. Making a mental note to call again later, she unpacked and resumed her coursework until Agnes knocked on the door.

"Alyssa, you've been in here studying for so long that you didn't come for lunch. I thought I'd bring it to you." The senior house manager rolled in a food cart filled with fruit, sandwiches, and a salad. Gesturing at the food, she said, "By the way, I know what Ben likes, but you haven't been here long enough for me to find out your diet preferences."

"Thank you, Agnes. You didn't have to go to all this trouble for me. I could have grabbed something from the kitchen."

"Oh no, that's not necessary. I'm here to prepare all your meals. You just tell me what you like to eat and when."

"Thanks Agnes. I'm not fussy I'll eat whatever you prepare for Ben," Alyssa smiled.

"I doubt you'll want the same," Agnes chuckled. Benjamin loves eating lots of red meat."

"Hmm, that's true. He ate a lot of steak at the resort as well."

"Yes, he increased his red meat intake when he was on the football team at Stanford, and he hasn't changed his diet since."

"Ben played football?" Alyssa asked, then quickly corrected herself when she saw Agnes's curious expression. "Oh yes, I forgot all about that. You know, on second thought, I usually eat a small sandwich or soup with salad for lunch. And yogurt with toast for breakfast. That's what I'll have."

The next morning, Agnes entered the library to let Alyssa know she had a visitor. Alyssa wasn't expecting anyone since Rosemary was away and Stanley was at work. She walked out to the great room to be greeted by a man she didn't recognize at first because he was smiling instead of scowling.

Andrew stood over six feet tall with a muscular build that left no doubt he worked out. He was also very handsome. Gloria's brother held out a beautiful large bouquet. "These are for you. I came to...." Andrew stopped abruptly when Agnes entered the room.

"Is there anything I can get for you, Mrs. Hallerman?" Agnes asked, eyeing Andrew with disdain.

"No, Agnes, I'm fine. Thank you," Alyssa replied.

Andrew smirked. "I don't think she likes me," he said after Agnes left.

"Well, you did punch Benjamin at his wedding. Thank you for the flowers, by the way. They're beautiful."

"You're welcome. I picked them out myself. Uh, is there someplace we can speak privately?"

"Sure, let's sit by the pool." Alyssa escorted Andrew outside where no one could overhear them.

"I wanted to apologize in person for frightening you, that wasn't my intention. I came to the wedding to cause a commotion and embarrass Benjamin because I thought he dumped my sister.

I had no idea Gloria arranged all this; she didn't tell me. I have to say, though, you guys were very convincing. When I saw you walking hand in hand with Benjamin at the restaurant, I wanted to knock him out right there. But with so many people around, I figured the restaurant would call the police and have me arrested. So instead, I asked around to find out what was happening, and I was shocked to discover Benjamin was getting married that Saturday.

"It was so disturbing to me; he was just over to my house a few days before. Maybe I should have asked Gloria if they suddenly broke up. But she was so nonchalant, going about her day as if nothing had changed, that I was afraid to bring it up. Anyway, that Saturday, I dressed up, drove to the house, and walked closely behind a group of people who I think were Benjamin's employees. No one checked the guests. They just pointed to a table where I could sign my name in the wedding book. I walked in with the other guests and took a seat.

"When I heard Benjamin say 'I do' and saw him kiss you, my blood boiled. The next thing I knew, you were screaming and running away. Ben's father and Stanley were coming for me, so I made my exit. When you were at the bottom of the stairs, I saw fear in your eyes. All I could think of was, why would such a nice-looking girl marry a two-timing bum like Benjamin?"

"I was really scared. I didn't know who you were, why you did what you did, or if you were going to come after me."

"I'm very sorry about that, it wasn't my intention to frighten you. I was just so angry because I thought he betrayed my sister. Hey, why don't I take you out to lunch to make up for scaring you?"

"That's not necessary. I'm fine now, and I understand why you did that. Besides, I have tons of studying to do. Thanks again for the flowers."

"Please, it would make me feel so much better. C'mon, Gloria told me you're new to the city. I'm sure there are some places you haven't seen yet. I can show you around—maybe we can start with my campus? I'm at UCLA?"

"Wow, UCLA? I'd love to see it."

"Great! We can go now," Andrew said as they both stood.

"I didn't know you were in college too. What's your major?"

"Business Management. When I'm done, I'll work for my father. And when he retires, I'll take over the company. Hey, why don't you grab your things, I'll wait for you in the car.

Weeks passed, and Alyssa settled into a routine. She began her day with an early jog on the beach. Alyssa and Benjamin would eat breakfast together before Benjamin left for work. Afterwards, before continuing her studies, she'd sometimes meet with Andrew, who would take her to different parts of the city. She still could not reach her cousin when she called, but Hazel'd surprised her one weekend with a morning call she made from her friend's house. She told Alyssa that she was having problems with her phone line.

When Benjamin returned home after work, they would eat dinner together, usually under Agnes' watchful eye, before retiring to their suite. Once inside, they'd relax or play video games they were both hooked on. At night, they'd wash up and go to their separate beds.

While Benjamin caught up with work, he also made plans to do something he hoped would make Alyssa happy. The next day, he picked up Stanley, and the two drove off to fulfill Ben's plan. "Do you think this is a good idea?" asked Stanley.

Benjamin looked puzzled. "I don't get you sometimes. Don't you want Alyssa to be happy?"

"Who said this would make her happy!? You don't know anything about her mother except that she abandoned Alyssa as a child. And now you're going to drive up to the woman's house and ask her to reunite with her daughter? What gives you, of all people, the right to interfere in her family relationships?"

"Ugh, you're so negative about everything I do! I have a very good reason to interfere," Benjamin retorted. "You didn't see Alyssa when she fell apart at the resort. She was so depressed when those kids were banished from the gate. I didn't know what to do! And I don't want to see her like that again. I don't know why her mother stepped out on her, but people can change. In this case, I'm hoping for the better. It would be great if Mrs. Holt wanted to reconnect or at least be there for Alyssa when she returns to Pitway, it would mean the world to her."

"I still don't understand why Alyssa wants to go back there. Didn't her cousin say it wasn't safe?"

"Alyssa's an adult now. We can't stop her from returning home. Trust me, I tried my best to talk her out of it, but she's determined to go after our marriage is over. And I plan to be there for her no matter what."

"You can count me in too. Just let me know when," said Stanley.

Benjamin nodded. "Great. I'm thinking if that pastor and his obtuse cousins see Alyssa's mother and the two of us, maybe they'll come to their senses and back off."

"Your plan's beginning to make sense to me now." Stanley checked the Henderson City map he had brought. "We should be close to the house. Wait, her address says Lot#, what's that?

I think we missed a turn. We're further than we're supposed to be," Stanley continued.

Benjamin pulled over, reached for the map and studied it. "She must be in that trailer park we passed. I'll turn around."

The Mustang drove slowly through the graveled road of the mobile home community. The men searched each unit for the right lot number until they came to an old dented trailer where an old man and a woman were arguing outside the door. The man demanded rent money, while the haggard, thin woman replied he'd have to wait till her husband returned from work. Eventually, the man threw up his hands in frustration and walked off as the woman stood defiantly with her hands on her hips. Finally, noticing the two onlookers, she shouted, "What are you creeps looking at?!"

Benjamin stepped forward. "Um, excuse me, ma'am. We're looking for Mrs. Linda Holt."

Her expression darkened. "Mrs. Holt? That's my old married name. Who are you, and how do you know my name? Whoever you are, I don't have any money. I'll tell you what I just told him—my husband pays the bills, and he'll be back in two weeks. Now get lost and leave me alone."

With that, she spun around and climbed the steps to her trailer, slamming the door behind her.

Stanley exhaled. "Looks like we drove four hours for nothing."

"I'm not giving up that easily," Benjamin replied.

"What are you going to do? Harass her into talking to you? You do realize that over 47% of adults in Nevada own firearms?"

Benjamin smirked. "I've got an idea. Follow me." They returned to the car and drove to the main trailer park office. The man who'd argued with Linda opened the door when they knocked.

"Whatever you guys are selling, I'm not buying," he said sourly.

"Wait," Benjamin said quickly. "We're not selling anything. We're here to help you with the woman you were arguing with."

"Well, just how are you going to help me with that one?"

"Can we come in, please?" asked Ben.

The old man hesitated, then stepped aside to let them in. Benjamin asked how much Linda owed. When the man told him the overdue amount, Benjamin pulled out enough cash to cover it. "I'll need a signed receipt for this, please."

The perplexed landlord eagerly obliged.

With the receipt in hand, Benjamin and Stanley drove back to the trailer and knocked on the door. Linda was clearly irritated to see the same two men she had dismissed earlier, but Benjamin spoke quickly.

"We have something for you." He handed the paid rent receipt to Alyssa's mother and then asked, "Can we please come in and talk to you?"

She looked at the receipt, then back at the young men, and then hesitantly opened the door. Linda moved empty beer cans from the couch to make space for them. Benjamin sat while Stanley stood, studying the pictures on the wall. There was one large frame with Linda's wedding picture along with many smaller pictures of other people and children. Stanley could not find any with Alyssa.

"My rent is usually paid up, but I lost my job a month ago. My husband doesn't stay here all the time, so I was stuck waiting for him to handle it. But why did you pay my rent? Who are you?" she asked.

"We're friends of Alyssa. By the way, she doesn't know we're here. I looked you up because your daughter helped me out a great deal, and I wanted to do something nice for her. Um, it's none of my business; but before I go any further, I wanted to ask, do you want to be in contact with your daughter? She told us you left when she was young," said Benjamin.

Linda exhaled slowly, and sat down gingerly. "That is a very personal question. But I guess you deserve a response since you helped me out. First of all, I didn't just leave my girl alone. I knew my cousin Hazel would take care of her. She'd often ask for Alyssa to stay with her anyway.

"Alyssa's father had passed a few years back. John was in the army. Initially, he had to go overseas occasionally, but for the most part, he was home with us. Alyssa adored him, and he loved her. They would spend a lot of time together hiking or going to the beach. I'm not much of an outdoorsy person, so I'd usually stay home. I don't have a picture of her father here, but Alyssa looks just like him.

"Anyway, the army wanted him to sign up for special ops. He was so excited, but I knew it meant less time with his family, so I told him not to take it. He signed anyway. We argued a lot about that. After his training, they sent him on so many missions that we hardly saw him. Finally, he got a three-month break. We planned a road trip to track down his biological family. We were to visit places and reservations where he believed they might be located.

"But before we could head out, he received a volunteer request for a covert mission that required more men. Again, I told him not to go. He went anyway, saying he had to back up his buddies. John was the only soldier who never made it back."

Her voice hardened. "I hated him for dying. For leaving me alone with a child who looked so much like him, sometimes I couldn't stand looking at her. I had a couple of boyfriends after that, but Jason, that's him in our wedding picture on the wall there—he was the one. He's not perfect, but he's a good man. One day, we had a really bad fight. I said some things he didn't like, and Jason got rougher than usual. He was really sorry afterward. He brought me flowers and a ring to the hospital, saying it was time for us to get married. But he didn't want me to bring the kid. I didn't like leaving my little girl like that, but I knew she was better off living with Hazel than she would be with Jason and me. So, I did the right thing and left her behind."

Linda peered out the trailer window. "That's a nice car you have out there, looks expensive. Alyssa's doing alright if she has friends like you. How's my girl anyway? Maybe I should visit her. It'd be nice if she's able to help her mama out sometimes."

Benjamin met Stanley's gaze. Stanley gave the slightest shake of his head.

"Oh, Alyssa's not in a good financial situation," Stanley said with a casual shrug. "We were actually hoping to find family members who could help her out. As for the car, my friend here recently won money in Vegas. The first thing he did was blow it all on that used Mustang."

Benjamin nodded. "Yeah, Alyssa did me a great favor, so I thought I could return it by finding family members who could help fund her college education. But it looks like you have your own financial issues, so we'll leave you alone. Have a good day."

Benjamin and Stanley quickly exited the trailer and returned to the car.

They drove in silence for over two hours before Benjamin asked, "What kind of mother was that?" The dismay was evident in his voice. "I hope I didn't make things worse. Do you think she'll look Alyssa up and start asking her for money?"

Stanley sighed. "It's a very sad situation. Sometimes we don't realize that not everyone's blessed with a mother who loves them. But it seems Linda knew what a horrible parent she was. Leaving town *was* the best thing she did for her daughter. I'd hate to imagine what Alyssa's life would have been like if her mother and her abusive husband had raised her. And I can't imagine Linda turning down the money the pastor would have given her to force her underage daughter into marriage."

"Anyway, I doubt you have to worry about her contacting Alyssa. You saw her face when you told her Alyssa is 'looking for funds.'"

"Get rid of all bitterness, rage and anger, brawling and slander, along with every form of malice. Be kind and compassionate to one another, forgiving each other, just as in Christ God forgave you."

Ephesians 4 31,32

Alyssa studied the calendar and counted nine days until the end of her marriage. The arrangement gave Alyssa extra time to study rather than work to save up for college. She imagined the remaining days would pass quickly, and she looked forward to the day she could stop living the lie. It wasn't all bad though. In fact, she found herself enjoying the beach house quite a bit.

Alyssa continued her routine of waking at daybreak to jog along the shore's edge while enjoying the tranquil beauty of a sunrise on the deserted beach. Benjamin was usually finished with their shared master bathroom by the time she returned. They continued to eat breakfast together and share the LA Times until Benjamin had to leave for work. Agnes also continued to watch them regularly. To keep up appearances, Alyssa would walk with Benjamin to the door and pretend to see him off with a kiss.

She was going to miss Agnes. The elderly woman was so kind to her and Ben. After they had returned from their faux honeymoon, Agnes had included heart-shaped toast with their breakfast for the remainder of the week. She had also left Gerber daisy bouquets in their bedroom because that was the flower Rosemary had chosen for Alyssa's bridal bouquet. Alyssa felt terrible for deceiving such a nice woman.

Just as she was about to leave for the library, the doorbell rang. Alyssa wondered who it could be. She hoped it wasn't Andrew again. She'd already told him she needed more time to study. The truth was, she never liked the way he talked badly about Benjamin. Andrew didn't believe Benjamin was good enough for his sister. She also sensed he desired to get closer to her, and she had no interest in that. Stanley was the only other person who visited, but he never came this early. A few minutes later, an excited Agnes entered the library.

"Excuse me, Mrs. Hallerman. You have a visitor."

Alyssa didn't understand the broad smile on her face. She walked into the huge great room where her guest was waiting. Alyssa saw a smartly dressed older woman with short brown hair smiling at her. Something about her features seemed familiar.

"Alyssa, I'm so happy to finally meet you. I'm Maureen—your mother in-law." The woman opened her arms and hugged a stunned Alyssa.

"I hope this isn't a bad time to visit. I wanted to see you earlier, but Ben doesn't return my calls. Well, I'm sure you know all about that. Agnes told me you're studying, so I won't get in your way. They're putting my things into the guest house."

"Guest house? There's a guest house?"

"Yes, of course. Didn't Benny show it to you?"

"Ahh, he's been so busy with the business. I'm sure he planned to get around to it."

"Excuse me, Mrs. Hallerman, but I have an idea," suggested Agnes. "Why don't you have lunch with Miss Maureen in the guest house? That way, you could get to know each other better."

"That's a wonderful idea, Agnes! I should be settled in by then," Maureen said, smiling kindly. "Well then, I'll let you get back to your studies for now. I'm looking forward to our lunch date."

Still stunned, Alyssa managed to reply, "Me too," before retreating to the library. After closing and locking the door, she promptly telephoned Benjamin's office. His secretary picked up the call.

"Hello, this is Alyssa Hallerman. Is Ben available?"

"Hello, Mrs. Hallerman. Mr. Hallerman is out of the office today on an errand."

"Oh, that's unusual. Did he say where he was going?"

"I'm sorry, Mrs. Hallerman. He didn't say."

Alyssa wondered aloud, "I wonder if he's with Gloria."

"Mrs. Hallerman?"

"Oh, sorry. I didn't mean it that way."

"Would you like to leave a message, Mrs. Hallerman?"

"Yes, please tell him it's very important that he calls me as soon as possible."

"Of course. I'll make sure he gets the message when he arrives. Have a good day."

Alyssa hung up, frustrated. Why would Benjamin disappear today of all days? And why had he never told her that the relative he spoke so badly about was his mother? Alyssa tried calling Stanley, but he was also out of the office. With Rosemary out of the country, she had no one else to speak to.

That afternoon, Agnes found Alyssa with her head in her hands. "Lunch is ready," she announced.

Alyssa plastered a smile on her face that probably looked more like a grimace. Somehow, she had to enjoy the company of a real mother-in-law without revealing the fact that the marriage was a sham. She also had no idea what Benjamin would not want her to mention.

Agnes showed Alyssa the path to the four-room guest house, which was cleverly tucked behind the guest parking area and separated by a row of tall hedges.

"Come in," Maureen called out when Alyssa knocked on the door.

She stepped inside, taking in the large open-concept living room and kitchen. The beach-themed décor included walls covered with white shiplap. Maureen sat in front of a projector screen, watching what looked like a home video.

"Please, come sit by me and make yourself comfortable. Agnes brought a ton of food." Maureen patted the couch seat next to her.

Noticing Alyssa's tension, Maureen gave her a reassuring smile. "Honey, I know my son doesn't want me here, but I'm hoping we can get to know each other despite his feelings. Please relax and eat. I'm not here to cause any trouble. Do you want to watch these with me, or would you like to watch something else?"

"What exactly are you watching?"

"These are home videos my father made. Look, there's Benny now! He was so happy that day."

Alyssa watched as a young Benjamin swam toward his mother in the pool. He couldn't have been more than five years old. When he reached Maureen, she gathered him in her arms and kissed him. *"Great job, Benny!"* she said cheerfully. Alyssa heard his tiny voice reply, *"I love you, Mommy!"* Little Benjamin then kissed his mother back before turning and continuing to swim in the long pool.

Alyssa could hardly believe what she was seeing and hearing. Benjamin had always vilified Maureen, warning her not to trust or even speak to her.

"The two of you had such a loving, close relationship."

Maureen sighed. "Yes, we were very close. Never in a million years did I think that would change. No doubt my son told you that I'm a very bad person and that you should stay away from me."

"Um, he hasn't said a lot about you. And I've asked. If you don't mind, can you tell me what happened between you two?"

"Phillip, my ex-husband—he's what happened." Maureen took a deep breath. "I'll explain. I thought we were happily married. I stayed at home raising Benny while Phillip worked in his construction company. He would come home late from work sometimes. I wasn't too bothered by that, but eventually, I noticed a pattern. He'd come home late and extra tired on specific days of the week. I became suspicious and hired someone to follow him. Turns out he was cheating on me.

"Well, I cried my heart out and then hired the best divorce lawyer I could find. Before he knew what happened, I had everything—the house, alimony, and joint custody of Benny, with me as the primary parent. Phillip was livid. He and his lawyer tried every trick in the book to get sole custody of Benjamin. As it was, he could only visit when I agreed to the time; I didn't make it easy for him.

"Unfortunately, my father was old-fashioned and abhorred divorce. He tried everything to make me stop the process. In the meantime, I met a good man named Nicholas in my divorce group. We started a relationship while my ex was still fighting me for sole custody of Benny. When Phillip found out I was dating someone, he did everything possible to disrupt my life. Many times, he would show up at the house uninvited until I called the cops on him. Then, he went to my dad and used my relationship with Nicholas against me. Somehow, he convinced my father that we both had affairs during the marriage and that, unlike him, I didn't want to work on getting our marriage back together. My father pleaded with me to break off my new relationship and return to the cheater for Benny's sake. I refused. That's when my father and I stopped talking.

"My new relationship blossomed into a marriage proposal. Nicholas is Greek and wanted to honeymoon in Greece on several small islands. He had a daughter from his previous marriage, and I had Benny, so we planned to bring our kids with us. I didn't bother telling my father about the wedding because I knew he would be against it. I had everything set and planned to leave the country. At the last moment, Phillip convinced a judge to stop me from taking Benny out of the country. So, I was forced to leave him behind with nannies, and that was tough.

"Nicholas and I got married on the island of Santorini. Then my husband surprised me by taking us to another island for our honeymoon. The island was very small, and there were no phones.

We had a wonderful time, but there was trouble back home. Benny had an allergic reaction to pistachios in an ice cream one of the nannies gave him. I'd never given him pistachios before, so I had no idea he was allergic to them.

"The nanny took Benny to the hospital and contacted Marilyn—Stanley's mother—who was my emergency contact. But Marilyn couldn't reach me. She tried calling Nicholas's family, but they had no idea which island we were on. I was oblivious to what was going on.

"Marilyn had no choice but to contact Phillip because a parent was required at the hospital. Phillip and his lawyer took advantage of the situation. He filed a trumped-up charge of child abandonment against me. My own father testified against me in court because Phillip convinced him it was the only way to force me back into our marriage. With my father's testimony, Philip won full custody of Benny. When I returned, I had to fight for visiting rights with my son.

Maureen's voice grew thick with emotion. "And that wasn't the worst part. During the time Benny stayed with his father, Philip somehow convinced him that I no longer cared about him. By the time my lawyer succeeded in obtain visiting rights for me, my eight-year-old despised me. Of course, I did everything I could to prove that I still loved and cared for Benny, but our relationship was never the same again. Ben refused to stay in my home, but I wouldn't take him back to his dad. I figured he'd eventually get used to staying with me and Nicholas.

Then Benny ran away. That was the scariest time of my life. We couldn't find him for a whole day. The next day, he showed up here at my father's house. I was so afraid he'd run away again that I gave up the idea of forcing Ben to stay with me.

"Eventually, Dad realized Philip wasn't home often, so he asked Phillip if Benny could live with him here instead. Phillip agreed on one condition—that I would not be in the house at the same time as Benny. He made sure my relationship with Benny never recovered. Benny stayed with Phillip from time to time, but it was my father who raised him.

"All these years later, my son still wants nothing to do with me. When I heard he was getting married, I thought he'd surely allow me to be there, but no invitation arrived. Maureen let out a heavy sigh before giving Alyssa a small smile. "You're probably wondering why I moved into a property where I'm not wanted. Well, my father's will states that the guest house is mine even after Ben inherits the house. Dad hoped that living nearby would bring us back together.

"I know it's a lot to ask, and I'm a stranger to you. But I hope you and I can become close despite this whole situation."

Alyssa didn't know how to respond to Maureen's request. She seemed like a nice person, but Alyssa was more disturbed by the fact that Benjamin had never told her about his mother. And now, their marriage was ending in just a few days. How could she and Maureen be friends?

"Um, I'll do whatever I can to help you and Ben get closer, I promise," said Alyssa. Maureen hugged and thanked her. They continued to watch home videos while they ate lunch. Maureen talked non-stop about Benjamin. Alyssa could tell that Maureen loved her son very much despite his behavior. For some reason, watching their bond made her feel an unexpected pang of jealousy, and her mind drifted to her own relationship with her mother.

"I'd better get back to my studies. Thank you for lunch," she said, turning quickly to leave so Maureen wouldn't notice the tears welling in her eyes.

Instead of heading to the library, Alyssa took the car keys and told Agnes she wouldn't be home for dinner. She was walking to her vehicle when Andrew's car drove up, blocking her path.

"Hey, I was just coming to see you. Where are you headed?" he asked.

"I don't know. I just need to get away."

Andrew could tell Alyssa was upset. "Looks like I arrived just in time, hop in." He reached over and opened the passenger door.

Alyssa hesitated for a few seconds before getting in. The moment he accelerated his Porsche, she regretted her decision. Maureen had stepped out to see Agnes when she watched in horror as her new daughter-in-law entered the young man's car. She quickly rushed to the main house to find Agnes.

"Agnes, Agnes!?"

The elderly house manager popped out of the kitchen. "What is it, Ms. Maureen?"

"A young man in a black Porsche just drove up to the house, and Alyssa got into the car with him!"

"Oh dear," Agnes said worriedly. "That's Andrew. He's the one who punched Benjamin at the wedding. He came by to apologize when the kids returned from their honeymoon, but he kept visiting to speak to Alyssa. The strange thing is, for the past few weeks, she told me to say she was busy whenever he called."

Maureen's mouth fell open. "Why would she get into his car? Oh, I hope I didn't say anything to upset her. We were talking about Benny and watching the home movies Dad made. Then she looked sort of sad and excused herself." She sighed. "I wish Ben would just talk to me. It's such a shame I must insert myself this way just to get closer to him," Maureen said tearfully.

"Now, Maureen, don't give up. You're not doing this just for yourself. You're doing this for your father too. This was his wish. He wanted so much for you and Ben to reunite as a family. And I can't count how many times he told me he regretted taking sides in the divorce." Agnes exhaled quietly. "I thought Benjamin would've grown out of this phase of trying to please his father all the time. That relationship Mr. Philip set up with Gloria was purely for business, and Ben knew it. Yet he still stayed in it, so I expected him to marry her. Then, unexpectedly, he brought Alyssa home and said they were getting married. I had no idea he was dating her."

"I know. It was a shock to me too," Maureen admitted. "You

know I keep regular tabs on Benny. Somehow, this relationship slipped by me. Once you gave me her name, I used my resources to check her out. She's from a very small town in Tulare County, and she started college here last year. Her father's deceased, and there's no record of what happened to her mother. A cousin raised her."

Maureen looked down sadly. "I really hope she comes home before Benjamin does. I don't like how this looks."

"Andrew, where are we going?" Alyssa asked a second time.

"Relax. I'm just taking you to lunch."

"That's not necessary. I just had lunch with Ben's mother."

Andrew chuckled. "Oh, that must have been exciting. You can tell me all about it. There's a park not far from here. I'll pull over so we can chat."

After parking, Andrew guided them to a bench outside the park entrance. He lit a cigarette as they settled down. "Now, tell me all about Ben's big bad mama," he said with a laugh.

"Maureen's not bad. She's actually pretty sweet, and she really loves Ben. We watched tons of home movies of him."

Andrew groaned. "That sounds so boring. But why were you looking so down when I saw you?"

Alyssa hesitated before answering. "I just discovered today that Maureen is Ben's mother. When we went to Mexico, I asked Ben about his mother, and he said nothing. I don't understand why he kept this secret from me. I thought we were friends. I entered this fake marriage to help him out, as a friend, and he promised to tell me everything I needed to know."

"He obviously doesn't trust you, although I don't know why. Personally, I think Ben's an idiot for running from his mother. If I were him, I'd befriend her just to gain the other 20% ownership of his grandfather's company. Then, I'd have full control." He smirked. "My dad says Ben doesn't know how to run his company well. Did you know he pulled out of a major real estate acquisition deal because some quack engineers claimed the builder didn't make the apartment complex safe enough to withstand a major earthquake? He could've made a ton of profit; he's such a coward."

"Well, I don't know much about business, but it sounds like he did the right thing," Alyssa replied.

Andrew then casually placed his arm around her shoulder. "Sounds to me like you've hung around Ben and his boring friends for too long. After this marriage thing is over, I'll teach you about business and introduce you to a much better crowd than that dull group you hang out with."

"My friends aren't boring. They care about me, and I care about them" she said as she shrugged Andrews arm off.

"Are you sure about that? None of them thought you were important enough to tell you that Maureen was Ben's mother. You need to face the facts; they're just using you."

Alyssa stood up suddenly. "I feel like taking a walk now. Maybe we'll talk another time."

Puzzled, Andrew called after her, "Wait, don't you need me to drive you back?"

"No, thank you. I'll find my way," she said impatiently as she walked away.

A fatigued Alyssa trudged through the gates of the beach house and up the inclined walkway after 5 PM. The walk was longer than she had anticipated, but that wasn't what exhausted her. Instead of heading directly home, she spent several hours on her campus, trying to clear her head. Andrew's statement echoed in her mind all afternoon, and she wondered why none of her friends had revealed Maureen's identity. Instead of going to the home's main entrance, Alyssa continued to the back entryway. She wasn't in the mood to see anyone. All she wanted was a hot shower.

After freshening up, she wrapped her wet hair in a towel and put on a robe before stepping out of bathroom.

"Alyssa? Where have you been?" Benjamin asked worriedly as she entered the bedroom.

Alyssa was ready to answer his question, but instead, she asked, "Where have you been? Didn't you receive the message I left for you at the office?"

"Ahh, no. I was away on business and came straight home. Agnes told me you left with Andrew hours ago. What's that all about?"

Alyssa ignored the question, sat down, and blotted her hair dry with the towel. "Ben, did you know that your mother, Maureen, is living in the guest house now?"

Benjamin sighed. "Yes, Agnes told me. Hey, I'm sorry about that. Legally, she can stay there, but she has no rights to our house, and I've reiterated that to Agnes. Unfortunately, Agnes has a soft spot for her because she raised my mother in this house."

"It would have been helpful to know that the 'Maureen' you kept talking about was your mother. I don't understand why you could not trust me with that information; I was blindsided. Your mother came in and hugged me, and I had no clue who she was to you."

"I'm sorry, Alyssa. Agnes told me she made you have lunch with her. You didn't have to do that. You're not obligated to spend any time with Maureen. I'm sorry that I wasn't here to keep her away from you."

"I like Maureen. We enjoyed each other's company. She's a very warm and friendly woman. Do you know what she was doing when I entered the guest house? She was watching home videos of you from when you were young. When I left, she continued watching those videos. She's not the monster you made her out to be."

"Alyssa, there's a lot you don't understand. I don't want you to waste your time with her. She's probably up to something."

"I promised to have lunch with her again."

"Well, break your promise. My mother knows all about breaking promises, so she won't mind when you break yours."

"But... I want to have lunch with her again."

"Alyssa, I'm telling you not to. You don't know her like I do, she's evil. Well, maybe not as evil as your moth...."

"What?" Alyssa's eyes narrowed. "What do you mean? You don't know anything about my mother. She could be dead for all you know!"

Benjamin remained silent, hoping Alyssa would let the topic drop, but she didn't. Alyssa stepped closer to Benjamin. In the short time she had known him, she could tell when he was avoiding a topic. "What else are you hiding from me? Or should I ask, why are you hiding things from me?"

Benjamin looked away from her gaze and remained silent.

Alyssa shook her head. "Andrew was right. You're not my friend, and I'm an idiot for thinking you were."

"Andrew? If you're listening to Andrew, you *are* an idiot!" he shouted.

Benjamin saw Alyssa tear up. "I'm so sorry," he said quickly. "I didn't mean to yell. I don't know why I did that."

But his apology didn't stop the tears.

"I don't want to be here anymore. I want to leave. Now!" That was all she could manage to say before running into the walk-in closet. Alyssa yanked her clothes out and stuffed them into her green duffle bag.

Benjamin followed her. "Alyssa, please stop. Let's talk about this."

"I don't want to talk anymore. This whole thing was a bad idea, and I feel like I'm the only one not in on a joke," she said, still packing furiously.

"Alyssa, I didn't mean to upset you. I wanted to tell you about my mother. You have to understand that it's difficult for me to talk about her. I know you want to leave because you're upset, but you must stop running away whenever there's a problem. This is a pattern with you. Every time something happens that you don't like, you bolt. Please, stop packing. I'm asking you to sit down with me and talk this through. What do you say? And it's late. Where are you going anyway?"

"I'm going to the dormitory."

"No, I don't want you to leave like this. You know what? I have a better idea. I'll leave. You can have the place to yourself."

"But you can't leave, it's your house!"

"Right now, it's *our* house." He grabbed a bag from the closet and threw in some clothing and toiletries. "You don't want to be around me, so I'll leave. You can spend the rest of your time with your new friends, Maureen and Andrew," he said angrily.

Ben stormed out, slamming the door behind him.

Alyssa stood frozen. She didn't understand what had just happened or why she wanted to run after Benjamin and make him stay.

Alyssa tossed and turned all night, replaying the argument in her head. The suite felt unbearably empty without Benjamin. One thing Benjamin said stuck in her mind: *You run away from problems.*

It was the last thought she had before crying herself to sleep.

Benjamin sat in his car, thinking about what had just happened. Alyssa was right, he should have told her Maureen was his mother; but he had hoped that he wouldn't have to. The more he thought about Andrew's frequent visits, the more enraged he became. He decided it was time to confront the man who had walked into his home uninvited and sucker-punched him in front of all his guests. He hoped Andrew would be there alone, without Gloria, so they could speak without interference.

Benjamin and Gloria hadn't met by chance, he was coerced into doing his father a favor, which entailed attending a luncheon with his father's business partner's daughter. Benjamin's initial plan was to subtly drop hints indicating he wasn't interested in a relationship. After all, he had promised his father that he'd meet the daughter of his business associate just once.

As he had approached the table at the bistro four years ago, and seen the back of his blind date's head, he overheard Gloria berating the waitress for adding ice to her drink when she hadn't asked for it. That was all Benjamin had needed to hear to confirm that she was not the woman for him. But then she had turned around. Gloria was gorgeous, and at that moment, he was determined to know her better.

They've been in a relationship for over three years. He learned early that Gloria had no filter. She would say whatever was on her mind without considering the feelings of others. Occasionally, that included him too. Normally, he'd shrug off the insults and do whatever it took to appease her. But somehow, tonight was different.

When he knocked on the front door of Gloria's house, one of the maids answered. She greeted him by name and casually told him that Gloria was in the game room. Andrew and Gloria's best friend was also there. Without acknowledging anyone, Benjamin strode straight to Andrew, pointing a finger in his face.

"I don't want you anywhere near my house or my friends ever again. You are never welcome in my home or on any of my properties. Stay away."

"Wait a minute, you can't talk to my brother like that!" Gloria snapped.

"Yes, I can. I never invited him. We're not close, and we never will be. He just shows up and causes problems."

"What problems has he caused?" Gloria demanded.

"You mean other than punching me in front of everyone I know? Today, after spending time with this jerk, Alyssa wants to leave."

Gloria turned to Andrew, exasperated. "Andrew, you can't mess this up! I really want that chalet. You can visit whenever you want once this marriage thing is over."

"No," Benjamin cut in. "I mean it. He's never welcome at any of my properties."

"Don't be silly. Once we're married, my brother can come whenever he pleases."

"No, he cannot. He has no respect for me, and I don't want to see his face in my home."

Gloria stood up, facing Benjamin. "And I say my brother is welcome wherever I am—even in your home. End of discussion!"

Andrew smirked, and Gloria's friend giggled.

Benjamin's face hardened. "So, this is how it's going to be if we marry? You'll disrespect me and joke about me in front of your friends and family? Okay, keep your brother and your jokes. Leave me out of it."

"What are you talking about? You're being ridiculous," Gloria replied.

"I'm talking about marriage, it's off. Find yourself another joker."

Gloria's face paled. "What? You're being crazy! You can't do that to me after all I've done to help you acquire those properties. That chalet is mine! I earned it!"

"If that's really all you care about, you can have it. Tell your father to make me a fair offer, and I'll sell it to you." Benjamin left the room without waiting for a response, though he caught the shocked expression on Gloria's friend's face.

Back in the car, Benjamin expected to feel remorse after the break up. Instead, he felt free. For a brief moment, he considered going back to apologize for how he had broken off their relationship. But after taking a deep breath, he started his car and drove off. This had to be one of the worst days of his life.

"I don't like this one bit. You're bunking with me while Maureen's at your house," Ben's father grumbled.

"Dad, she's not in the main house; she's in the guest home."

"What was your grandfather thinking, deeding the guest house to her? That's a rotten move. The inheritance should be for the whole property. If I were you, I'd sell it the second the title transfers to your name."

Benjamin sighed. "Knowing grandfather, it was probably his way of trying to bring Maureen and me back together."

"Well, that's never going to happen. That woman is no good, she never cared about you. No doubt she's putting ideas into Alyssa's head. You'd better hope that girl doesn't spill the beans and tell Maureen the truth." Philip shook his head. "If you'd married Gloria like you were supposed to, we wouldn't be dealing with this mess."

Benjamin frowned. "Don't you care that Gloria didn't love me? She only wanted the chalet."

"I'll tell you again, people don't marry for love, they marry people who are on their level. You and Gloria were a perfect match, and her father would've helped you run your grandfather's company. And with my construction firm, the three of us could've made a lot of money."

Benjamin sighed. "Money's not everything, Dad."

Phillip shook his head disapprovingly. "I don't know where you get that thinking from. Sometimes you sound just like your mother."

In the past, such a comparison would have infuriated him. But now, he was too emotionally drained to care. All he could think about was Alyssa not wanting him around anymore. Benjamin stood up. "Dad, I'm tired. I had a long drive this morning, and I have tons of work to catch up on tomorrow. Let's continue this conversation later."

"Oh yeah, that's right. I called you this morning. Your secretary had no idea what client you had an all-day meeting with. Who did you meet?"

Benjamin sighed. "Let's just say the person I met with wasn't worth the effort. Goodnight Dad."

The next day, Maureen insisted that Alyssa join her and her husband, Nicholas, for lunch. Remembering what Benjamin had said made Alyssa hesitate, but Maureen was so kind that she couldn't refuse.

She had a great time with the couple. They were warm and friendly. Alyssa couldn't help feeling guilt-ridden for pretending to be their daughter-in-law. Not only was the charade ending in a few days, but also, she feared Benjamin would end their friendship because she had befriended his mother. This, and their recent argument, worried Alyssa so much that she called him as soon as she got home.

"Hi, Ben. Look, I'm sorry for arguing with you yesterday. Finding out who your mother was shocked me, and I wasn't prepared for it. Also, Maureen's been so nice to me. I can't bring myself to be rude or avoid her. Do you understand?"

Alyssa heard Benjamin sigh on the other end.

"Alyssa, it's my fault for putting you in that situation. I didn't tell you because I don't like talking about my mother. It brings up too many painful memories. I swear, I wasn't trying to keep you in the dark. I'm sorry I made you feel like you had to get away from me. That's not how I want you to feel. If it's okay with you, I'd like to come home."

"Of course you can come back! This is your home. Besides, I miss sharing the newspaper at breakfast."

"Thanks, I want us to have a long talk so that I can tell you everything. I promise never to keep you in the dark again. Listen, I have a lot of work right now, so I'll stay at my father's tonight because it's closer. But I'll be home by dinner tomorrow. In fact, why don't we

go out for dinner? You can tell Agnes to take the night off. How does that sound?"

"That sounds wonderful! I'd love that."

"Great. Can't wait to see you tomorrow. Goodnight."

Benjamin was so relieved that Alyssa was no longer angry with him that he couldn't stop smiling.

CHAPTER
SIXTEEN

"...but if he neglects to hear the church, let him be unto thee as a heathen man and a publican."

Matthew 18:17

Alyssa felt so much better after speaking with Benjamin the previous day. She stretched as she put her laundered clothes in the walk-in closet. The wall calendar reminded her of how little time she had left at the beach house.

She ate breakfast alone again. Instead of sharing the newspaper with Ben, she began reviewing her class registration pamphlet. Agnes entered to inform her that Andrew was on the line, but Alyssa relayed a message that she was unable to come to the phone. She'd made up her mind to stay clear of Andrew as Benjamin had requested.

On her way to the library, Agnes approached again. This time, it was a call from Sarah. Alyssa happily picked up the line.

"Hi, Sarah. I've been meaning to call you. I know Hazel had phone line problems, but I thought the telephone company should have fixed the line by now. I've called several times and, I'm still not able to get through. I keep getting this weird message saying the line is unavailable."

She waited for Sarah's chirpy response, but it never came. "Sarah... are you there?"

"Yes, I'm here. Alyssa, I don't know if I should tell you this because Hazel doesn't want me to tell you anything, but I think you

should know. When I drove by your home yesterday, there was a fore-closure notice on the door."

Alyssa sat down, stunned. "Foreclosure?! That can't be right. Cousin Hazel never said anything was wrong when she called from her friend's home."

"Did you know she lost her job at the school four months ago? I've heard rumors that Pastor Bryant was responsible for her being let go. Apparently, he blames Hazel for you leaving Pitway. People are also saying that Hazel's phone service was cut off for non-payment."

"She lost her job? Hazel never said anything... Why didn't she tell me?"

"Well, she warned me not to tell you anything. I don't think she wanted to worry you."

Alyssa replied slowly while wiping away tears. "I have to go back. I'm coming home today."

"But Hazel doesn't want you to come back. Besides, what can you do now? These things have already happened."

"I have money saved for college. I'll go to the bank with the money to stop the foreclosure."

"What if it's not enough?"

"I don't know. But I'll do whatever it takes to keep our home; work two or three jobs, anything. That house was built by my great-grandfather. We can't lose it."

"But what about college?"

Alyssa wiped her tears again. "That's not important right now. I must take care of my family." She glanced at the clock. It was past ten in the morning. "Sarah, I have to get ready to leave. Thanks for telling me."

"Alyssa, wait! What are you going to do about Pastor Bryant?"

"I honestly don't know. Pray for me."

Alyssa hung up and rushed to the bedroom to pack. When she was done, she searched the house for Agnes but couldn't find her. She called Benjamin, but he wasn't in the office. So she told his secretary she'd like to leave a message on his answering machine.

"Ben, I just found out that Pastor Bryant made Hazel lose her

job, and now my home is in foreclosure. I can't get through to Hazel, so I must go home to help her. Ben, you were right—I have to stop running away from my problems. Maybe this wouldn't have happened if I'd somehow stood up to the Bryants last year. I'm driving home today. Sorry, but I must borrow your car. I promise to bring it back as soon as I can. I know there are a few days left for our arrangement. Please don't be angry that I'm leaving now. I'll tell Agnes I have a family emergency and have to see my cousin today."

With that, Alyssa grabbed her bag to leave the bedroom. As she looked behind her, Alyssa wasn't sure when she'd be back, so she removed the wedding band and placed it on Benjamin's dresser.

She then stowed her luggage into the trunk of the Ford Taurus Benjamin had given her to drive. Alyssa decided to say a quick goodbye to Maureen. When she knocked on the guest house door, Agnes opened it.

"Oh, Mrs. Hallerman! I'm sorry, were you looking for me?" Agnes quickly noticed her puffy eyes. "Mrs. Hallerman, you've been crying. Is something wrong?"

At that moment, Maureen came to the door.

"Alyssa, come in. Tell us what's wrong," said Maureen.

"I'm sorry, but I must leave in a hurry. There's a family emergency with my cousin back home. I just came to let you know I was leaving."

"Oh no! Alyssa, is there anything I can do? Maybe I can hire a driver so you don't have to drive while you're upset."

"No, that's not necessary. My bag is packed. I just have to make a stop at the bank before getting on the freeway. Ben wasn't in his office when I called, so I left him a message. Please don't worry."

Both women hugged her and begged her to call when she reached her cousin.

As Alyssa drove off, Agnes turned to Maureen. "She's such a sweet girl. I wish there was something more I could do."

"So do I, but she didn't give us any details. If her cousin is ill, we could send flowers," said Maureen.

"That's a good idea! Let me check her room, maybe she left a note or clue about the emergency. I'll be right back."

The house manager hadn't spent much time in the couple's suite because Alyssa insisted on keeping it clean herself. When she walked in, it was just as neat as ever. There were no papers or documents left out, but as she turned to leave, she saw the wedding band on the dresser.

Panicked, Agnes quickly ran back to Maureen.

"Ms. Maureen!!" she yelled while knocking frantically on the guesthouse door.

"Agnes, what's going on? Why are you out of breath? Come, sit down until you catch your breath."

"The ring!" Agnes blurted out as she sat. "She left her wedding band on Benjamin's dresser. I think she's left Benjamin!"

Benjamin strolled casually down the hallway to his office, having just returned from a commercial property closing that seemed to take forever. Now, he finally had time to return Stanley's call.

"Hey buddy, I'm sorry about your breakup. But you know how Rose and I felt about Gloria."

"I know, I know. You always said we weren't a good match. I did care for her, though. Maybe that's why it took a while for me to realize that she not only did not love me but had no respect for me. Her baby brother came first in everything. Of course, Dad doesn't care about my feelings, he wants me to go back and grovel."

"And are you certain you're never going back?"

"I'm certain. That relationship is dead. Now, on to more pressing things, I'm going to sit down with Alyssa tonight and tell her about the meeting with her mother."

"Wow, that's going to be tough. Let me know how it works out."

"I'll do better than that, I want you there with me."

"Oh, come on, Ben. Alyssa's not Gloria. You won't have to duck under a table."

"I know. Alyssa's the opposite, and that's exactly why I need you with me. I made her cry the other night because I said things without thinking. I don't want to upset her again, and I need you there to keep me in check."

"Well, alright. I'll do it for Alyssa. But what did you say to make her cry?"

"I'm not going into that. I'm getting a call now; I'll call you back later."

Benjamin quickly hung up when he saw the number from his home on the phone console screen.

"Hello, Alyssa?"

"No, Ben. It's Agnes."

"Agnes, is everything alright? You sound flustered."

"I don't know, Benjamin. Alyssa's gone. She said goodbye to me and your mother. She told us there was a family emergency and that she had to go back home. But Ben, she left her wedding band in the room. I don't know what that means. She also said that she left you a message."

At that moment, Benjamin noticed the message light blinking on the console.

"Agnes, I'm coming home now!"

As he hung up, he pressed the button to listen to the message. Alyssa relayed the details about Hazel losing her home because she ran away from Pitway. Then, Alyssa said something that made him panic. She said that he was right about her running away from her problems, and she was going back to face this one.

He cringed at the thought of Alyssa confronting the pastor and his family on her own. And she was doing this because of what he said.

Benjamin quickly called Stanley.

"Stan, I really messed up. Alyssa's on her way to confront her pastor, and it's all my fault. I told her to stop running away from her problems. I'm driving up there as soon as I get home. I must find her before she meets him."

"Oh no! Ben, how are you going to find her? We don't know her address!"

"You're right. I don't know how to find her home. I could look it up in the Pitway phone book, but I don't know her cousin's last name."

"Look, Ben, I can't leave work now. You go ahead, and I'll drive up in the morning to the inn we stayed at and check for you. Leave a message for me at the desk. If you haven't found her by then, we'll canvas the town together. Don't worry, we'll find her before anything bad happens."

"Thanks, buddy; I'm heading home now."

Back at home, Benjamin left the engine running as he sprinted from his car toward the entrance. Before he reached the door, he watched Agnes and Maureen hurrying to Maureen's car. Maureen popped the trunk open, and Agnes threw in an overnight bag. Then Agnes noticed Benjamin and rushed toward him.

"Oh, Benjamin, I'm so glad you're here! Oh, you poor thing. Alyssa left about an hour ago, and she left this behind." Agnes pulled out the wedding band and placed it in Benjamin's palm, studying his face. "I'm so sorry, Ben, but don't worry. Your mother's going after her. She called her office to look up Alyssa's address. Your mother will do her best to bring her back to you."

Benjamin's head snapped up. "Wait, she has Alyssa's Pitway address?"

He then walked over to the parent he had refused to face for years. "Um, excuse me. Can you give me the address to Alyssa's cousin's house? I'm leaving for Pitway now."

Shocked and elated that her son spoke to her, Maureen forced herself to reply calmly. "Benny, I'd be happy to drive you there. I'm going to support Alyssa in any way I can."

"That's kind of you, but it's not necessary. She's my wife, I'm the one who should support her. Now, please give me the address. We're wasting valuable time."

"No, I'm not giving you the address, but I'd be happy to drive you there. It's your decision, but I'm leaving now." With that, Maureen entered her car, turned on the engine, and waited.

Benjamin was livid, but he gave in. "Fine!" he snapped. "Give me a few minutes." He hurried to the house and threw some clothes into a travel bag.

Overhearing the conversation, made Agnes approached Maureen's car. "You and Benjamin in the same car together. I never thought I'd see this day!" gushed Agnes.

"Shh, Agnes, don't get too excited. He was furious. I'm afraid he still hates me."

"Oh, but you should be happy! Your son hasn't acknowledged you for the past eighteen years. Now, you'll have him all to yourself for the next four hours. Make the most of it!"

Benjamin returned and shut off his car's engine. Then, he angrily threw his bag into the back seat of his mother's car before entering through the passenger side. He rolled his eyes at the sight of Maureen studying a map. "Look, I've been to Pitway before. At least let me drive. You obviously don't know where you're going."

"I do know where I'm going," Maureen said, folding the map. "I'm just finding the best route to avoid heavy traffic." She handed the map to Benjamin and motioned for him to put on his seatbelt. She then waved to Agnes before they took off for the freeway.

They drove together in silence. Benjamin kept his arms crossed as he continued to fume. Occasionally, Maureen looked Ben's way, hoping to start a conversation, but he just stared out the window to avoid eye contact. Then, unexpectedly, Benjamin spoke.

"Tell me something, how did you find Alyssa's cousin's address?"

This wasn't how Maureen had hoped to start a conversation with her son, but she was still thrilled he was talking to her.

"Oh, that was easy. You know I manage many rental properties, which means I need to check backgrounds before leasing a property. I have a company that does that for me. I called them to look up Alyssa's last known address."

"Still, you just found out today that Alyssa was leaving. I don't know of any company that works *that* quickly."

Maureen decided to change the subject. "Benny, I know you and Alyssa are having problems. If you believe I'm part of the problem, I'll leave. If that's what you want."

Benjamin turned and stared at Maureen. "You'd leave just like that? All I have to do is ask?"

"I would do anything for you, Benny. You're my son."

Benjamin let out a cold laugh. "Let's not go there. We're not close, and we never will be."

Maureen had had enough. "Benjamin, it's been eighteen long years. I'm tired of you shutting me out of your life! I've never done anything to hurt you..."

"YOU LEFT ME!" Benjamin shouted. "You don't remember what you did, but I'll never forget! You left me with a bunch of strange nannies you just hired. They didn't know me, and I didn't know them. And why? So you could run off with your new husband for three long weeks! Dad said you decided to leave me behind because I would be a drag on your honeymoon. While you were having fun, I ended up in the hospital because YOU never told the nannies I had a life-threatening allergy. I lay in the hospital for a week. Every single day, I waited for you to show up, but you never came. So don't you dare sit here pretending you never did anything wrong!"

Flustered from his rant, Benjamin closed his eyes and massaged his forehead. He wished he could be anywhere but here, sitting next to the mother who had abandoned him.

At first, he heard sniffing. Then tears rolled down her cheeks as she sobbed. When Maureen finally broke down completely, Benjamin looked out the passenger window, hoping the crying would stop soon. But it didn't.

She had made him angry. Still, he shouldn't have yelled like he did. It became difficult to ignore his mother's sobbing, and he felt guilty for how he behaved. While searching for the right words to apologize for his outburst, the car suddenly veered toward the guardrails.

"Mom!" Benjamin yelled, grabbing the steering wheel. He yanked it back, steadying the vehicle.

Though crying loudly now, Maureen's foot was still on the gas.

Benjamin spoke as calmly as he could. "Mom, slow down. I need you to steer into a road shoulder when you see one. I've got the wheel." Benjamin spotted a shoulder on the road. "Slow down and pull over to the right, over there."

She did as he asked. When Maureen hit the brakes, Benjamin reached down, turned off the ignition, and applied the emergency brakes. He exhaled loudly as he sat back in his seat.

Still shaking and sobbing, Maureen quickly pulled Benjamin into a tight hug. "I'm so sorry, Benny! I would never abandon you! You were supposed to be with me at the wedding. But at the last minute, your father refused to let me take you out of the country. His divorce lawyer got a judge to sign a court order. I swear, there was nothing I could do to stop your father! This was his way of getting back at me for divorcing him."

"I had a choice to leave you with a nanny or give you to your father, and I didn't want to hand you over to him, so I hired the nannies. I swear, there was no phone on the island. That's why no one could call to tell me what happened. I never abandoned you, and I never knew you had an allergy!"

Everything Maureen said contradicted what his father had told him.

Benjamin's mind reeled back to the day Phillip Hollerman had taken him home from the hospital. *"Your mother wanted a break from taking care of you, so she went to another country to marry her boyfriend and left you behind."*

As long as he lived, Benjamin would never forget the crushing sadness he felt that day.

No, he didn't believe her. But she was crying so hard that Benjamin didn't have the heart to correct her statement. He imagined that over the years, she had made up this lie to make herself feel better. So he decided not to argue, for now. When they returned to LA, he'd investigate his parents' divorce case and confront Maureen with the facts.

Still clutching her son, Maureen looked up at Benjamin's face and then down at his white button-down shirt.

"Oh no! I've ruined your shirt. I'm so sorry, Benny. I'll buy you a new one."

Benjamin looked down at his tear-dampened shirt smeared with his mother's makeup. Then, he looked up at the typically confident and sharp-witted Maureen. She looked so unsettled that he put his arm around her shoulders and pulled her close to his chest again.

Some time passed before Benjamin could successfully console his mother. He switched seats and took over the driving.

She said nothing for the rest of the journey. Occasionally, she'd gently rub his arm, still astonished that her son allowed her to touch him.

Maureen took another look at the address she'd written down, then glanced back at the house in front of them and the condition it was in. Anyone could see it needed maintenance. Paint peeled in spots, and cracks lined the driveway. The foreclosure notice sat prominently on the front door.

"Doesn't look like anyone's home, and Alyssa's car isn't here," she said.

"I'll knock on the door, just in case," Benjamin said as he stepped out. He hoped Alyssa would be there without her cousin because he didn't know how to keep up the marriage sham in front of Maureen without shocking Alyssa's cousin.

No one answered. He peeked through the window and saw no lights or signs that Alyssa had been there. *Could she be at the church?* The thought of Alyssa surrounded by the Bryant family members stressed him. He walked back to the car and drove through town.

Benjamin and Maureen scanned the roads as the car rolled down the streets of Pitway. He passed by the church several times, hoping to spot Alyssa or her car. They finally gave up just before dark and checked into the Pitway Inn. Maureen promptly called Agnes, but the house manager informed them that Alyssa hadn't called.

That night, Benjamin was in agony, wondering where Alyssa was and whether she was safe.

Earlier that morning, Alyssa made good time on Interstate 5. She pulled into the driveway of her Pitway home in less than four hours after leaving the bank.

The garage was open and empty. As she walked up the steps of her home, she saw the huge foreclosure notice pasted on the front door. Just looking at it made her queasy. Her great-grandfather had built this house. It was Cousin Hazel's inheritance from her deceased grandmother. Cousin Hazel had taken excellent care of it until her husband wrecked her finances. Then, she had taken on the responsibility of financially supporting her young cousin. And now, Hazel was losing the home because of her.

Since her cousin wasn't home, Alyssa decided to take care of business on her own. She got back into the Taurus and headed straight to the only bank in town.

People did double takes when Alyssa walked into the Pitway branch of Sequoia Regional Bank. She greeted those who acknowledged her and kept moving to the bank officer's desk. Ed Bryant sat with his mouth open, amazed that a woman who looked like his cousin's runaway fiancée was heading straight toward him. This wasn't the shy, mousey teen he remembered. This woman was confident, with a professionally cut hairstyle and a designer outfit.

"Good afternoon, Ed. Can I speak with you?"

"Well, sure!" "My goodness!" Ed said as he scratched his balding head. "We haven't seen you around for a long time, Alyssa. How've you been?"

Alyssa informed him that she was attending college as planned. Then, she got straight to the point, discussing the foreclosure and asking how she could stop it. She told him how much money she had available to put toward it.

Ed told her there was nothing she could do to stop the foreclosure because the deadline had passed. Then, he shocked her with his next statement. "You know, if you go reconcile with Tim as soon as possible, I'm certain he could straighten things out for Hazel." Alyssa was so angry that she left without saying another word.

Alyssa retreated to her car, feeling defeated and unsure of how to save her home. She wished she knew where Hazel was. Finally, she decided to take care of some matters in the meantime. Alyssa walked down the street to the utility office. Again, she was recognized and greeted warmly. They immediately knew why she was there. Alyssa used a small portion of her college money to pay off her cousin's overdue phone bill. Fortunately, the service would be restored the same day.

Back in the car, she headed toward home but then changed course, steering to another home she had been dreading to visit. Two cars were parked outside Tim Bryant's home when Alyssa pulled up. She remained in her car for a long time before her nerves allowed her to get out.

In her head, Alyssa had rehearsed what she was going to say, but when a woman in a tight dress and too much makeup opened the door, she was speechless.

The woman eyed her suspiciously. "Who are you?"

"Um... I'm here to see Pastor Bryant."

"And you are?"

"My name is Alyssa Holt."

"I'll see if the pastor is available. Wait here."

She waited patiently at first. But after five minutes passed, she rang the doorbell again. No one came to the door this time. Alyssa had turned to leave when the door opened.

The pastor stood in the doorway with a smirk on his face. "Well, well, well... if it isn't my missing fiancée! Ed told me you might drop by. I thought Hazel would've brought you back a long time ago. It's a pity you waited so long to come out of hiding, things could have been different...."

Alyssa's temper flared. "Why are you doing these things to Hazel? You made her lose her job, and now you've got Ed foreclosing on her house. She's never done anything against you!"

Tim raised an eyebrow, clearly surprised at her boldness. Then, he smiled smugly. "Oh yes, she *has* done something against me. The two of you made me look like a fool in front of the whole town! Everyone knew about the wedding, but you and your cousin decided to play games. I know Hazel made you leave town; you don't have the guts to do something like that on your own. So, what's going on now? Your cousin wants her house back? Well, for starters, I'd need a huge apology from her. And you'd have to apologize to Tammy." A slow, satisfied grin spread across his face. "Then maybe, just maybe, I'll give you a second chance to marry me. I'm sure I can get Ed to work some magic and find a way to let Hazel stay in her home."

Alyssa shook her head. "Hazel had nothing to do with me leaving town. That was my choice! I told you 'no' a long time ago. I'm never going to marry you. I am asking you as a pastor and a man of God to do the right thing and reverse everything you did against my cousin."

The pastor placed his hands on his hips and looked down at Alyssa. "'I'm *never* going to marry you?' Those aren't the magic words needed to save Hazel's home. Guess you don't care enough about all the old girl's done for you. She'll be put out on the street, and it will be your doing. Maybe she'll find a nice cardboard box to live in, and every time you visit, you'll be reminded that her bleak living conditions are your fault. The foreclosure's perfectly legal, so don't go bothering Ed again. I thought I knew who you were, but you're dumber than I thought. You're a nobody who had a great opportunity to become an important person in this town, but you threw it all away."

The pastor's callousness infuriated Alyssa. "How can you be so evil? Don't you have a conscience? You're a pastor! Ezekiel 34 says you're supposed to take care of the flock, not tyrannize it. But here you are, punishing my family because I don't want to marry you."

Tim scoffed. "Who do you think you are to speak to me like that? I don't know where you've been, but you've changed for the worse. And you're right, I *am* your pastor! You're supposed to speak to me with respect! I don't have time for your foolishness. Go crawl back under the rock you came from—and take your old cousin with you."

The pastor slammed the door in her face.

Dejected, Alyssa returned to her vehicle. This wasn't how she'd planned for things to go. Not knowing if Cousin Hazel had returned, Alyssa decided to drive to Sarah's house.

When she arrived, they were having dinner, and Sarah's mother insisted she stay to eat with them. After the meal, Alyssa relayed everything the pastor and his family did against her and Hazel to Sarah's parents. They were disturbed by what was going on, though even they admitted the pastor's character was the main reason they had stopped attending services at Pitway Baptist.

"I've been telling everyone, including the students who remember Hazel from school, about what the pastor did to her since I saw the foreclosure notice," said Sarah. "Lots of people are upset about it. What's strange is that many of them are former members of Pitway Baptist. They've had bad experiences or witnessed others being mistreated before deciding to leave. It's not right. These things should not be happening in a church of God."

"I appreciate all you've done for Cousin Hazel, Sarah," said Alyssa.

"I wish I could do more. Hazel shouldn't be treated this way."

"Well, I should go home and help my cousin sort things out. I'm not certain when we'll have to leave."

"Are you still dropping out of college?" Sarah asked.

"Yes. I know Hazel will fight me on it, but I'm not giving her an option. After I finish packing, I'll return my friend's car and tell the college I'm not returning this fall."

When Alyssa returned to the house, she was relieved to see Hazel's car in the garage. She rang the bell and saw her cousin hesitantly peer out the window. The moment she saw Alyssa, the door swung open, and Hazel scooped her inside.

"Oh, Alyssa!" Hazel cried, wrapping her in a hug. "I missed you so much." Hazel stood back and looked at her young cousin. "It's only been a year, but you look so grown-up! I like your hair like that, and I'm so happy you're doing well in college. But it's dangerous for you to be here."

"No, not anymore. That's settled. After visiting the bank, I drove to the pastor's house. I looked him straight in the eye and told him that leaving town was my doing. He still refused to stop the foreclosure unless I married him. Then I reminded him that I already told him 'no' last year. He wouldn't listen to me after that."

"You did what?" Hazel gasped. "Weren't you afraid of him?"

"No, not anymore. I experienced some anxiety in the car, but I calmed myself down before ringing his doorbell. I'm not afraid of him anymore. My friend Ben told me that I run away from my problems, and he was right. So, I've decided to do whatever needs to be done, even if I'm afraid when I do it.

"Speaking to the pastor made me realize that he doesn't care about following God, whatever he does is for his own glory. I had to confront him because I was worried about you. Why didn't you tell me they took your job away or that they put the house in foreclosure? I could have helped you."

"There was no way for you to help, Alyssa. Besides, you were in college. It made no sense to worry you. I wanted you to stay focused on your studies."

"Cousin Hazel, college will always be there. At this time, it's a luxury we can't afford. I can always go back later. But right now, I'm staying with you. Tomorrow, I'll start looking for a few jobs. I'm willing to work seven days a week if necessary, and I have all my savings with me. Together, we can pool our money and try to buy the house back when it's auctioned."

"No, no, no!" Hazel protested. "You are not dropping out of college! It's not just your dream, it's mine too. Alyssa, you must stay in Los Angeles. I have a plan. I'm working two jobs outside of Pitway. I'll get an apartment away from this town, and you can come home during breaks without worrying about the Bryants."

Alyssa's eyes filled with tears. "Cousin Hazel, how can you give up on your home so easily? It's been in our family for generations. I won't let you lose your home because of me."

"Alyssa, be sensible. There's nothing we can do. The house is already in foreclosure, and they'll want more than what we can offer. We must let it go, honey."

Alyssa broke down. "It's not fair! What Pastor Bryant did is wrong! Why doesn't anyone stand up to him?" Her voice cracked as tears streamed down her face. "This is all my fault," she whispered.

Hazel embraced Alyssa. "This isn't your fault; it's my ex-husband's fault. He's the one who took out the loan on the house, and I'm the idiot who signed my approval of it. The bank foreclosed because my payments were late too many times. Normally, Ed gives me time to catch up, and I always do. But when the Bryants laid me off from my school job and the part-time work at the Inn, I couldn't find another job that paid me nearly enough. The phone's been cut off. The money I saved to give you for school, that's all gone."

"As far as the town goes, most people don't bother attending Pitway Baptist anymore. They have no clue what's going on with the pastor. The others either don't know or don't care to find out. I love this old home, but I will not allow this building to steal your dream. So, you will go back to college when classes start this fall."

Alyssa was tired and didn't want to argue anymore. But she was determined about one thing: she had to find a way to save her home, even if she had to do it alone.

It had been over a year since Alyssa had last slept in her bed. She didn't know if it was from the long drive or the stress of the day's events, but her bed felt very comfortable. She looked up at the pink flowery wallpaper Hazel had hung for her. Alyssa still remembered the day her cousin had asked her to pick out whichever wallpaper made her happiest. She had done so much to make Alyssa comfortable after her mother deserted her.

A row of aging stuffed animals lined the back of her old armoire. Alyssa remembered how her father had won them all at the Fresno Fair. Every summer, they would visit the fair, and he would save the shooting game for the end of the day so they wouldn't have to carry the stuffed animal around all night. Her father was a great marksman, so they never left the fair without a stuffed animal.

The second-hand bookshelf next to the armoire was filled with books Hazel had bought for her. She never wanted to part with them. *The Island of the Blue Dolphins*, a story about a Native American woman stranded on an island off the coast of California, was one of her favorites. Everything in this room had helped her survive the pain of being abandoned by her mother.

For the first few years after her mother left, Alyssa received birthday cards from Linda. None of the envelopes had a return address. Yet, in every letter, Linda would ask how she was doing. The last and final card she received on her 16TH birthday had a Nevada postmark. Alyssa had secretly taken the envelope to the library and asked the librarian if there was a way to track the sender's address. Together, they located the Nevada town from where the post office was located, but nothing more.

Alyssa yawned but fought sleep. She wondered if she should start packing her belongings in the morning. Thinking of losing her home made her want to cry again. Instead, her mind kept searching for a solution to save their home. Several hours passed by, and she couldn't come up with any ideas. Eventually, her eyelids drooped, and sleep took over.

CHAPTER
SEVENTEEN

"For there is nothing hidden that will not be disclosed, and nothing concealed that will not be known or brought out into the open."

Luke 8:17

Alyssa jolted awake. The clock said 6:10 a.m. She had a plan. It would take a miracle to work, but it was her only hope. *That's not true*, she thought. And in that moment, she knelt beside her bed and asked God for a miracle.

Now fully dressed, Alyssa walked down the hallway, passing Hazel's bedroom. She hesitated and wondered if she should wake Hazel and share her plan. Alyssa decided not to. Hazel had already given up on saving their home, so she'd only try to talk her out of it.

Alyssa turned off the ignition as she parked in front of his house. She could think of a thousand reasons to turn the car around and start packing. After all, he was a Bryant, and Bryants stick together, right or wrong. But he was also the head deacon, responsible for making sure the church was running well, and he was also responsible for supervising all the staff.

The drive to Deacon Barry's home had been quite short. Alyssa sat in the car, waiting. 6:45 a.m. was too early to knock on someone's door. Her stomach growled, encouraging her to go back home, to eat and think this over. She ignored the noises.

At 7 a.m., Alyssa left the car without a plan.

Deacon Barry took a while to open the door. He was dressed but unshaven. "Hello? Alyssa, is that you?"

"Good morning, Deacon. I'm sorry for knocking so early on a Saturday. I hope I didn't wake you?"

"You did, but that's alright. This must be important. Why don't you come in?" He gestured for her to have a seat on the couch. "It's good to see you back home. Please give me a few minutes to freshen up."

"Please, take your time, Deacon."

The semi-retired lawyer resided in a beautiful, spacious, mid-century modern home. It was filled with sculptures likely left by his artist wife, who had passed away a few years ago. She scanned the family photos of his adult children and grandchildren. There were also photos of what looked like Bryant family gatherings. Alyssa's heart sank when she saw Pastor Bryant in a few of them.

"Those pictures on the left are my kids," said the deacon as he re-entered the room.

"Oh, I've never seen them before. Do they live close by?"

"No, they've all moved to the city to find jobs. I don't see them often enough since my wife passed."

"I'm sorry to hear that. Family is very important. I hope you get to see them more often."

"Speaking of family," the deacon said as he sat down, "I thought you were going to be part of mine. I remember telling Tim that young people like you were going to make a positive difference in Pitway. What happened? Why'd you leave?"

Alyssa was so happy he'd asked that question, as she didn't know how to start.

"That's part of the reason why I came here. Deacon, there was never a wedding planned, at least, not by me. I never desired to marry the pastor, and I told him so, but he made plans to marry me anyway. That's why I left town so suddenly."

Deacon Barry looked confused. "I don't understand. I was told that you wanted to marry but your cousin prevented it."

"That's not true; I prevented it. After the argument with Tammy at the Pitway Inn, I left my job. Tammy was telling all the guests that I was marrying the pastor. When I told a guest that I wasn't, Tammy argued with me. After that, I was so frightened that your family would force me to marry the pastor that I sneaked out of town. It wasn't Cousin Hazel's plan, she didn't know I was gone until she woke up.

"I've been in Los Angeles ever since, attending college like I had planned. I've only returned because the pastor made Hazel lose her job. Then, he had Ed foreclose on her house. Yesterday, I confronted the pastor about it, and he admitted to everything. He said Cousin Hazel and I had made him look like a fool. Then, he told me that if I agreed to marry him and Cousin Hazel apologized, she'd get her job back and Ed would stop the foreclosure."

Barry sat shaking his head. "I heard rumors about all this, but I had no idea they were true. I'm so sorry, Alyssa. I want to help you, but Tim doesn't listen to me or the board anymore. Others have made valid complaints about his behavior and his many relationships. Tim doesn't understand that these things hurt the church, he just does what he wants to do."

"But you can stop him. You need to discuss this with the church board and remove Pastor Bryant."

"Oh no, no," Barry said, shaking his head vehemently. "I cannot do that. Tim's family, he's my cousin."

"Yes, he is related to you. But this is not about your family, it's about the church; and the church family belongs to Christ. According to leader qualifications in 1 Peter 5, our pastor is not doing what he is supposed to. I've confronted him, and he made it clear that he will not change what he did against my family. You've also said that others have complained about the pastor. Look, I understand that you're close to your family members, but as the senior church elder, you have an obligation to do something. The people in this town come to church to worship God, not Pastor Bryant."

"Enough!" Barry bellowed. "You have no right to dictate what's done in our church! Tim is the pastor, and he is to be respected as such. I'm sorry, but it's time for you to leave, young lady."

As the deacon led Alyssa to the door, he felt remorseful for his outburst. "Alyssa, I regret speaking to you that way. I shouldn't have lost my temper. It's just... what you're saying goes against who I am. Tell me, what do you and Hazel plan to do now?"

"Deacon, we're going to do what so many others have done, we have no choice but to pack up and move far away from this place," she said before turning to leave. The deeply distressed deacon frowned, then grimaced from his painful ulcer.

Benjamin had been parked outside Hazel's house since seven in the morning, hoping Alyssa would return soon from wherever she had gone. Knocking on the front door wasn't an option, as he had no idea if she told her cousin about him.

A few minutes later, the Ford Taurus pulled into the driveway. Benjamin was excited to finally see his friend. He waited, expecting Alyssa to get out, but she stayed inside. He left his car, walked over to the Taurus and tapped the passenger-side window. Alyssa was shocked and elated to see Benjamin when she lifted her tear-streaked face from her hands. Without hesitation, he opened the passenger door and got in. She immediately embraced him.

"Ben, I'm so happy you're here. My friend Sarah told me about Pastor Bryant being responsible for getting cousin Hazel fired and forcing the foreclosure on our home. You would have been proud of me," she said through tears. "I stood up to Pastor Bryant yesterday. I was afraid, but I did it anyway. This morning, I pleaded with the head deacon for help. It was a waste of time; we're still being kicked out."

She took a few deep breaths, trying to compose herself. "Do you mind if I keep the car for a few more days? I must help Hazel pack and find a new place to live. I'll bring your car back and let my college know that I'm leaving."

Ben shook his head. "No, you're not packing, and you don't

have to find a new place to live. You're coming back to LA with me. You will stay in college, and your cousin will continue to live in her home."

"Ben, didn't you see the foreclosure notice on the door? They're auctioning off our house!"

"Alyssa, Maureen and I drove up here yesterday looking for you. We saw the notice. I've already spoken with my team. They'll start working on the foreclosure next week. I promise you; your cousin can stay in her home."

"But... how?"

"You do realize you're married to a real estate attorney, right? Everything will be settled Monday when the banks open."

"Oh, Ben... can it really be settled just like that? Wait, what do we have to pay? I emptied my bank account, so I have some money to give the bank."

"Keep your money. You don't have to pay anything."

Alyssa was confused. "But what about the mortgage debt?"

"Trust me, your cousin won't owe a dime; I promise. The foreclosure process will be stopped."

"Really? Ben, that's wonderful news! I must tell Cousin Hazel. I'm so glad you followed me... wait, did you say Maureen came with you? The two of you are speaking again?"

"Yes. There were some arguments in the car, but we're on speaking terms now."

"I'm really glad to hear that because I like your mom," She placed her hand on his. "Come with me. Let's tell Hazel the good news right away!"

Hazel found the news of the mortgage being settled difficult to believe, but Alyssa insisted that her friend Benjamin knew the real estate business well. Alyssa explained in detail how Benjamin's grandfather had started the real estate company and how Benjamin's been running it on his own. Hazel remained skeptical about the bank not needing any money from her to stay in her home.

Hazel was also skeptical about Alyssa's friend. She wished she had never allowed her phone service to be terminated because she now felt like she had missed out on a lot in Alyssa's life. Watching Alyssa and Benjamin interact was like watching a married couple. *Why doesn't Alyssa want to tell me he's her boyfriend?* she wondered. Hazel didn't understand the secrecy, but with so much going on, she figured Alyssa was waiting for a good time to tell her about the relationship. In any case, she liked how the young man treated Alyssa.

The three of them had lunch together, during which Hazel asked Benjamin many questions about his work. He answered them all effortlessly and continued the conversation by explaining what his company does. Benjamin then used Hazel's phone to let Maureen know that he was with Alyssa and her cousin. He assured her that Alyssa would be returning to LA with him. Maureen passed the phone to Stanley, who'd driven up early that morning. During their conversation, another call came through on Hazel's phone, so he passed it to Alyssa.

"Alyssa, you are not going to believe this!" said an excited Sarah. *"Deacon Barry and the board are having an emergency meeting at the church to vote on expelling Pastor Bryant. This is blowing my mind! Someone overheard your conversation with Ed at the bank yesterday and spread the news around. The whole town's been talking about what the pastor did to Hazel, and others are speaking up about their bad experiences. Get this, Deacon Barry is the one who requested this emergency meeting. I'm told, former church members are headed to the church to demand Pastor Bryant's removal. My family and I are on our way to the church now!"*

"Sarah, are you serious? How did this happen?"

"It must be you, Alyssa. Most people didn't know what was happening to your cousin until you came home. Also, once people began

talking, they realized just how many members had run-ins with the pastor. You must go to the church now!"

"I'll meet you there in a few minutes!"

"Great!"

"Cousin Hazel, Ben; that was Sarah. She said the church board is meeting at Pitway Baptist right now to vote on removing Pastor Bryant. I have to be there!"

"Oh my goodness, this is so unexpected! I want to be there too; let's go," replied Hazel.

Benjamin called his mother again and told her to grab Stanley and meet him at the church as soon as possible.

By the time Benjamin pulled up to the church, a sizable crowd had gathered outside. Some were shouting at each board member as they walked up the steps. All requests were the same: Pastor Bryant had to go. Many people and vehicles were gathered around the church. The overflow of vehicles lined the nearby streets, and people stood together in clusters. Benjamin dropped Alyssa and Hazel off before continuing to search for a parking spot.

Both current and former congregants greeted Hazel and Alyssa warmly. When Maureen and Stanley arrived, Alyssa greeted them with hugs and introduced them to her cousin.

Despite the scorching August sun, the townspeople stood unwavering, waiting to hear the outcome of the board vote. Some thought Alyssa should be present at the meeting, and they encouraged her to walk up the steps of the church.

Suddenly, they all heard loud shouting from behind the church doors. A fuming, red-faced Tim Bryant abruptly yanked the church door open. He appeared temporarily stunned to see so many people standing outside, then he snarled when a few applauded his exit. When his eyes locked on Alyssa, he swiftly marched toward her.

He jabbed a finger in her face. "I should have known you'd be here. This is all your doing! You ungrateful troublemaker, who do you think you are? I'll tell you what you are. You're a stupid, witless, meddling nobody! Your own mama didn't want you because you're not worth wanting!" he shouted.

A frightened Alyssa backed up as she wiped Bryant's spittle from her cheek. Then, out of nowhere, Benjamin ran up the stairs and wedged himself between Pastor Bryant and Alyssa.

"Hey! You *do not* talk to my wife like that! She's not a nobody; she's a kind woman who was bullied by a joker pretending to be a man of God! You'd better leave. Now!"

Tim's mouth fell open. "W–w–wife?" He uttered in amazement.

Seeing Benjamin's expression made him step back and walk away from the couple. He quickly exited by a different flight of stairs while occasionally glancing over his shoulder to ensure Benjamin wasn't following. There were cheers, applause, and hoots from the crowd as they watched him leave.

Benjamin took Alyssa's hand. "Alyssa, don't listen to anything he said. None of it is true. You did a great thing here, and I'm very proud of you," He wrapped her in a hug.

Hazel's mouth hung open as she stared at Alyssa and the friend who had just claimed to be her husband, locked in an embrace.

Noticing Hazel's expression, Alyssa quickly pulled away and hurried down the stairs to speak to her. She pulled Hazel away from Maureen and whispered, "I'll explain all this later. It's not what you think."

But as Hazel looked back at Benjamin, who remained in a combative stance as he watched Tim retreat, she wasn't so sure.

One by one, the board members began to leave the church building. They confirmed what everyone already assumed: Pastor Bryant had been relieved of his duties. The townspeople surrounded Alyssa, thanking her for convincing the deacon to do what many believed should have been done a long time ago. Some also congratulated her on her marriage. Alyssa tried to correct them, but no one paid any attention.

When Sarah and her family congratulated her, Maureen and Stanley were standing behind them, so she chose not to refute the marriage at that time. Alyssa then excused herself and ran over to Benjamin, who was in the parking lot, watching Tim Bryant back out and drive away.

"Ben! Thanks so much for standing up for me...."

Alyssa didn't finish her statement because Benjamin pulled her close and asked,

"Are you alright?" his voice filled with concern.

"I'm fine, Ben. But you seemed very upset. Are you better now?"

"Yes, and I'm sorry for blurting out that you're my wife in front of everyone. I was so angry when I heard him speak to you that way, and I lost my temper. Sorry, I wasn't thinking clearly. I'll find a way to fix it somehow, I promise. But, Alyssa, I'm so proud of all that you did here. You put your fears aside and accomplished so much in just one day. You're an amazing woman."

"Thanks, that means a lot coming from you. I would never have stood up to the pastor without your encouragement," she said with a smile. "Let's go inside. I want to thank the deacon for firing his cousin. I know that must have been very difficult for him."

As they opened the church door, Alyssa turned and waved for Hazel, Stanley, and Maureen to join them. Sarah tagged along, hoping to talk to Alyssa about her marriage. More board members exited as the group walked inside the sanctuary and made their way to the board room. Inside, they found Deacon Barry slumped in his chair, sitting with a grim expression at the head of the table. The deacon looked up as they entered.

"Deacon Barry? I just wanted to thank you for calling the meeting. I know it wasn't easy going against a family member, but everything will work out."

"No, Alyssa, it won't." He sighed. "For the first time ever, there will be no Sunday service tomorrow, and I have no idea if these church doors will open again. Pitway Baptist will remain closed indefinitely until we find a new pastor willing to work on a small salary."

"Oh no! Deacon, there must be a way to keep Sunday services going. Isn't there anyone who could fill in temporarily?"

"Unfortunately, no. Tim was supposed to have a pastor understudy to cover him whenever he's away, but he never liked any of the people we suggested."

"Cousin Hazel, are you still in touch with Pastor Darrell?" Alyssa asked.

"I am, but he holds Sunday service at a different church over 100 miles from here. Sorry, I don't think he will be able to help."

There was nothing left to say. Alyssa and the others were just as sullen as the deacon. Suddenly, Alyssa turned to Stanley and placed her hand on his arm. He instantly knew what she was asking.

"No, I can't. I'm not an ordained pastor; I'm just a Bible study teacher," he said, shaking his head.

"Neither was Pastor Bryant when he took the job. Stanley, you are well qualified for this. In fact, you're more qualified than Pastor Bryant because you minored in Theology at college. I've listened to your Bible study class every week over the past year, and I've learned so much. You have a gift for scripture interpretation. You keep people engaged, and your class size has grown in the short time I've been there. You're great at what you do! I know this is a lot to ask, but it won't be forever. Can you commit to maybe, six Sundays?" she asked pleadingly.

"We do offer a modest salary that should cover your expenses, and all our townspeople would greatly appreciate you doing this for us," the deacon added.

Stanley sighed. "Well, I guess six Sundays is not bad. It will at least keep the church doors open. I'll do it, but I have conditions," said Stanley.

"Great!" cried Alyssa. "What conditions?"

"Well, first, I want to take part in the interview process for the new pastor. Second, I want to review the church bylaws and make some changes to prevent this situation from happening again. And third," Stanley turned to Benjamin, "I would like Benjamin to accompany me every Sunday I'm here."

Alyssa lost all her enthusiasm when she heard the last condition.

"Huh? What do you need me here for? Am I your driver?" Benjamin asked, crossing his arms.

"No, not as my driver. I need your help to rebuild the congregation and correct the church's policies. Also, whether you realize it or not, you need this opportunity."

Stanley pulled his confused friend aside. "Based on what Alyssa has told me, Pitway Baptist hasn't functioned correctly for many years. Ben, I need you to be my Executive Pastor. With your knowledge of the Bible and business organization skills, you'd be a tremendous asset in getting this church back on track so it can operate as it should. Together, we'll bring this church and its policies in compliance with the teachings of Christ. I'll minister, and you'll oversee operations. What do you say? Are you in?"

"Stan, I don't know anything about churches," Benjamin protested.

"That's not true. You know enough to recognize when a church or its leaders are going the wrong way. Every time we talk about you attending church, you mention how corrupt churches are and list all the negative things you've seen written about them. That's why you refuse to step foot in one. You're the one who's constantly telling me how a church should function. Now you have the opportunity to fix one, for God."

"Oh, come on, Stan. God doesn't need me to fix this church. Any one of the members could do that," Benjamin countered.

"That's not true. Remember, it took Alyssa's involvement to get Pastor Bryant out; the members didn't do it," Stan replied.

"But I don't enjoy church. I went often as a kid because my

grandfather forced me to go with him. I really don't want to be involved."

Stanley became frustrated. "Really, Ben? Whenever I ask you to my Bible study, you complain about the corruption in churches. Do you want to know how evil is allowed to thrive in those churches? I'll tell you how. Those churches are filled with too many people like you; people who know the Word of God and yet when they see a church leader taking advantage of a member or spreading false doctrine, they turn and run instead of using the gifts God gave them to keep the church on the right path. People like you exclude themselves from the congregation and leave the other members to suffer harm. You're who Christ referred to in Matthew 9:37 when He said, 'the harvest is plentiful, but the laborers are few.'"

"Look, we can't do anything about the church tragedies that happened in the past, those crimes have already taken place. But we have an opportunity to help this church spread the gospel without hurting its members. Think about it: many people in this congregation were hurt by their leader. If you, Benjamin Hallerman, were a member of this congregation, would you just sit in the pews and stay silent about corruption, or would you speak up? I know the answer is the latter. You would never stand by and allow someone to be hurt."

"Ben, you identify as a follower of Christ, but standing on the sidelines and pointing fingers at church problems doesn't help Him. He wants you to be engaged, worshiping with other followers of Christ. Remember, Hebrews 10 says '...let *us consider how to stir up one another to love and good works, not neglecting to meet together, as is the habit of some.*' That means you, a follower of Christ, are supposed to congregate with other Christians."

Stanley sighed and softened his tone. "Ben, you know all about church problems, here's your chance to be part of the solution. Take six weekends and help restore a fallen church into one that Christ would approve of. I know you've got more free time now that you've broken up with Gloria."

"You broke up with Gloria?" Alyssa blurted. At her outburst, the men realized everyone could hear their hushed conversation.

"Wait, what breakup? You two are married!" asked a confused Maureen.

Benjamin acted fast, guiding Alyssa by the shoulders and raising his voice just enough for the others to hear. "Uh... sweetheart, of course, you remember when I broke up with Gloria before we got married. It's been a very stressful weekend for you. Why don't you sit and relax? Stan and I will sort this out soon."

Alyssa leaned in and whispered, "Sorry for saying that out loud. Good save though."

"That's okay," he whispered back. "I'm sorry for bringing this marriage mess to your hometown." He then motioned Stanley to move away from the crowd before continuing their conversation. "Stan, how can I be an executive anything? I've never worked in a church. I don't know what's required of me."

"Ben, remember, the church, or ecclesia, is not the building. It's the people, and these people need you. Deacon Barry will fill us in on the basics. Look, I've never preached in front of a congregation either, and just thinking about it makes me nervous, but I'm pushing my nervousness aside because I believe this is something God wants me to do. And though I think it can be done without you, I know running this church will be so much better with you by my side. You remember what Proverbs 27:17 says?"

"Iron sharpens iron," Benjamin quoted.

"I need you to keep me sharp and keep this ecclesia on the right path. What do you say? Are you with me?"

"Please Ben," Alyssa chimed in. "I know this town doesn't look like much now, but when this church was the center of the community, it was vibrant. People were friendlier, and they cared more about each other. Please, help us bring it back to what it used to be."

"Now you guys are teaming up on me." He shook his head with a half-smile. "Well... if you both think this will work, six weeks isn't too much to ask. I'll do it." A wave of excitement rippled through the small crowd when they heard the news. Several people came over to shake Benjamin and Stanley's hands.

"Ben, I'm so happy you said yes!" Alyssa gushed. "Thank you so much for doing this for my church. I promise you won't regret it." She threw her arms around him in a quick hug. "You're the best friend ever!"

Alyssa continued talking as Benjamin looked into her eyes. He'd grown to love the way her eyes lit up when she was happy. Alyssa talked more about how Pitway Baptist used to be and what she could do to help him and Stanley revive it. Benjamin hoped his smile masked the severe pain he felt when Alyssa had referred to him as a 'friend' because he didn't want her to know how he really felt.

A relieved Deacon Barry approached, thanking the men profusely. He steered them both to the newly evacuated pastor's office.

"Deacon," Stanley said. "Besides the interview, I'd like to spend time with the new pastor once they arrive. I want to ensure that the hard work Ben and I put into fixing the church doesn't go to waste."

Meanwhile, the excited townspeople broke into small groups, eagerly discussing who they would invite to the service now that they had a new pastor.

Hazel and Maureen started a conversation about the married couple, while Sarah pulled Alyssa aside and demanded to hear everything about her secret marriage to the handsome Benjamin. Alyssa looked around to ensure Maureen wasn't near and then lowered her voice. "Sarah, you have to promise to keep this to yourself." While Alyssa filled Sarah in on the scheme, she could see the confusion and disappointment on her friend's face.

"I know what you're thinking. You're probably wondering why I would do such a thing. In the beginning, it felt like I was helping Ben with a minor legal issue. But it's complicated now because his mother believes the lie. Time's almost up, and I don't know how

Maureen will handle the truth. She'll probably never speak to me again."

"Oh Alyssa, I don't know what to say. You definitely fooled me. Your marriage looked so legit, especially when Ben confronted Pastor Bryant. That was real anger."

"I know. I was so afraid he'd punch Pastor Bryant. Ben's been a really good friend, and he's always protected me."

Sarah studied her carefully. "So... how are you going to feel when you move out of his house?"

"Honestly, I don't know. I love it there. Ben's so funny in the mornings... I could watch him all day. And Agnes, his house manager, she made me feel so welcomed." Alyssa sighed. "She'll probably hate me when she finds out the truth. When I agreed to this arrangement, I didn't realize how deceitful we had to be, but I'm glad you know the truth now."

CHAPTER
EIGHTEEN

"Then you will know the truth, and the truth will set you free."

John 8:32

"Stanley, don't be nervous. The Pitway people are easygoing, and trust me, they all know Pastor Bryant was fired," said Alyssa.

"Deacon Barry told me the church is normally only 25 percent filled. Did you look out there? It's packed!" Stanley replied nervously.

"Stan, this is a good sign! Word got out that there's a new pastor, so the people who left because of Pastor Bryant came back. They're here for you, isn't that great?" Alyssa said.

"Great for whom?" Stanley muttered. He peered out from the edge of the curtains again, looking past the choir members. More people were being ushered in, and there were several groups of people searching for empty seats. Stanley looked down at his ill-fitting robe with too much material in the midsection and thought, *how did I get here?*

"Stan, you're wonderful at Bible study, and you've been doing it for years. I know you can handle this," Alyssa reassured him.

"I agree," Benjamin chimed in.

"You agree? You've never been to any of my Bible studies! How do you know I'm great at it?" Stanley retorted.

"Shh, the choir just started singing. Ben, I've reserved front seats for us, but the church is filling up. We should go now. Stanley, stop worrying. They'll love you. I just wish Rosemary were here to see your service."

"Yeah, Rosemary returns soon, so she'll be here for next Sunday's service. That should calm him down," Benjamin whispered.

Alyssa left for her seat, but Stanley pulled Benjamin's arm, holding him back. "We need to talk," he said.

"About what?"

"I spoke with Alyssa this morning. Why did you tell her the bank made a mistake and her cousin won't owe any money on the mortgage? We both know there's no way you could have obtained any information on the foreclosure that quickly. Why are you lying to her?"

"Shh, keep your voice down. I'm going to pay off the mortgage first thing Monday morning."

"Okay, but you don't even know how much they owe. And why lie? You're doing a great thing, why not tell her you're paying it off?"

"I know Alyssa. She won't take the money. She still refuses to accept tuition money for the marriage. Look, I didn't want her to drop out of college. I want her to stay enrolled and be happy. Promise me you won't tell her the truth."

"I don't know, Ben. I'm happy you're doing this, but it seems like these lies are getting out of hand. I won't tell her, but you must promise me that you'll tell the truth once the foreclosure has been stopped." Stanley exhaled. "I'll be so relieved when this fake arrangement of yours is over."

The congregation watched the interim pastor intently; this only increased Stanley's nervousness as he flipped through the Bible and instructed them to turn to a specific chapter and verse. He read from Acts 2:42 and Proverbs 27:17, then spoke about the importance of fellowship and praying together. Stanley went on to explain the verses in detail, in the same manner as he does for Bible study. Somewhere along the way, his nervousness diminished and he lost track of time. When he did notice the time on his watch, he promised to continue the interpretation next Sunday. He then signaled the choir to return as he took a seat next to the deacon. The elder was very pleased with Stanley's sermon.

At the end of the service, Stanley was shocked at the number of people who waited by the door to shake his hand. From a distance, Benjamin and Alyssa both smiled as they watched Stanley converse with the church members.

"You know, I've never seen Stan this enthusiastic about anything," said Benjamin.

"That's because you've never seen him at Bible study. Stanley's knowledge of the Bible is extensive, and he thoroughly enjoys discussing scripture with people."

"I see that now. I also see that we're going to be late going home if he doesn't wrap it up. Are you ready to come home and register for classes?"

Alyssa hesitated. "I wish I could stay longer. Cousin Hazel and I had a long discussion about our 'fake marriage.' She's very disappointed in me, especially since she's befriended your mother. Hazel thinks we're wrong for lying to Maureen. I must admit, the deception was so much easier when I didn't know who Maureen was. Now, I feel rotten about it." Alyssa purposely left out the rest of the conversation with her cousin, especially the part where Hazel said she's convinced Benjamin isn't 'playing' husband anymore. She also expressed her disapproval of them sleeping in the same bedroom.

"Alyssa, did you hear me?" said Benjamin, touching her shoulder.

The little electric shock happened again. The more it happened, the more she realized Ben's touch gave her a tingle that made her feel flushed.

"S—sorry, Ben. My mind was somewhere else."

"I see that. You've been through so much these past few days.

You must be exhausted. I promise, when this whole marriage charade is over, I'll apologize to your cousin for everything. We'd better head home now so you can get some rest."

Alyssa experienced so many emotions when Benjamin said the word 'home.' "Ben, you know I must start packing to move out of your house. Did you figure out how we're going to tell Maureen that we're not really married?"

"Don't stress over that now. When the time comes, I'll figure out a way to deal with my mother. And I'll explain that you were kept in the dark about the details. You're not to blame for anything. Now, let's grab Stanley and hit the freeway."

Stanley, Benjamin, and Alyssa arrived back at the beach house by mid-afternoon that Sunday.

"Stanley, you did a wonderful job as interim pastor! How do you feel? The people really took to you," Alyssa said.

"I don't know how to explain it... Umm, thrilled? That's how I feel. The people actually listened to my sermon and asked questions afterward. And the staff, they were so accommodating. Deacon Barry thanked me repeatedly."

"Stanley, they were amazed you read from the Bible and quoted scripture. These are things Pastor Bryant rarely did. You already did so much for the church. You have no idea how much you're going to help the community of Pitway. I can't thank you enough for what you're doing."

"It's really been my pleasure, you don't have to thank me," Stanley replied.

"And Ben, I'm so happy you're helping Stanley with restructuring Pitway Baptist policies. The work you're doing will be very much appreciated for years to come. Thank you. Now, if you'll excuse me, I'm going to review the courses I need to register for tomorrow."

Stanley waited for Alyssa to leave before turning to Benjamin. "So, time's almost up. How are you going to end this marriage?"

"Alyssa asked the same thing today. Funny thing is, when I started this fake marriage, I wasn't even concerned about telling my mother when it ended. I had planned to let the lawyer handle that."

"That would have been very cold, even for you. But something's changed between you two. You're not calling your mother by her first name anymore. That must have been some car ride."

"It was. She revealed some things about my dad and their divorce; things I don't want to believe. She said she never left me. I remember her saying that repeatedly when she returned from her honeymoon. Back then, I thought she was lying just to befriend me so I'd agree to live with her again. But when she said it again in the car, a part of me believed her. I mean, she knows how easy it would be for me to access the court documents, so why would she lie? First thing in the morning, I'll sort out the foreclosure. Then, I'll go to the court and get copies of my parents' custody case. If what she said is true, my mother deserves to know my marriage is fake."

"But if you tell her before the 60-day period, you'll lose everything," said Stanley.

"I've made my mother an enemy for so long based on what my father told me. I don't want to lose my home or the other properties. But if what my father told me is a lie, nothing I do can make up for all the hurtful things I've said to her over the years; and I don't deserve any inheritance."

"Now I'm in shock. You, Benjamin Hallerman, are willing to give up the properties you've drastically altered your life to acquire? I feel like I'm missing something important. What's happened to you?"

"I don't know. Maybe it's Alyssa's influence. She's developed a close relationship with my mother and Agnes. They both love her. Agnes will be heartbroken when she finds out the truth."

"Speaking of Alyssa, when are you going to tell her you know where her mother lives?"

"I had planned to tell her before she left for Pitway, but she's been through so much, and she's happy now. I don't want to take her joy away."

"Um... I don't know how to ask this question without upsetting you, but... are you part of her joy now?"

"What do you mean?"

"Oh, let's see... there was that gallant display of chivalry when you threatened the pastor, the way you look at Alyssa when she's not looking at you, and the fact that you guys are hugging a lot more than necessary. I don't know what happened during the honeymoon, but you two have become very close. Are you paying off the mortgage to make sure she doesn't move away from you?"

"No! I would have paid it regardless of my recent feelings. She's my friend."

"Okay, but I'm still worried about these 'recent feelings.' "Stanley said inquisitively.

"Worried? Why?"

"You know why."

"What are you saying? I can't believe you're accusing me of taking advantage of Alyssa. I would never do anything to hurt her! Is this coming from Stanley the interim pastor or Stanley my friend?"

"Both. I'm also Alyssa's friend, and I don't want either of you to get hurt. Secondly, we accepted the responsibility of correcting and spiritually cleaning a church that had ineffective or nonexistent moral policies. We can't be effective if our morals are compromised."

Benjamin exhaled. "You have nothing to worry about. This arrangement is almost over. And anyway, Alyssa doesn't have feelings for me. She only sees me as a friend."

"Ben, I know you would never intentionally hurt Alyssa, but being in love with a beautiful young woman who shares your bedroom suite at night is too much temptation for any man. You know I was against this arrangement from the beginning, despite you and Rosemary believing 'it's not a big deal.' It's not good for Alyssa to live with you. Listen, I know you're going through a lot right now with Maureen and the foreclosure problem. I only ask that you change this situation with Alyssa sooner rather than later. Rosemary's flying back in the morning. I'll bring her over tomorrow; I know she'll want to catch up with Alyssa.

"Call me when you find out the truth about the divorce. But Ben, regardless of what the documents say, I know your mother never stopped loving you."

The first thing Benjamin did on Monday was call the bank about the foreclosure. He was shocked to learn that his mother was already at the bank working on the foreclosure, and she wasn't alone. The homeowner, Hazel Cummings, was also present, and the property was no longer available for auction. The bank employee refused to provide any additional information.

Benjamin banged his fist against the desk, chastising himself for not staying in Pitway to resolve the foreclosure himself. He could have let Alyssa go home with Stan while he stayed to visit the bank. Now that his mother had paid off the mortgage with Hazel, he dreaded what might have been said between the two women about his marriage. But for now, he had to push those concerns aside and focus on the divorce documents.

Benjamin wished he could pass this task to someone else. Anything would be better than reading the details of his parents' custody hearing. But he found himself driving to the courthouse anyway. He also found himself wishing Alyssa were with him.

Fortunately, the records department wasn't busy. The clerk made a copy of every document, and Benjamin gladly took the court transcripts back to his office to examine them in private.

Reviewing the records took him back to that dark period in his life when his father told him that his mother didn't want to take him with her. As Ben continued reading through the papers that detailed every aspect of the custody battle waged by his parents, he became overwhelmed with emotion. Each page revealed more painful truths. His mother's lawyer presented credible evidence of his father's infidelity. His father's uncaring, flippant response was that she was "well cared for" and that he was always discreet with his relationships. He went on to plead that his wife didn't know how to keep him happy. Ben's eyes teared up as he turned the pages. He'd read enough to verify that his mother had told him the truth. Still, his father's lawyer convinced the judge to grant him full custody of Benjamin.

Benjamin was numb with disbelief. His father had purposely made his life miserable by keeping his mother away. He sat in his office, ignoring the calls his secretary attempted to pass to him. So many thoughts ran through his head; he felt disgusted at his father and regretful for how he had treated his mother. Benjamin remembered all the times she reached out to him, and he responded by turning away. He shook his head, thinking of all the years he had wasted by pushing his mother away when she should have been a part of his life.

His secretary, who had buzzed the intercom several times to reach him, was startled to see Benjamin appear at her desk, briefcase in hand.

"Please cancel all my appointments for today. I have to go home; I'm not feeling well."

She did as he requested, though she couldn't help but notice that he left with the same morose expression he wore when his grandfather died.

Benjamin tried his best to stay focused on the road as he drove home. He was happy to find that Alyssa had already returned from registering for her courses.

When the door to the study opened, Alyssa was surprised to see Benjamin home so early. Then, she noticed his expression.

"Ben? What's wrong? You don't look well. Are you ill?"

He perked up when he saw the face of the woman he'd grown to loved but then he remembered she would be leaving soon.

"Alyssa, you're going to hate me. I'm so sorry for everything I put you through," he said solemnly.

Alyssa's concern deepened. "Ben, I don't understand what you're talking about. You didn't put me through anything. Let's sit. Tell me what's on your mind."

Benjamin told Alyssa the lie his father made him believe all these years and how he had encouraged Benjamin to stay away from his mother. He also explained that he was not going to claim the properties inherited via the marriage. He would allow them to be deeded to his mother. That meant their phony marriage had not been necessary.

"Benjamin, that's wonderful! I'm so happy you're reuniting with your mother. I know that's all Maureen ever wanted. Everything will work out." Alyssa's voice was filled with warmth. "When I watched those home videos of the two of you, I saw a loving relationship between a mother and her son. To be honest, I was jealous because you have something I prayed for but never received. My mother never loved me the way Maureen loves you. I felt bad about hiding the truth from Maureen after I got to know her. I'm certain she'll never speak to me again when we tell her what we did."

"No, telling my mother the truth is something I must do on my own. This was all my plan. I want the two of you to remain friends." He hesitated, then added, "Also, I wonder if you could help me find a new home. I'd appreciate your opinion when I start looking at properties."

"You want *me* to help you find a new home? *You're* the real estate attorney."

"Alyssa, you're always so supportive. Just being there with me would help a great deal."

"...but his mother treasured all these things in her heart."

Luke 2:51

Maureen

"Congratulations, Hazel! There's no more debt on your home," Ed said with a nervous grin.

Hazel and Maureen kept their unsmiling expressions as Ed handed over the paperwork that declared the loan was paid in full. Less than an hour ago, this same Edward Bryant had refused to accept the full loan payment check from Maureen, claiming someone else had put money down toward the purchase of the home. But after Maureen made one quick call to her office, Ed's phone rang.

The caller introduced himself as the VP of his bank's headquarters before making statements that made Ed sit up straight and stare apologetically at the woman sitting across from him. Ed excused himself and returned with papers for Hazel to sign. Maureen intercepted the papers, briefly reviewing the terms before handing them to Hazel for her signature. Then, she confidently slid the signed check across the desk to the anxious bank executive, who quickly carried it to one of the tellers to process.

The women waited until they were outside the bank entrance before celebrating. Hazel shed tears of relief.

"Thank you so much for doing this! I promise I will pay you back."

"No, I told you before, this is a gift, not a loan."

"But I told you, Alyssa and your son are not really married."

"And as I said before, I know they're living a lie, and I understand why. It's because of my father's will. Benjamin felt he had to marry to secure his inheritance. I assume he wasn't ready to marry his girlfriend and asked Alyssa instead to satisfy the sixty-day marriage clause. She's not my real daughter-in-law, but I'm paying off this loan anyway because I like Alyssa."

Hazel shook her head. "I'm still very upset that Alyssa would do something like this."

"I don't blame her for going along with Benny's plan. They seem close."

"Still, I didn't raise her that way," Hazel muttered.

After they left the bank, Maureen dropped Hazel off at her home and proceeded to the highway. She had some thinking to do. How was she going to discuss this with Benjamin? Not long ago, he had called her "mom" for the first time in eighteen years.

For years, Maureen had dreamed of reuniting with her son, but it never happened. She had moved into the guest house with high expectations; still, Benjamin treated her like a stranger. The way she saw it, if not for Alyssa's influence, her son would still be a stranger to her. The young woman who masqueraded as her daughter-in-law was the only person who had made Benjamin acknowledge her. For that gift, she would have paid off ten foreclosures.

Her Benny calling her "mom" again? That was priceless.

So many years have passed since her son had been taken away from her. Not being able to raise him herself had left Maureen constantly worrying about what kind of influence her ex-husband would have on him. Thankfully, she had Agnes, who kept her abreast of all the events that took place in her son's life.

Her ex had many girlfriends moving in and out of their home. If any stayed with Phillip longer than a month, he would haphazardly tell his son, "Ben, this is your new stepmother." But even at his young age, Benjamin knew he did not want to be around these strange women, much less refer to them as his mother.

With Benjamin constantly nagging to visit his grandfather, and with Phillip realizing that his dating life improved whenever his son wasn't around to interrupt, her ex-husband allowed Benjamin to live with her father full-time under the condition that Maureen never stepped foot inside the house when their son was present.

Maureen celebrated with her husband the day Benjamin moved into her father's home. It was a step in the right direction, a step closer to her. She stuck to the terms: Maureen never set foot inside her old home while Benjamin was there. However, she thought of ways to close the gap. Maureen sent birthday gifts and toys, but Benjamin refused to open them. All the cards and packages were returned unopened. Next, phone calls were made, but when her son heard who was on the other end, he'd hang up.

Maureen would cry all the time. Years passed and still nothing changed; her only child no longer loved her. Her husband, Nicholas, weary of seeing his wife suffer, had insisted she stop pursuing a relationship with her son for the sake of her mental health and the health of their marriage. "Let's leave it in God's hands," he had advised.

Maureen focused on the family she had, Nicholas and his adult daughter. Agnes made life better by funneling tidbits of information through phone calls and letters. Maureen knew when Benjamin went on his first date and when and where he played football games. Agnes also supplied copies of updated photos whenever she could. But Maureen's best gift was watching her son walk across the stage to accept his degree from Stanford. Through some searching, Nicholas managed to purchase a graduation ticket for his wife as a gift. To date, Benjamin has no idea his mother has a video recording of his graduation ceremony.

As Maureen exited Sierra Drive, she hesitated a few moments before turning south to Los Angeles. When her father was staying at the chalet, she'd turn north, back to her home in San Francisco, but Los Angeles was her temporary home for now. She felt guilty for leaving Nicholas for such an extended period, but he was an understanding husband. He knew her son meant the world to her. Those few hours they spent together in the car had given Maureen so much hope.

But where would they go from here? And how would she tell him that he doesn't have to pretend to be married anymore?

Sometime after Benjamin and Alyssa returned from the honeymoon, Agnes had confided in her about something odd she had noticed. Only one person seemed to sleep in the king-sized bed. The covers on one side were creased, while the spread on the other side remained smooth. The pillows on that side remained fluffed too.

One day, Agnes decided to check the linen closet in the master suite to make sure it was well stocked. That's when she found a folded cot with linen, tucked away in the back of the walk-in closet. She checked several times since that day, when the couple was out, and the setup was the same every morning. That and the fact that Gloria made calls to Benjamin leading up to the wedding day made Agnes wonder if the couple was truly married. She did have fun teasing Benjamin and Alyssa with romantic table settings and watching them greet each other.

Maureen wanted to see things for herself, so she had decided to make use of her guest house ownership. It had saddened her to find out that Alyssa had no idea who she was. She had hoped Benjamin would have at least shown her a picture. Once she got to know Alyssa, however, she quite liked her. She thought it was a pity this girl wasn't really her daughter-in-law.

Later, Agnes began questioning her own observations. Benjamin began behaving like a jealous husband when Alyssa was around Andrew, and the senior housekeeper didn't understand it. Agnes also noticed subtle changes in Benjamin; he smiled more at Alyssa and seemed more relaxed. And now, their greetings appeared genuine. Maureen had witnessed her son's behavior toward the ousted pastor firsthand. She remembered holding her breath, thinking her son was about to strike the pastor. Was he behaving this way for just a friend?

So, when Hazel gave Maureen confirmation that the marriage was fake, it came as no surprise. However, Hazel's opinion mirrored Agnes's, both agreed the hoax marriage was in the process of becoming real. What she didn't agree with was Hazel's insistence that Alyssa move out as soon as possible before something happened between the two. But Maureen kept her thoughts to herself. She respected Hazel's strong moral values; without them, Alyssa wouldn't be the person she was today.

Maureen planned to call Nicholas as soon as she entered the guest cottage to update him on everything. She had planned to return home to San Francisco next week, but now, that seemed too soon. Maureen needed confirmation of her son's feelings towards her before she could return home a happy woman.

Her dear Nicholas had been a godsend, bringing joy back into her life when she was at her lowest point. Maureen met Nicholas at a divorce support group; his wife had abandoned him and his daughter for an affair, leaving him with deep trust issues. But somehow, their friendship had helped them open their hearts again. And since they both were family-oriented, they married within a year of dating.

Maureen thought about her father, and the years she wasted being angry with him for siding with her ex-husband. She was so happy he survived the stroke because it gave them a chance to reunite. Maureen will never forget the day she came to her father's bedside at the hospital. He couldn't speak, but he was so happy to see her; she held his hand and they both cried. Now she wondered how Benjamin will respond when she arrives to speak with him.

The hours passed quickly, and Maureen made the trip in good time. As she entered the driveway to the parking area, she saw Stanley's car and thought it was good that Benjamin's close friend was there. Maureen had been amazed by Stanley's sermon at Pitway Baptist, and she was so proud of her son for helping him.

As she exited her car and walked toward the main house,

another car entered the driveway and parked beside hers. When she saw Andrew casually stepping out of the Porsche, Maureen became enraged.

"What are you doing here?" she asked sternly.

"Um, I'm here to see Alyssa."

Maureen stepped into Andrew's path. "Alyssa doesn't want to see you, and I don't want my son's attacker walking on my property. You are trespassing."

"Look, lady, I've called, but the old maid always says Alyssa's not available. I'm only here to ask Alyssa to take a drive with me. Once she comes out, I'm gone."

"Wrong. You leave now or I'm calling the police!"

"Sure, I'll go," he snapped. "You know something? You're a heartless old broad. Now I know why your son hates you!" Andrew retreated to his car and sped off.

Maureen exhaled sharply, relieved she was able to chase the young man away without Alyssa's knowledge. She was certain it was the right thing to do and had no regrets about calling Agnes from Pitway, and instructing her to continue blocking any future calls from Andrew. But his words did sting. Did Benjamin really hate her? Had she overstepped with the foreclosure payment and put their relationship in danger? It did prove that he had lied to Alyssa. Maureen was ready to apologize or even grovel, anything to bring Benjamin back to her.

When she reached the house, Stanley opened the door. "Oh, Stanley, I wanted to ask Ben if we could talk in the guest house. It's so nice to see you again, I really loved your sermon! You must bring your family next time so they can hear you."

"Thanks Maureen. Rosemary has already convinced my brother and sister to join us when we go back next Sunday. It'll be good to see you again too; the more friendly familiar faces, the better. Well, Benjamin went for a stroll on the beach. I'll tell him that you're waiting for him. Rosemary's in the bedroom with Alyssa, we'll be leaving shortly, but I look forward to seeing you on Sunday." With that, he kissed her on the cheek and went back to helping Alyssa pack.

CHAPTER

TWENTY

"Instead, speaking the truth in love, we will grow to become in every respect the mature body of him who is the head, that is, Christ."

Ephesians 4:15

Earlier that afternoon, when Rosemary and Stanley arrived to see Alyssa. Ben took a stroll along the beach and enjoyed the scenery; something he hadn't done for a long time. Now that he had to give up living in the beach house, he wondered why he took it for granted for so long.

Benjamin struggled with what to say to his mother when she arrived, and how to make Alyssa accept his apology. Hazel called earlier, and told Alyssa that Benjamin lied about her not owing money. Maureen paid off the mortgage that morning and was on her way back to Los Angeles. Alyssa was furious with him and he couldn't blame her.

As he walked around the beach house, Ben saw the open trunk of Stanley's car. His heart sank when he peered inside. It was filled with Alyssa's things. When he entered the house, Stanley emerged from the library with a box of Alyssa's books.

"Hey, Ben, didn't hear you come in. Rosemary's still in the bedroom helping Alyssa pack. We're driving her to the dorm tonight. How was your stroll?"

"It was fine, until I came home. Does she really have to leave tonight? I can drive her tomorrow.

"Ben, Alyssa asked us to move her back to the dorm tonight. She said there's no reason for her to stay, and it seems her cousin wants her to leave this... situation as soon as possible. Of course, you know I agree with this, but it's not like you won't see her again. It'll be like before; we'll still hang out together. And anyway, Alyssa will be over at Rosemary's more often to help with our wedding plans."

"How's that going, by the way?"

"It's coming along. We tried to keep it small, but Rosemary's parents added more guests, so we're up to 175 and counting. I shouldn't complain though since they're paying for it. The banquet hall is reserved, and we've booked our honeymoon in Maui." Stanley paused. "Oh, you may want to sit down for this.

"Maureen's been waiting for you in the guest house. She wanted to speak with you when you came in."

Benjamin sank onto the couch and sighed. "Seems like everything is happening so fast. I want to talk to Alyssa before I speak with my mother. I have to make her understand why I lied about the mortgage, and I want to drive her to see her mother this Saturday."

"Uh... you mean you'll tell her about her mother and ask if she wants to see her first, right?"

"No. I've given this a lot of thought. Me describing Alyssa's mother isn't the best idea, especially because I have nothing good to say. She should visit Linda for herself and make her own judgment."

"Hmm... seems more complex than just telling her the details, but it's your call."

Just then, they heard a knock on the front door. With Agnes gone for the night, Benjamin stood to get it, but Stanley motioned for him to stay.

"That must be your mother. Why don't you wait for her in the library so the two of you can hash things out in private. I'll let her in and send her to you. You guys may be a while, so we'll let ourselves out when we're done packing. He patted Benjamin's shoulder. "I have a good feeling it'll all work out for both of you."

"Thanks, buddy. I hope you're right."

The following Saturday, Alyssa sat stiffly in the car with her arms folded, looking everywhere but at Benjamin. She was still upset with him for lying to her about the mortgage. Benjamin had to beg Alyssa to drive with him somewhere important. She gave him a terse hello when he picked her up from the dormitory, but they drove for several hours in near silence.

"You're still angry with me, aren't you?" Benjamin finally asked.

"How can I be anything else? After I found out Maureen was your mother, you promised no more lies. But you did it again! Why couldn't you tell me the truth, that you planned to pay the foreclosure debt?"

"I wanted to, but I knew you were too proud to accept the money. You would have said no and dropped out of college to help your cousin. Am I wrong?"

Alyssa remained silent because he was right, but she was still angry with him.

"Why can't you tell me where we're going? Is this trip part of another lie?"

"Not exactly. I planned to tell you about it the night you left for Pitway. But you had so much going on that I decided to wait until things calmed down."

They passed a sign that read, *"Welcome to Nevada."*

Alyssa blinked. "Wait—Nevada? We're going to Vegas? Oh, Ben, I appreciate that you want to take me somewhere, but it's not necessary. You and your mother have done so much, too much already. And I'm really grateful, but I have so much unpacking to do. And driving back and forth from Vegas is a lot for you. I don't want you to be too tired to help Stanley at church tomorrow."

Benjamin shook his head. "We're not going to Vegas. I'm taking you to see someone important."

Fifteen minutes later, the Mustang pulled up in front of Linda's trailer.

Alyssa turned to her friend. "What is this place?"

"Alyssa, I brought you here because I didn't know how to tell you this. Your mother lives in that trailer. Before we got married, my father looked her up, don't ask me why. Anyway, he gave me the address. Stanley and I drove here a few weeks ago, and I was waiting for a good time to tell you, but too many things got in the way..."

"Wait, you knew where my mother was all this time, and you didn't tell me? Ben, I trusted you! I told you all about my life. After everything I shared with you on our honeymoon, you didn't tell me my mother was alive? How could you?!"

"I'm sorry... I didn't want to see you get hurt. I know I haven't handled things the way I should have, and I regret that. But I'm trying to change, for you."

Frustrated, Alyssa stormed out the car, slammed the door, and hurried up the trailer steps. Before knocking, she smoothed down her clothes and hair. Just as she raised her hand to knock, a sudden fear gripped her. *What if she doesn't want to see me?* Alyssa stood frozen for a moment, trying to muster the courage to knock.

Then, she felt a hand on her shoulder.

"Do you want me to go in with you?" Benjamin asked gently. Somehow, Ben's presence gave her the confidence to continue.

"That's okay. I'll take it from here, but thanks for the offer." She turned to face him. "Ben, I'm sorry for getting angry earlier. I know you were just looking out for me."

He gave her a slow smile before retreating to the car. Alyssa turned and knocked on the door. When it opened, Alyssa saw a version of her mother she didn't expect. Linda's beautiful long hair was short and dry. Deep wrinkles and a slightly disjointed nose accompanied the frown on her face. At first, Linda looked at Alyssa curiously. Then, the shock of recognition set in. Linda stood in awe of the tall young woman standing in front of her.

"Mama, I missed you so much," Alyssa cried, throwing her arms around her mother's thin frame.

Slowly, Linda's arms lifted to embrace Alyssa, who was weeping on her shoulder.

"Alyssa? I can't believe it! Let me get a good look at you!" Linda stood back, taking in her daughter's appearance. "You look so pretty and healthy. Hazel did a great job with you. Well, come in and sit down. Do you want anything to drink?"

Linda walked over to a small refrigerator and retrieved a beer. That was when Linda spotted the red Mustang parked outside. "Is that your man out there?" she asked.

"Um, no. Benjamin's just a good friend."

"Oh? Well, your good friend paid my rent last time he was here. That makes him okay in my book. He told me you were in college? How'd you manage to swing that? Did Hazel come into some money?"

"No, Cousin Hazel doesn't have any money. In fact, she almost lost her house in a foreclosure a few days ago. I received a college grant from the Children of Veterans Association, and I work to pay my other bills."

Linda sipped her beer and peered through her blinds at the Mustang again. "Bet if you play your cards right, you could get your friend out there to pay those school bills for you."

Alyssa felt a little uncomfortable after her mother's statement. She looked around the dimly lit, well-worn trailer and tried to think of something else to talk about. Her eyes landed on about a dozen pictures hanging on the wall.

"Who are the people in those pictures?"

"Oh, those are Jason's kids from his first and second wives. They're all adults now. He tries to stay in touch with them when he can." She then pointed to one frame. "This one's from his son's wedding. Jason and I are on the right; see, I still look good when I put a little makeup on," she said with a reminiscent smile. "That one over there is our wedding photo, and that small frame at the bottom is of Jason's first grandchild. The woman in the picture on the left is his oldest daughter from his first wife."

Alyssa searched the wall, scanning each frame, but she didn't find a single picture of herself.

Outside, Benjamin pushed his car seat back as far as it would go, so he could take a nap. He imagined Alyssa would be inside for a while. The convertible top was already up, keeping the sun out of his eyes as he drifted off into a light sleep.

The conversation he had with his mother Monday night gave him a great deal of peace. A smile formed on his lips as he thought of how many times she had hugged and kissed him. Benjamin had spent so much time dreading what his mother would say about his fake union, but ultimately, she didn't care about it or anything he did against her in the past. She had only wanted him. In the end, he was upset with himself for not speaking with her for so long. Benjamin thought of all the Christmas holidays he could have spent with his mother and her new family instead of sharing his father with strange women he hardly knew.

The peaceful nap was interrupted by a noisy, well-worn pickup truck that pulled up directly behind his car. Benjamin squinted to see a tall, middle-aged man with an ample beer belly and a faded baseball cap step out of the truck. He walked up the trailer stairs and let himself in.

Benjamin could hear the man's loud complaint before he shut the door behind himself: "Hey, who's the idiot who parked in my spot?"

Inside the trailer, Jason went quiet when he saw the young woman sitting on his couch. He nodded in her direction and swiftly walked to the back of the trailer. Linda hurried after him.

"Who's that sitting on our couch? You know I don't like strange people in the house," Jason complained.

The sight of Jason brought back a flood of unwelcome memories for Alyssa. Those memories made her stand up and move closer to the door.

"Jason, that's my girl, Alyssa. Don't you recognize her?" she heard her mother reply.

When they returned to the living room area, Jason took a long look at her. "That's Alyssa? The skinny girl who was always crawling out her window? Well, well!" Jason said as his gaze traveled up and down her figure.

Alyssa didn't like the way he was looking at her.

"Look at you, you certainly filled out well," he remarked.

Feeling self-conscious, Alyssa glanced down at her jeans and white tee, making sure nothing was awry. When she looked up, she saw the frown return to Linda's face after Jason's comment.

"I... I guess I should be going now. It was good to see you, Mama," she said, moving toward the door.

Alyssa expected her mother to protest her leaving so soon, but there was only silence and an unmistakable coldness in her unwelcoming face. Linda stood fixed, with arms crossed, making no attempt to kiss or hug her daughter goodbye.

Alyssa slowly stepped through the door and closed it behind her.

Benjamin, who had been alert and listening for trouble since Jason entered the trailer, sighed with relief when Alyssa came outside and entered the car. He was dying to ask how it went, but the look on Alyssa's face answered his question. Benjamin drove slowly away from the trailer and headed for the highway.

Some time had passed before Alyssa blurted out, "She still doesn't want me. My own mother doesn't want me."

Benjamin pulled over, giving her his full attention as she continued. "I waited. I waited for her to ask for my phone number or my address. I got nothing, no answers as to why she abandoned me. She wasn't apologetic. She hasn't changed. My mother loves Jason and no one else, not even herself. I can't believe she married him. She's the worst mother ever!"

Alyssa turned and looked at Benjamin. "There's so much anger and hate inside me. I know it's wrong to feel this way, but why doesn't she love me? What's so wrong with me that my own mother doesn't care about me?"

Benjamin sighed. "I made a mistake. I shouldn't have brought you here."

"No, you did the right thing. I wanted to see my mom. It's good to know she's not dead. I expected her to be happy to see me because she missed having me in her life. We did talk a little, but she became cold once Jason arrived." Alyssa hesitated for a moment. "Ben? I know the Bible says God wants us to honor our parents, but how do you honor a parent who wants nothing to do with you?"

"Well," Benjamin said gently, "you start by letting go of the anger and hate. Ephesians 4 says, 'Let all bitterness and wrath and anger be put away from you... Be kind to one another. Forgive one another, as God in Christ forgave you.' My grandfather quoted that verse to me after I refused to invite my mother to my graduation party. I wish I had taken that advice and not wasted so much time being angry with her. I have a lot of regret now because, despite what my father told me, my mother never stopped loving me.

"Your mother, on the other hand, may not know how to love you. Jesus said we are to love others the way we love ourselves. Can anyone who willingly stays with a physically abusive man love themselves? Mark 12:30–31 says, 'You can't pour from an empty cup.' So, if love doesn't exist in your mother's cup, she's unable to share it with you, because a person can't share something they don't have."

"Please don't think your mother's inability to love has anything to do with you. And don't do what I did, waste time and energy carrying bitterness in your heart. I know from experience that it will hurt you more than anyone else. Alyssa, you're a kind, smart, loving person, and I hope you never change—because I love you just the way you are."

Alyssa's eyes softened. "Benjamin, you always know what to say to make me feel better." She reached out and hugged him like she'd done so many times before. But this embrace felt different. She looked up and realized Benjamin was staring directly into her eyes. He abruptly dropped his arms and sat back.

"Here," he said, reaching into the glove compartment. "I need to give you something to destroy before I ask a favor of you." He handed her their marriage license. "This marriage certificate was never filed; so, the state has no record of us being married. When you destroy this, you'll be completely free of me."

Alyssa took the document, carefully folded it, and placed it back in the glove compartment.

"I thought you'd be ripping it to shreds by now," said Benjamin. "I know you endured more than you expected."

"You make our marriage sound horrible," she teased. "There were some fun times, right? Like having breakfast together with Agnes peeking at us. Remember all the times she waited for us to hug before you left for work?"

They both laughed at the memory.

"And playing against you on your Nintendo console. I'm going to miss beating you at Donkey Kong," Alyssa recalled fondly.

"Wait, we have to schedule a rematch so I can finally defeat you," Benjamin demanded. "I'm going to miss having you to come home to, Alyssa," he said, pushing stray strands of hair from her face.

His touch gave her the familiar tingling sensation she had gotten accustomed to and no longer recoiled from.

"And I'm going to miss seeing you every morning," she murmured.

She hesitated before speaking again. "Ben, there's something I must tell you. Something embarrassing. The reason I moved out so quickly is—"

"Wait, there's something I need to tell you first while I have the nerve." He took a deep breath. "I didn't tell you earlier because I wasn't sure how you'd feel about it. Here goes... I'm in love with you. I've been in love with you for a while now. It's been extremely difficult living with you while hiding my true feelings, but I knew it wouldn't be right to tell you this while we were sleeping in the same room."

"Oh, Ben, I moved out in a rush because I'm in love with you! I didn't know you felt the same way; I expected you to get back with Gloria."

"Alyssa, you don't know how happy I am to hear you say that."

Benjamin didn't wait for approval as he cupped her face before kissing her lightly on the lips. When he pulled back to look into her eyes for a response, she wrapped her arms around him and kissed him back.

The couple drove until they spotted a diner. As they waited for service in a booth, Benjamin continued to kiss Alyssa until they were interrupted by the waitress.

"Good afternoon! What can I get you folks? You seem so happy. Are you celebrating something?"

"Yes, we are!" Benjamin replied excitedly. "I'm on my first date with my wife!"

TWENTY-ONE

"Blessed are the meek, for they shall inherit the earth."

Matthew 5:5

10 Years Later

The announcer stepped up to the microphone as the huge crowd of townspeople became quiet, their clapping faded but their excitement was still intense.

Near the stage, local and regional reporters waited eagerly in their designated media area with cameras poised. The stage, newly assembled in Pitway's town square, was a rare sight; few could remember the last time it had been set up. Municipal staff made last-minute checks on the seating arrangements, ensuring everything was in place.

Several years ago, Pitway residents had come together to clean and restore this spot and other public areas throughout the town. Volunteers and local businesses had even taken the time to clean and repair the town statues. Now, the well-manicured turf in Pitway's town square is maintained by salaried employees who used to be those volunteers who prided themselves in keeping the town clean.

The turnout for the event was unprecedented. Pitway's police were forced to close all roads leading to the roundabout, and redirect traffic because of record number of residents gathered around the square. The townspeople flooded into the streets, standing shoulder to shoulder, anxiously waiting for the ceremony to commence.

Then, the speaker's voice boomed through the sound system. "This lady is so well known, she needs no introduction, but I'll give one anyway, as we all need to be reminded of her accomplishments."

"She was born and raised right here in Pitway." Cheers and hoots erupted from the crowd, they stared at the announcer, waiting for more.

"As a high school student, she worked several jobs while still making time to volunteer her services to the community. After graduating at the top of her class with a bachelor's degree in Social Work from Mount Saint Mary's University, she returned to our humble town and spearheaded the re-establishment of the Pitway Baptist Church children's ministry.

"Most Pitway scholars who left for college never returned, because they found more lucrative jobs elsewhere. But this scholar came back to our humble town and used her skills to uplift our community."

"Many of you remember those difficult times when Pitway had seen better days. Jobs were scarce, children had no programs to attend, and crime was rampant. But when Alyssa came home, she hit the ground running; pouring all her energy into reviving her church and community. Within a year, Alyssa, along with her friends and family, tripled membership at Pitway Baptist. Today, the church has grown so much that they've planted sister churches in other towns. But Alyssa didn't stop there. She initiated many community programs: the food bank, facilities for Alcoholics Anonymous meetings, and free computer training, just to name a few.

"Through numerous calls and meetings with elected officials and government staff, our heroine secured funding to open the John Holt Regional Veterans Administration Center, right here in town! Through her family's involvement with the Chamber of Commerce, many new businesses and hotels opened, this brought more jobs to the community. The old factory that had been abandoned for many years was transformed into valuable loft space with multiple units.

"You know, I could stand here all day and talk about her accomplishments, but you didn't come to hear me speak. Ladies and gentlemen, without further ado, I present to you our new leader, Mayor Alyssa Holt-Hallerman!"

The townspeople erupted in cheers, clapping and whistling.

"I'm so proud of you, honey," Benjamin whispered and kissed his wife on the cheek.

Alyssa smiled at her husband of ten years before handing him their two-year-old daughter. Her friend Sarah, who sat next to her; gave Alyssa a congratulatory hug. Their seven-year-old twins, Raymond and Johnny, sat between Benjamin and Maureen, while Hazel sat on the other side of Maureen with their two teenage sons; Emelio and Antonio, whom Ben and Alyssa adopted through an open adoption arrangement with the boys' mother in Acapulco. Nearby, Stanley, Rosemary, and their children sat with Maureen's husband and stepdaughter.

Alyssa shook hands with several people on her way to the stage. The cheering only grew louder as the new mayor stepped up to the podium. Scanning the sea of familiar faces giving her a standing ovation, she spotted the pastor whom Benjamin and Stanley had selected for Pitway Baptist, young voting adults whom she had instructed as kids through the children's ministry, and so many other longtime friends.

Before speaking into the microphone, her gaze settled on her husband. Somehow, looking at Benjamin always provided Alyssa with the confidence she needed to speak freely and boldly. She thought of the many victories they shared as husband and wife in the past ten years; victories she never imagined possible without her family and community.

It was Maureen who had helped her locate her father's family, something Alyssa always wanted to do. Now, her father's sister, who told her all about their Yokut tribe heritage, was seated with her other family members. Having five children meant their home was constantly busy, but Hazel and Maureen provided endless hours of babysitting and support without Alyssa ever asking. Stanley and Rosemary were frequent visitors to Pitway, and both played a huge part in Alyssa's mayoral campaign.

Alyssa began her speech by expressing her deep love for the town of Pitway. She thanked God, her husband, family, and friends before proceeding. She then acknowledged many others for their prayers and support. The hushed crowd listened intently to every word as she spoke about her vision for Pitway's future. She announced plans for reinstating a local Child Services Facility so children in need wouldn't have to be sent so far away from their community. She also informed them of the possible addition of a Senior Living facility by the riverfront, which would create more jobs and strengthen the local economy.

As Mayor Alyssa Holt-Hallerman spoke, a lone figure turned away from the enthusiastic crowd. Stunned by his defeat, Alyssa's rival walked past many young adults he did not know. Some were once kids who grew up in the children's ministry that Alyssa had re-opened. Others were newcomers who had recently moved to the area for work.

It had been hard for him to keep up with the many new residents who now called Pitway home. The real difficulty, however, was that these new faces did not know or care who the Bryants were. They showed no respect to the family who had run Pitway for generations. Also, they weren't deterred by the fact that their new mayor came from nothing and was once a poor orphan. Things would have been different had Hazel's foreclosure gone through, Tim Bryant thought bitterly.

For years, the Bryants assumed that when William Bryant passed, his son Tim would take his place as town mayor. That was how things had always been in Pitway, no one dared to run against a Bryant. But when Alyssa's busybody friends nominated her, the town went crazy. When Tim first saw the "Alyssa Holt-Hallerman for Mayor" signs posted around town, he laughed until his belly ached. But soon, everywhere he went, people were talking about how much the Hallermans had done for Pitway.

Ed and the other Bryant cousins were worried and had warned him to take action, but Tim remained confident. He was a Bryant. He never imagined an orphaned mother of five could beat him.

And yet, Alyssa Holt-Hallerman received over 80% of the votes. When the poll results were up, all the townspeople walked to the town center as was custom in Pitway. Tim's cousins shook their heads and walked away, leaving Tim alone, staring at the podium in disbelief.

As the former pastor drove in silence to his struggling dealership, his mind raced. The new businesses and housing brought in by the newly formed Chamber of Commerce, which also included Benjamin Hallerman, had welcomed rival dealerships into Pitway. Competition had never been a concern before. Now, it was threatening everything.

Back at the town center, Alyssa invited the now-retired Pastor Darrell to the stage. She informed the crowd that without the help and prayers she received from Pastor Darrell and the members of the Pitway Baptist children's ministry, she would not be their mayor today.

The elderly pastor humbly accepted her compliment before joining hands with Alyssa. All her family members were now onstage, with joined hands. In the crowd, the townspeople followed suit. With heads bowed, Pastor Darrell led all in prayer, asking for blessings over their new mayor, her family, and the town of Pitway.

AFTERWORD

There are a few concepts mentioned in this book that some may find questionable. The following paragraphs will provide some clarity and answers.

The first verse mentioned in this book, "Blessed is anyone who does not stumble on account of me," can also be translated as "Blessed is the one who is not offended by me." This was one of Jesus' replies to John the Baptist, who had sent his followers to ask Jesus, "Are you the one?"

John had witnessed and heard of the many miracles Jesus performed, but this statement suggests that John expected something more from the savior; perhaps a bold act of judgment against King Herod, who had placed John in prison.

Today, many followers of Christ are like John, disappointed. They are disheartened because Jesus did not act in the way they expected, whether in their lives or the lives of others. As a result, some refuse to attend a church or any gathering of Christ's followers (except for weddings and funerals). But Christ never promised a life without suffering. In fact, he said the opposite. John 16:33 states, "In the world, ye shall have tribulation: but be of good cheer; I have overcome the world."

There are other followers who refuse to enter a church because of the actions of a pastor or clergy member. Jesus also knew that not all who claim to be prophets or spiritual leaders are to be trusted. In Matthew 7:15, He states, "Beware of false prophets, who come to you in sheep's clothing, but inwardly they are ravenous wolves." Benjamin was one such believer. He refused to enter a church out of fear and loathing; fear of being taken advantage of and loathing for the evil acts performed by unscrupulous clergymen.

Some may wonder, why should we go to church if it's written as a suggestion and not a command in the Bible? We can compare attending church to visiting a doctor. You're not forced to get medical checkups, but regular visits can help detect problems that could lead to serious illnesses or even death. Medical checkups help us monitor our cholesterol levels to prevent heart attacks, glucose levels to prevent diabetes, and blood pressure to ward off strokes.

Likewise, attending church helps us maintain our spiritual health. Ephesians 4:16, 1 Corinthians 12:12–27, and Hebrews 10:25 explains this. Also, our participation in church helps spread the gospel faster and farther. As a group, we can do so much more to show the love of God than we could individually.

In 1 Corinthians 5, Apostle Paul rebukes the church for failing to correct a brother living in sexual sin. He goes on to say that we, in the church, are to judge each other and not those outside the church. So, if you are like Benjamin, a follower of Christ who's upset about sin within the church, shouldn't you do something about it? And how can Christ use the talents God has blessed you with to help keep the church holy and without blemish (Ephesians 5:27) if you remain on the outside?

Apostle Paul is not saying we should judge a sinner who has just come to Christ. Also, his words are not a license to push political agendas or harass and bully good leaders who fall short of your personal expectations. Most people can't imagine calling someone out for sinful actions within the church. It's not an easy task, and you run the risk of being shunned or rebuffed by the individual and/or congregation. Thankfully, Matthew 18:15–17 outlines the proper steps for handling such situations.

In late 2024, a Middle Eastern country proposed an amendment allowing girls as young as nine years old to be married. I imagine that most Americans who read about this were appalled, and are likely unaware that young girls can marry adults in their own country.

As of 2024, there is **no** minimum age for marriage in California and three other states. And yet, despite allowing minors to marry, the law requires individuals to be at least eighteen to obtain a divorce.

In these four states, any adult can marry a child, regardless of age, as long as there is parental consent and/or court approval. This means it is entirely legal for an unloving parent to offer their child to an adult for marriage. Furthermore, parents are not legally required to report any gifts or assets received after giving consent for their child's marriage. According to unchainedatlast.org, while most underage marriages involve children aged 16 to 17, some children as young as ten have been married.

Alyssa's father is a fictitious character, but the forced enrolment of Native American and Native Canadian children into the foster care system was a tragic reality.

Before the 1978 Indian Child Welfare Act (ICWA), many Native American children were systematically removed from their tribal homes, often without cause, and placed in foster care. Many parents never saw their children again, and it was not uncommon for the children to grow up unaware of their roots.

Sadly, history reveals that many of these children suffered abuse or faced untimely deaths. These forced placements occurred in the United States and Canada.

The subjects of child marriage and forced native foster care in the United States may seem improbable to some; so, I've listed the following links for anyone who wants more information on these topics. Please keep in mind that these sites are active and valid as of 2024.

CHILD MARRIAGE IN THE UNITED STATES

Unchained At Last

www.unchainedatlast.org/
united-states-child-marriage-problem-study-findings-april-2021

Equality Now

www.equalitynow.org/learn_more_child_marriage_us

Unicef USA

www.unicefusa.org/how-help/advocate/how-we-work/
child-protection-inclusion/end-child-marriage

Girls Not Brides

www.girlsnotbrides.org/articles/
new-federal-law-aims-to-accelerate-action-to-end-
child-marriage-in-the-us/

Journal of Adolescent Health

www.jahonline.org/article/S1054-139X(21)00341-4/fulltext

NATIVE AMERICAN/NATIVE CANADIAN CHILDREN IN FOSTER OR ADOPTIVE HOMES

National Native American Boarding School Healing Coalition

www.boardingschoolhealing.org/education/
us-indian-boarding-school-history

The Indian Residential School Survivors Society (IRSSS)

www.irsss.ca

CBS News

www.cbsnews.com/news/
canada-residential-schools-unmarked-graves-indigenous-children-
60-minutes-transcript-2023-05-28

Ohio State University

https://news.osu.edu/
the-grief-of-native-american-mothers-whose-children-were-
separated-from-them

www.ingramcontent.com/pod-product-compliance
Lightning Source LLC
Chambersburg PA
CBHW030023200726
48283CB00012B/808